全民英檢 初級 聽力 閱讀

全真模考+詳解

擬真版1 試題本

GEPT Mock Tests

U0105897

GEPT 完全命中

全民英檢 初級 聽力閱讀
全真模考＋詳解

擬真版 **1** 試題本　*GEPT Mock Tests*

發 行 人　鄭俊琪

社　　長　阮德恩

總 編 輯　陳豫弘

責 任 編 輯　林芸儀

英 文 編 輯　Jerome Villegas

封 面 設 計　羅靜琪

美 術 編 輯　羅靜琪

出 版 發 行　希伯崙股份有限公司

　　　　　105 台北市松山區八德路三段 32 號 12 樓

　　　　　劃撥：939-5400

　　　　　電話：(02)2578-7838

　　　　　傳真：(02)2578-5800

　　　　　電子郵件：Service@LiveABC.com

法 律 顧 問　朋博法律事務所

印　　刷　禹利電子分色有限公司

出 版 日 期　2014 年 7 月 初版一刷

　　　　　2018 年 10 月 初版五刷

目　錄

檢測程度

通過全民英檢初級測驗者，具有基礎英語能力，能理解和使用淺易日常用語。

分項能力說明

通過初級檢定者的英語能力：

聽	能聽懂與日常生活相關的淺易談話，包括價格、時間及地點等。
讀	可看懂與日常生活相關的淺易英文，並能閱讀路標、交通標誌、招牌、簡單菜單、時刻表及賀卡等。
寫	能寫簡單的句子及段落，如寫明信片、便條、賀卡及填表格等。對一般日常生活相關的事物，能以簡短的文字敘述。
說	能朗讀簡易文章、簡單地自我介紹，對熟悉的話題能以簡易英語對答，如問候、購物、問路等。

一般行政助理、維修技術人員、百貨業、餐飲業、旅館業或觀光景點服務人員、計程車駕駛等，宜具備初級能力。

檢測對象

國中（含）以上學生及一般社會人士。

測驗項目

初試：聽力及閱讀測驗
複試：寫作及口說測驗

成績計算

	測驗項目	題型		題數		作答時間
初試	聽力測驗	第一部份	看圖辨義	5 題	30 題	2 項合計 約 1.5 小時
		第二部份	問答	10 題		
		第三部份	簡短對話	10 題		
		第四部份	短文聽解	5 題		
	閱讀能力測驗	第一部份	詞彙與結構	15 題	35 題	
		第二部份	段落填空	10 題		
		第三部份	閱讀理解	10 題		
複試	寫作能力測驗	第一部份	單句寫作	15 題		約 1 小時
		第二部份	段落寫作	1 題		
	口說能力測驗	第一部份	複誦	5 題		約 1 小時
		第二部份	朗讀句子與短文	6 題		
		第三部份	回答問題	7 題		

測驗計分

1. 聽力與閱讀能力測驗採電腦閱卷，以標準分數計分，滿分 120 分。寫作及口說能力測驗採人工閱卷，使用分級制，分為 0~5 級分，再轉換為百分制。各項成績通過標準如下：

	初試		複試	
測驗項目	聽力測驗	閱讀能力測驗	寫作能力測驗	口說能力測驗
滿分	120 分	120 分	100 分	100 分
通過標準	兩項測驗成績總和達 160 分，且其中任一項成績不低於 72 分。		70 分	80 分

2. 凡應考且合乎規定者一律發給成績單。初試及複試各項測驗成績通過者，發給合格證書。本測驗成績紀錄自測驗日期起保存 2 年。

聽力測驗答對題數分數換算表					
答對題數	分數	答對題數	分數	答對題數	分數
30	120	20	80	10	40
29	116	19	76	9	36
28	112	18	72	8	32
27	108	17	68	7	28
26	104	16	64	6	24
25	100	15	60	5	20
24	96	14	56	4	16
23	92	13	52	3	12
22	88	12	48	2	8
21	84	11	44	1	4

閱讀能力測驗答對題數分數換算表							
答對題數	分數	答對題數	分數	答對題數	分數	答對題數	分數
		30	103	20	69	10	34
		29	99	19	65	9	31
		28	96	18	62	8	27
		27	93	17	58	7	24
		26	89	16	55	6	21
35	120	25	86	15	51	5	17
34	117	24	82	14	48	4	14
33	113	23	79	13	45	3	10
32	110	22	75	12	41	2	7
31	106	21	72	11	38	1	3

全民英檢初級聽力測驗
第一回 模擬試題答案紙

准考證號碼：521-17-00123　　　　　考生姓名：＿＿＿＿＿＿＿＿＿＿＿＿＿

注意事項：

1. 限用 2B 鉛筆作答，否則不予計分。

2. 劃記要粗黑、清晰、不可出格，擦拭要清潔，若劃記過輕或汙損不清，不為機器所接受，考生自行負責。

3. 作答樣例：正確方式　錯誤方式

聽 力 測 驗

題號	A	B	C		題號	A	B	C
1	A	B	C		26	A	B	C
2	A	B	C		27	A	B	C
3	A	B	C		28	A	B	C
4	A	B	C		29	A	B	C
5	A	B	C		30	A	B	C
6	A	B	C					
7	A	B	C					
8	A	B	C					
9	A	B	C					
10	A	B	C					
11	A	B	C					
12	A	B	C					
13	A	B	C					
14	A	B	C					
15	A	B	C					
16	A	B	C					
17	A	B	C					
18	A	B	C					
19	A	B	C					
20	A	B	C					
21	A	B	C					
22	A	B	C					
23	A	B	C					
24	A	B	C					
25	A	B	C					

全民英檢初級聽力測驗
第一回模擬試題

一、聽力測驗

本測驗分四個部份,全部都是單選題,共 30 題,作答時間約 20 分鐘。作答說明為中文,印在試題冊上並經由光碟放音機播出。

第一部份:看圖辨義　　🎧 Tracks 1~5

共 5 題,每題請聽光碟放音機播出的題目和三個英語句子之後,選出與所看到的圖畫最相符的答案。每題只播出一遍。

■ **Question 1**

■ **Question 2**

■ **Question 3**

■ **Question 4**

■ **Question 5**

第二部份：問答　🎧 Tracks 6~15

共 10 題，每題請聽光碟放音機播出的英語句子，再從試題冊上三個回答中，選出一個最適合的答案。每題只播出一遍。

6. A. I want to take violin lessons.

   B. I like to listen to music when I have free time.

   C. My uncle owns a music store.

7. A. I sometimes help my mom grow vegetables.

   B. I know. I'm the shortest in the class.

   C. I think I want to be an animal doctor.

8. A. Yeah, please do me a favor.

   B. Sure. What's the problem?

   C. That's OK. I don't like rice.

9. A. Yes, you can either have steak or a baked potato.

   B. Yes, you can get a baked potato with it.

   C. No, I asked for French fries.

10. A. Really? I thought John liked math class.

    B. That's true. John needs to study more.

    C. I know. John is very good at math.

11. A. Sorry, I'm really busy right now.

    B. Sure. It's a quarter past nine.

    C. Yes, the meeting will take more than ten minutes.

12. A. Yes, cooking is one of my favorite activities.

    B. Yes, that restaurant has delicious food.

    C. Yes, I love to eat birthday cake on my birthday.

13. A. Sorry, I have other plans.

    B. Yes, I don't want it to get stolen.

    C. No, I go to school by bus.

14. A. Really? What is she going to do?

    B. Yes, she just left for the party.

    C. Oh? I didn't know she likes summer.

15. A. I usually go swimming or hiking.

    B. I will never shop there again.

    C. I am seldom late for school.

第三部份：簡短對話　🎧 Tracks 16~25

共 10 題，每題請聽光碟放音機播出一段對話和一個相關的問題後，再從試題冊上三個選項中，選出一個最適合的答案。每段對話和問題播出一遍。

16. A. Played a joke on the woman.

   B. Said something that isn't true.

   C. Stole something from the woman.

17. A. The woman will send her brother to the hospital.

   B. The man will drive the woman to the hospital.

   C. The woman will meet the man at the hospital.

18. A. There are only a few computers in the classroom.

   B. You can learn how to cook on the Internet.

   C. Students must eat and drink outside of the classroom.

19. A. One.

   B. Two.

   C. Three.

20. A. They could never see each other again.

   B. They lived happily ever after.

   C. They beat the bad guy and saved the world.

21. A. It is far away from where the woman lives.

   B. The woman should take a taxi.

   C. It is nearby.

22. A. No, the woman is the boss.

   B. No, the man is not the boss.

   C. Yes, the man is the boss.

23. A. He's going to take a vacation.

   B. He doesn't care.

   C. He's very excited.

24. A. His classmates make fun of him.

   B. He gets along well with his classmates.

   C. All of his classmates want to play with him.

25. A. A pair of pants.

   B. A pair of socks.

   C. A pair of gloves.

第四部份：短文聽解　🎧 Tracks 26~30

共 5 題，每題有三個圖片選項。請聽光碟放音機播出的題目，並選出一個最適合的圖片。每題播出一遍。

■ Question 26

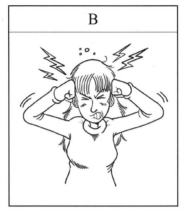

■ Question 27

■ Question 28

A	B	C
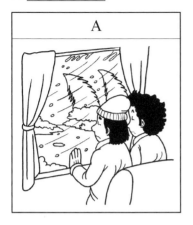	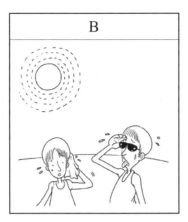	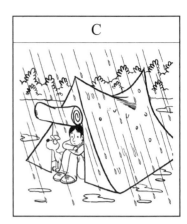

■ Question 29

A	B	C

■ Question 30

A	B	C

全民英檢閱讀能力測驗
第一回 模擬試題答案紙

准考證號碼：521-17-00123　　　　　考生姓名：＿＿＿＿＿＿＿＿＿＿＿

注意事項：

1. 限用 2B 鉛筆作答，否則不予計分。

2. 劃記要粗黑、清晰、不可出格，擦拭要清潔，若劃記過輕或汙損不清，不為機器所接受，考生自行負責。

3. 作答樣例：正確方式　錯誤方式
　　　　　　　■　　☑ ☒ ▢ ◖

閱 讀 能 力 測 驗

	A B C D		A B C D
1	A B C D	26	A B C D
2	A B C D	27	A B C D
3	A B C D	28	A B C D
4	A B C D	29	A B C D
5	A B C D	30	A B C D
6	A B C D	31	A B C D
7	A B C D	32	A B C D
8	A B C D	33	A B C D
9	A B C D	34	A B C D
10	A B C D	35	A B C D
11	A B C D		
12	A B C D		
13	A B C D		
14	A B C D		
15	A B C D		
16	A B C D		
17	A B C D		
18	A B C D		
19	A B C D		
20	A B C D		
21	A B C D		
22	A B C D		
23	A B C D		
24	A B C D		
25	A B C D		

全民英檢初級閱讀能力測驗
第一回模擬試題

二、閱讀能力測驗

本測驗分三部份，全部都是單選題，共 35 題，作答時間 35 分鐘。

第一部份：詞彙和結構

共 15 題，每個題目裡有一個空格。請從四個選項中選出一個最適合題意的字或詞作答。

1. I want to give my girlfriend a _____. I'm going to send her roses on her birthday.

    A. future   B. control

    C. surprise   D. knowledge

2. I am _____ a dress to wear to my sister's wedding.

    A. looking for   B. putting off

    C. giving up   D. running over

3. Wendy was upset because she studied very hard but still did _____ on her final exams.

    A. shortly   B. hardly

    C. poorly   D. generally

4. Jill had a great time at the class reunion _____ she saw many high school friends.

    A. if   B. so

    C. therefore   D. because

5. This _____ shows what my grandparents looked like when they were young.

    A. menu   B. voice

    C. photo   D. idea

6. It's going to rain. You had better _____ an umbrella.

    A. brought   B. been bringing

    C. to bring   D. bring

7. Tammy is very generous; she always _____ her toys with her friends.

    A. hangs   B. shares

    C. checks   D. accepts

8. Let's go to Taipei 101 and watch the fireworks, _____?

    A. do we   B. don't you

    C. will you   D. shall we

9. It's so dark in the room that I can't see _____. Could you please turn on the light for me?

    A. thing   B. something

    C. anything   D. nothing

10. Can you give me some advice about _____ for my vacation?

    A. I should go where   B. to where I go

    C. where should I go   D. where to go

11. _____ about shopping at the new mall this Friday?

    A. What   B. Why

    C. When   D. Whether

12. I tried to ignore the people who were talking _____ on the bus.

    A. loudly   B. bravely

    C. silently   D. easily

13. We decided to hire Adam, _____ can speak both English and Japanese.

    A. that   B. which

    C. who   D. whose

14. I am still waiting for a response to the e-mail I _____ Helen two weeks ago.

    A. sent   B. send

    C. have sent   D. were sending

15. It was _____ to leave the window open when you knew rain was coming.

    A. generous   B. patient

    C. foolish   D. humble

第二部份：段落填空

共 10 題，包括二個段落，每個段落各含四到六個空格。每格均有四個選項，請依照文意選出最適合的答案。

■ Questions 16-20

    Bill has a new skateboard. His friends think it is really cool. They all want to ride it, but Bill does not want to share. __(16)__, he lets Jim ride it. However, Bill tells him he cannot ride it __(17)__ more than ten minutes. Jim loves the skateboard. He imagines __(18)__ one, too. Jim thinks about having a new skateboard __(19)__ that he becomes careless and falls to the ground. He knows that is not very smart. Jim is lucky that he __(20)__ break his leg or Bill's new skateboard.

16. A. Whenever   B. Finally

    C. Next   D. Although

17. A. for   B. by

    C. until   D. during

18. A. to buy   B. bought

    C. buying   D. buys

19. A. very   B. enough

    C. so much   D. too much

20. A. can't   B. won't

    C. hasn't   D. doesn't

■ Questions 21-25

Mr. Smith is chatting with his students. He is wondering __(21)__ they would like to be when they grow up. One of his students, Barry, says that he hopes __(22)__ a lot of money when he is older. He wants to be a successful businessman. Mr. Smith __(23)__ Barry that it can be a challenging and stressful job. Barry knows that it won't be easy, but he __(24)__ watching his father for many years, and his father assures him that it is a very rewarding profession. __(25)__, Barry will do his best to make this dream come true.

21. A. what   B. why

    C. how   D. where

22. A. earning   B. will earn

    C. to earn   D. earns

23. A. had reminded   B. reminds

    C. will remind   D. was reminding

24. A. has been   B. was

    C. is   D. can be

25. A. Since   B. After

    C. Although   D. Therefore

第三部份：閱讀理解

共 10 題，包括數篇短文，每篇短文後面有三至四個相關問題。
請由四個選項中選出最適合的答案。

■ **Questions 26-28**

> ### Love of Drama Acting Class
>
> **Do you want to be an actor / actress? Love of Drama acting classes can teach you how to be a success in the movie business. Let your friends and family see you in the end of summer show!**
>
> ☺ *Morning Classes: Tuesday and Thursday 9-12*
> ☺ *Evening Classes: Monday-Friday 5-9*
> ☺ *Weekends: 8-12*

26. How many days a week can you go to a class held in the morning?

   A. Two.

   B. Three.

   C. Four.

   D. Five.

27. What time of the day can you not go to class?

   A. Night time.

   B. Afternoon.

   C. Morning.

   D. Evening.

28. What month might you be able to see the show?

    A. March.

    B. June.

    C. November.

    D. August.

■ **Questions 29-31**

> March 24, 2013
>
> Dear Wendy,
>
>   Hi, I'm Richard. We are in the same history class. I am tall with brown hair. I am not very smart, but I always try my best. Do you know who I am? I hope so!
>
>   Are you free this weekend? I am on the baseball team and we have a game. Maybe you can come and watch us. I think we will win. We have a good team.
>
>   I think you are smart and pretty. Will you be my friend? Maybe you can write back to me and tell me.
>
> Sincerely yours,
> Richard

29. How does Richard know Wendy?

    A. They live next door to each other.

    B. They are in the same class.

    C. They are on a team together.

    D. They play baseball together on weekends.

30. What is NOT true about Richard?

    A. He is not very good at history.

    B. He has brown hair.

    C. He doesn't work hard.

    D. He wants to be friends with Wendy.

31. What does Richard ask Wendy to do?

    A. Watch him play baseball.

    B. Help him with his homework.

    C. Go on a date with him.

    D. Play baseball with him.

■ Questions 32-35

Most children look forward to celebrating Halloween, which takes place on the last day of October every year. Children love this special day because they are able to do many interesting activities which they can't normally do. They can go trick-or-treating, wear interesting and frightening costumes, and stay out late at night.

The most common tradition during Halloween is when children go out at night to knock on doors and ask for candy. While most girls like to dress up as Snow White or other Disney princesses, boys like to put on scary masks and frighten people. Besides dressing up in many different styles of clothing, children also like to play tricks on their friends to have a good Halloween. Even though Halloween is a time for fun, it is important for parents to take care of children and keep them safe.

32. Which of the following is NOT a Halloween tradition?

    A. Give money to each other.

    B. Trick-or-treat.

    C. Wear costumes.

    D. Play tricks on people.

33. Why do children enjoy Halloween so much?

    A. They can have fun at Disneyland for free.

    B. They don't need to go to school.

    C. They can stay up late and eat candy.

    D. They like to be scared at night.

34. According to the passage, what should parents do on Halloween night?

    A. Dress up in a costume and go trick-or-treating with their kids.

    B. Keep an eye on their children to make sure they are safe.

    C. Eat candy and watch TV with their children all night long.

    D. Put on a mask at night and scare the neighbors.

35. What might be a good title for this passage?

    A. What Parents and Children Can Do Together on Halloween

    B. Things Kids Shouldn't Do on Halloween

    C. How to Frighten People on Halloween

    D. Halloween Fun for Kids

全民英檢初級聽力測驗
第二回 模擬試題答案紙

准考證號碼：521-17-00123　　　　　　　考生姓名：＿＿＿＿＿＿＿＿＿＿＿＿＿

注意事項：

1. 限用 2B 鉛筆作答，否則不予計分。

2. 劃記要粗黑、清晰、不可出格，擦拭要清潔，若劃記過輕或汙損不清，不為機器所接受，考生自行負責。

3. 作答樣例：正確方式　錯誤方式

聽力測驗

	A B C			A B C
1	☐ ☐ ☐		26	☐ ☐ ☐
2	☐ ☐ ☐		27	☐ ☐ ☐
3	☐ ☐ ☐		28	☐ ☐ ☐
4	☐ ☐ ☐		29	☐ ☐ ☐
5	☐ ☐ ☐		30	☐ ☐ ☐
6	☐ ☐ ☐			
7	☐ ☐ ☐			
8	☐ ☐ ☐			
9	☐ ☐ ☐			
10	☐ ☐ ☐			
11	☐ ☐ ☐			
12	☐ ☐ ☐			
13	☐ ☐ ☐			
14	☐ ☐ ☐			
15	☐ ☐ ☐			
16	☐ ☐ ☐			
17	☐ ☐ ☐			
18	☐ ☐ ☐			
19	☐ ☐ ☐			
20	☐ ☐ ☐			
21	☐ ☐ ☐			
22	☐ ☐ ☐			
23	☐ ☐ ☐			
24	☐ ☐ ☐			
25	☐ ☐ ☐			

全民英檢初級聽力測驗
第二回模擬試題

一、聽力測驗

本測驗分四個部份,全部都是單選題,共 30 題,作答時間約 20 分鐘。作答說明為中文,印在試題冊上並經由光碟放音機播出。

第一部份:看圖辨義　　🎧 Tracks 31~35

共 5 題,每題請聽光碟放音機播出的題目和三個英語句子之後,選出與所看到的圖畫最相符的答案。每題只播出一遍。

■ **Question 1**

■ **Question 2**

■ Question 3

■ Question 4

■ Question 5

第二部份：問答　　🎧 Tracks 36~45

共 10 題，每題請聽光碟放音機播出的英語句子，再從試題冊上三個回答中，選出一個最適合的答案。每題只播出一遍。

6. A. I'm glad they could help you study.

   B. They must be really angry with you.

   C. You must feel happy about that.

7. A. I really studied a lot.

   B. Our teacher is helping us prepare.

   C. Great! I'm glad I did so well.

8. A. I don't have to go to school on weekends.

   B. I ride my bike to school.

   C. I am never late for school.

9. A. He looks like my grandfather.

   B. He always looks happy.

   C. I think he likes Michelle.

10. A. I just heard a funny joke.

    B. I haven't slept much recently.

    C. I was trying to surprise you.

11. A. I agree. It doesn't work well, and it was so expensive.

    B. I can't believe it only cost NT$5,000.

    C. Yeah, I'm so glad we got it.

12. A. He is going to get a pay raise.

    B. His report was rejected by the boss again.

    C. He just won first place in the talent show.

13. A. Your total is NT$999.

    B. We hope to see you again.

    C. Sure. What's your name, please?

14. A. No, it's not. You can have it.

    B. Could I have a seat in the back, please?

    C. Yes, this way, please.

15. A. Yes, I'd like to pay cash.

    B. No, I'm single.

    C. Yes, it's under the name of Larry Chen.

　　共 10 題，每題請聽光碟放音機播出一段對話和一個相關的問題後，再從試題冊上三個選項中，選出一個最適合的答案。每段對話和問題播出一遍。

16. A. At 12:25 p.m.

　　B. In January.

　　C. On December 23.

17. A. At a gym.

　　B. At a clothing store.

　　C. At a supermarket.

18. A. It's too big.

　　B. It's too expensive.

　　C. It's the wrong color.

19. A. The man.

　　B. The woman.

　　C. They will go together.

20. A. She gave Allen her homework.

　　B. She did Allen's homework for him.

　　C. She looked at Allen's homework and wrote the same.

21. A. One.

　　B. Two or three.

　　C. None.

22. A. A lower-priced phone.

　　B. A colorful phone.

　　C. A smaller phone.

23. A. Taking a break.

　　B. Cleaning the living room.

　　C. Using the computer.

24. A. She did well.

　　B. She did poorly.

　　C. She doesn't know.

25. A. It's after eight.

　　B. It's before eight.

　　C. It's eight.

第四部份：短文聽解　🎧 Tracks 56~60

共 5 題，每題有三個圖片選項。請聽光碟放音機播出的題目，並選出一個最適合的圖片。每題播出一遍。

■ **Question 26**

A	B	C

■ **Question 27**

A	B	C

A	B	C
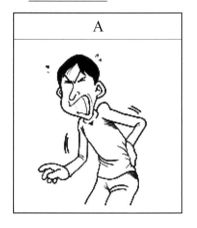	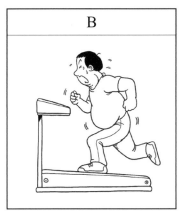	

■ **Question 29**

A	B	C
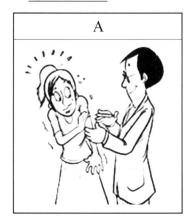		

■ **Question 30**

A	B	C

全民英檢閱讀能力測驗
第二回 模擬試題答案紙

准考證號碼：521-17-00123 　　　　　考生姓名：＿＿＿＿＿＿＿＿＿＿

注意事項：

1. 限用 2B 鉛筆作答，否則不予計分。

2. 劃記要粗黑、清晰、不可出格，擦拭要清潔，若劃記過輕或汙損不清，不為機器所接受，考生自行負責。

3. 作答樣例：正確方式　錯誤方式

閱 讀 能 力 測 驗

	A B C D		A B C D
1	A B C D	26	A B C D
2	A B C D	27	A B C D
3	A B C D	28	A B C D
4	A B C D	29	A B C D
5	A B C D	30	A B C D
6	A B C D	31	A B C D
7	A B C D	32	A B C D
8	A B C D	33	A B C D
9	A B C D	34	A B C D
10	A B C D	35	A B C D
11	A B C D		
12	A B C D		
13	A B C D		
14	A B C D		
15	A B C D		
16	A B C D		
17	A B C D		
18	A B C D		
19	A B C D		
20	A B C D		
21	A B C D		
22	A B C D		
23	A B C D		
24	A B C D		
25	A B C D		

請沿虛線剪下

全民英檢初級閱讀能力測驗
第二回模擬試題

二、閱讀能力測驗

本測驗分三部份，全部都是單選題，共 35 題，作答時間 35 分鐘。

第一部份：詞彙和結構

共 15 題，每個題目裡有一個空格。請從四個選項中選出一個最適合題意的字或詞作答。

1. I like Tim's ____. He always tells the truth.

　A. humor　　　　　　　B. respect

　C. courage　　　　　　D. honesty

2. Jeremy won the race, so his father was very ____ of him.

　A. nervous　　　　　　B. selfish

　C. proud　　　　　　　D. bright

3. The shoes were of poor ____. The bottoms fell off the first day I wore them.

　A. diet　　　　　　　　B. quality

　C. health　　　　　　　D. price

4. Bill is so strong that he can ____ 100 kilograms.

　A. lift　　　　　　　　B. cancel

　C. praise　　　　　　　D. revise

5. The restaurant is ____ here, so we should leave early or take a taxi.

　A. ahead of　　　　　　B. in front of

　C. far from　　　　　　D. across from

6. Before you buy that carton of a dozen eggs, make sure ____ of them are broken.

    A. no   B. neither

    C. either   D. none

7. Lori's mother makes her ____ her teeth before she goes to bed every night.

    A. brush   B. brushes

    C. to brush   D. brushing

8. Someone's cell phone ____ on the bench in the park.

    A. left   B. leaves

    C. was left   D. is leaving

9. Tony ____ to your birthday party if he has time tomorrow.

    A. will go   B. has gone

    C. goes   D. went

10. The knife is ____. You may cut yourself if you are not careful.

    A. quick   B. useful

    C. modern   D. sharp

11. Monica always keeps her mother's words ____.

    A. at head   B. in mind

    C. to heart   D. by brain

12. Jeremy and his friends played basketball ____ Saturday afternoon.

    A. in   B. at

    C. for   D. on

13. The clerk said we need to _____ of the hotel before twelve o'clock.

    A. check out   B. break up

    C. run away   D. leave for

14. I left a message for Fred, but he didn't _____.

    A. record   B. recover

    C. repair   D. reply

15. Mr. Hanks fell _____ in his chair because he was so tired.

    A. sleeps   B. sleeping

    C. asleep   D. slept

第二部份：段落填空

> 共 10 題，包括二個段落，每個段落各含四到六個空格。每格均有四個選項，請依照文意選出最適合的答案。

■ Questions 16-20

    Andy wants to ask the most beautiful girl in school, Monica, out on a date. He is shy, __(16)__ he asks his friend, Greg, to help him. Greg composes a beautiful love song and tells Andy to sing it under Monica's window. Monica thinks he is very sweet after __(17)__ the song. Next, Greg writes a love letter and asks Andy to sign his name at the bottom and __(18)__ it. Monica thinks the letter is beautiful and she decides to __(19)__ Andy. Andy is very happy and thanks Greg __(20)__ all his help.

16. A. or   B. so

    C. therefore   D. however

17. A. hear   B. hears

    C. hearing   D. heard

18. A. throw   B. lend
    C. return   D. mail

19. A. give up   B. point at
    C. go out with   D. put up with

20. A. for   B. by
    C. with   D. because

■ Questions 21-25

James is the best student in school. He is so __(21)__ that he gets an A in every class. He uses a computer database at his school to search __(22)__ information. He also likes to search the Internet. Reading nonfiction books __(23)__ him think of new ideas. He believes that there is always room for improvement. That is the reason __(24)__ he studies so hard. He wants to become a teacher __(25)__. He thinks education is one of the most important things in life.

21. A. silly   B. careless
    C. intelligent   D. jealous

22. A. on   B. for
    C. over   D. into

23. A. help   B. which help
    C. and helping   D. helps

24. A. why   B. where
    C. which   D. what

25. A. next time   B. one day
    C. on time   D. the other day

第三部份：閱讀理解

共 10 題，包括數篇短文，每篇短文後面有三至四個相關問題。
請由四個選項中選出最適合的答案。

■ **Questions 26-28**

Room for Rent in Shared Apartment

- *Close to campus, bus stop, parks, supermarket*
- *Own room + bath, share kitchen + living room*
- *Comes with bed, desk, chair; no closet*
- *NT$6,000 per month - Female student only*

Interested? Contact Ms. Sarah Chen today 6421-9824

---

26. What can you NOT find near the apartment?

　　A. A theater.

　　B. A place to relax.

　　C. A school.

　　D. A place to shop.

27. Who can rent the room?

　　A. Anyone that is interested.

　　B. Only men that are students.

　　C. Anyone that is single.

　　D. Only women that are students.

28. What is NOT included in the room?

    A. A bed.

    B. A chair.

    C. A closet.

    D. A desk.

■ **Questions 29-31**

May 19, 2013

Dear Annie,

My favorite season is spring. In spring, I can ride my bike in the park with my friends. I also like to play Frisbee with my dog there. In addition, the air always smells nice because of all of the flowers. I like the weather, too. It is always warm. Well, except when it rains.

Baseball starts in spring, too! I love baseball so much. Oh, and finally, I also like spring because my birthday is in spring. It's later this month, and it's coming soon!

How about you? What is your favorite season?

Sincerely,
Charlie

29. What is the main idea of this letter?

    A. Asking for help.

    B. Talking about his best friend.

    C. Making up a funny story.

    D. Talking about a season.

30. What does Charlie do in the park?

    A. Play baseball.

    B. Ride his bike.

    C. Walk his dog.

    D. Enjoy the rain.

31. What will Charlie do this month?

    A. Play Frisbee with his friends.

    B. Ride his bike to school.

    C. Celebrate his birthday.

    D. Visit Annie.

■ Questions 32-35

A bully is someone who uses their power to scare or hurt someone who is weaker. In school, "bullying" happens all the time, especially when there are no teachers or adults around.

Usually, bullies are mean to kids that are a little different from everyone else. If you have ever been "bullied" in school, you are not alone. About half the kids you know have been bullied, too. If you need help, the best thing you can do is talk to an adult about what is happening to you.

32. What best describes a bully?

    A. He is a funny guy.

    B. He is a smart kid.

    C. He is a little strange.

    D. He is a mean person.

33. According to the passage, when does "bullying" usually happen?

    A. When no kids are around.

    B. When classes begin.

    C. When no grown-ups are around.

    D. When kids leave school.

34. How many kids have been bullied before?

    A. Less than ten percent of kids.

    B. Around fifty percent of kids.

    C. Only a few kids in a class.

    D. Almost every kid.

35. What can you do if you have been bullied?

    A. Tell your parents.

    B. Discuss it with your classmates.

    C. Ask a bigger kid to protect you.

    D. Talk to the person who is bullying you.

全民英檢初級聽力測驗
第三回 模擬試題答案紙

准考證號碼：521-17-00123　　　　　考生姓名：＿＿＿＿＿＿＿＿＿

注意事項：

1. 限用 2B 鉛筆作答，否則不予計分。

2. 劃記要粗黑、清晰、不可出格，擦拭要清潔，若劃記過輕或汙損不清，不為機器所接受，考生自行負責。

3. 作答樣例：正確方式　錯誤方式

聽 力 測 驗

	A B C			A B C
1	A B C		26	A B C
2	A B C		27	A B C
3	A B C		28	A B C
4	A B C		29	A B C
5	A B C		30	A B C
6	A B C			
7	A B C			
8	A B C			
9	A B C			
10	A B C			
11	A B C			
12	A B C			
13	A B C			
14	A B C			
15	A B C			
16	A B C			
17	A B C			
18	A B C			
19	A B C			
20	A B C			
21	A B C			
22	A B C			
23	A B C			
24	A B C			
25	A B C			

全民英檢初級聽力測驗
第三回模擬試題

一、聽力測驗

本測驗分四個部份,全部都是單選題,共 30 題,作答時間約 20 分鐘。作答說明為中文,印在試題冊上並經由光碟放音機播出。

第一部份:看圖辨義　🎧 Tracks 61~65

共 5 題,每題請聽光碟放音機播出的題目和三個英語句子之後,選出與所看到的圖畫最相符的答案。每題只播出一遍。

■ **Question 1**

■ **Question 2**

■ Question 3

■ Question 4

Trip Packages

Destination	Length	Price
Korea	4 nights / 5 days	NT$17,500
Japan	7 nights / 8 days	NT$35,000
Hong Kong	2 nights / 3 days	NT$9,999

★ *Packages include flight and hotel* ★

■ Question 5

第二部份：問答　　🎧 Tracks 66~75

共 10 題，每題請聽光碟放音機播出的英語句子，再從試題冊上三個回答中，選出一個最適合的答案。每題只播出一遍。

6. A. Yes, I love reading books.

   B. No, I don't like to study in the library.

   C. Please tell me how to apply for a card.

7. A. I just moved to a new house.

   B. My house is as big as John's house.

   C. My parents built our house.

8. A. I like blue the best.

   B. I'm a medium.

   C. I love ice cream very much.

9. A. It is made of wood.

   B. It is pretty small.

   C. It's NT$800.

10. A. Just keep walking and you will see one on the right.

    B. Yes, I usually keep my money in the bank.

    C. The bank is open until 3:30 p.m.

11. A. Yes, it's faster to get there by bus.

    B. I have been to many stores before.

    C. No, but I will go next week.

12. A. Twice a week.

    B. With my brother.

    C. In the park.

13. A. Yes, Joe sent me a letter.

    B. No, I called him on the phone.

    C. Actually, Joe is my cousin.

14. A. Then you should see a doctor.

    B. I'm glad that you feel better.

    C. Yes, it was raining hard this morning.

15. A. Arthur is my friend.

    B. Arthur Smith wrote it.

    C. It is a book on King Arthur.

共 10 題，每題請聽光碟放音機播出一段對話和一個相關的問題後，再從試題冊上三個選項中，選出一個最適合的答案。每段對話和問題播出一遍。

16. A. She doesn't like to run.

    B. They won't be on time for the movie.

    C. She doesn't want to see the movie.

17. A. The man thinks he is taller than the boss.

    B. The boss did not like his work.

    C. He is going to have a hard day at work.

18. A. She likes to eat.

    B. She likes to read.

    C. She likes to exercise.

19. A. At 6:00 p.m.

    B. After the movie.

    C. Before they see the movie.

20. A. From her mother.

    B. At the bakery.

    C. She made it herself.

21. A. Everything closes early.

    B. Too many people come to the city.

    C. The weather is too hot.

22. A. Tonight.

    B. At lunch time today.

    C. Tomorrow.

23. A. She really enjoys watching TV.

    B. She feels bored when she watches TV.

    C. She feels like buying a new TV.

24. A. She bought it herself.

    B. It's a present from her mother.

    C. Her grandmother gave it to her.

25. A. Fish.

    B. Beef.

    C. Pork.

第四部份：短文聽解 🎧 Tracks 86~90

共 5 題，每題有三個圖片選項。請聽光碟放音機播出的題目，並選
出一個最適合的圖片。每題播出一遍。

■ **Question 26**

■ **Question 27**

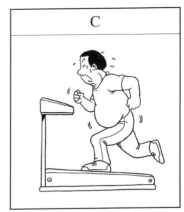

■ Question 28

A	B	C
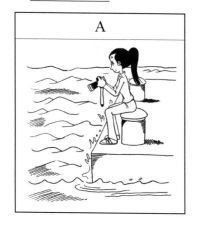		

■ Question 29

A	B	C
		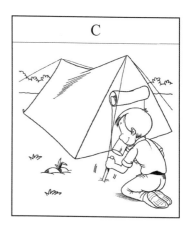

■ Question 30

A	B	C

全民英檢閱讀能力測驗
第三回 模擬試題答案紙

准考證號碼：521-17-00123　　　　　　考生姓名：＿＿＿＿＿＿＿＿＿＿＿

注意事項：

1. 限用 2B 鉛筆作答，否則不予計分。

2. 劃記要粗黑、清晰、不可出格，擦拭要清潔，若劃記過輕或汙損不清，不為機器所接受，考生自行負責。

3. 作答樣例：正確方式　錯誤方式
   ■　☑ ☒ ☐ ◦

閱讀能力測驗

	A B C D		A B C D
1	A B C D	26	A B C D
2	A B C D	27	A B C D
3	A B C D	28	A B C D
4	A B C D	29	A B C D
5	A B C D	30	A B C D
6	A B C D	31	A B C D
7	A B C D	32	A B C D
8	A B C D	33	A B C D
9	A B C D	34	A B C D
10	A B C D	35	A B C D
11	A B C D		
12	A B C D		
13	A B C D		
14	A B C D		
15	A B C D		
16	A B C D		
17	A B C D		
18	A B C D		
19	A B C D		
20	A B C D		
21	A B C D		
22	A B C D		
23	A B C D		
24	A B C D		
25	A B C D		

請沿虛線剪下

全民英檢初級閱讀能力測驗
第三回模擬試題

二、閱讀能力測驗

本測驗分三部份,全部都是單選題,共 35 題,作答時間 35 分鐘。

第一部份:詞彙和結構

　　共 15 題,每個題目裡有一個空格。請從四個選項中選出一個最適合題意的字或詞作答。

1. Jimmy will bring his teddy bear ＿＿＿ on the camping trip.

　　A. back
　　B. up
　　C. along
　　D. about

2. We usually go to the park to fly our kites on ＿＿＿ days.

　　A. helpful
　　B. funny
　　C. painful
　　D. windy

3. Sabrina bought a ＿＿＿＿ of Jay because he's her favorite singer.

　　A. plant
　　B. poster
　　C. planet
　　D. prize

4. Whenever John talks, he has trouble ＿＿＿ his audience interested.

　　A. keeping
　　B. to keep
　　C. keeps
　　D. kept

5. It is better to buy fruit and vegetables in ＿＿＿.

　　A. year
　　B. period
　　C. season
　　D. month

6. I'm going to _____ a DVD. What kind of movie do you want to see?

   A. beat   B. rent

   C. greet   D. treat

7. I'm very thirsty. _____ you get me a glass of water?

   A. Whether   B. Should

   C. Must   D. Could

8. Edward pressed the button to _____ the computer.

   A. look into   B. break into

   C. turn on   D. call on

9. The new teacher is smart as _____ as handsome.

   A. good   B. many

   C. long   D. well

10. Helen has two brothers. One is a pianist, and _____ is a lawyer.

    A. other   B. the other

    C. the others   D. another

11. _____ if you are angry, you should never hit anyone.

    A. Even   B. Yet

    C. Still   D. Once

12. _____ students in Cindy's class wear glasses.

    A. Every   B. A lot

    C. Several   D. Much

13. The poor boy wishes that he _____ a million dollars.

    A. could win   B. will win

    C. has won   D. wins

14. Debby was talking on the phone _____ the doorbell rang.

    A. then   B. since

    C. that   D. when

15. Here are two balloons. You can have _____ the blue one or the red one.

    A. both   B. also

    C. either   D. not

第二部份：段落填空

        共 10 題，包括二個段落，每個段落各含四到六個空格。每格均有四個選項，請依照文意選出最適合的答案。

■ Questions 16-20

    Most children and adults like to watch television. In fact, every child and adult has a __(16)__ cartoon. These shows don't have special effects, but they are still popular. Many children enjoy __(17)__ shows with funny or cute characters. Some adults like these, __(18)__. Many adults __(19)__ to watch older cartoons like Bugs Bunny and Daffy Duck. Adults are __(20)__ that these characters are still appearing on screen, like in the movie Looney Tunes: Back in Action. This is a movie that children and adults can enjoy together.

16. A. most favorite   B. better favorite

    C. favorite   D. best favorite

17. A. watching   B. to watch

    C. in watches   D. watch

18. A. nor   B. neither

     C. too   D. either

19. A. occur   B. regret

     C. prepare   D. continue

20. A. jealous   B. excited

     C. greedy   D. surprising

■ Questions 21-25

Ralph likes to shop. All of his friends know that he is a picky __(21)__ . Ralph likes expensive clothes that are stylish, but he never has __(22)__ money. He is always looking for clothes that are __(23)__ sale. Ralph __(24)__ a small, but he usually buys a medium because he likes baggy clothes. At this time, Ralph has enough shirts. However, he will go to the menswear section soon to buy a few new __(25)__ of pants. Ralph will definitely make sure that they are brand-name.

21. A. seller   B. eater

     C. driver   D. shopper

22. A. many   B. much

     C. few   D. lot

23. A. on   B. in

     C. for   D. up

24. A. worn   B. wore

     C. was wearing   D. wears

25. A. pieces   B. packs

     C. pairs   D. plates

第三部份：閱讀理解

共 10 題，包括數篇短文，每篇短文後面有三至四個相關問題。
請由四個選項中選出最適合的答案。

■ **Questions 26-28**

> # *Mama's House*
> ## *Steak & Seafood*
> ### *All you can eat!*
>
> Adult--------------------------------------$450
> Child (6-12)---------------------------$250
> (Under 6)-----------------------Free
>
> ☻ Save $50--Coupon in Daily Times
> ☻ Our spots in Taipei:
> ☆Ximending: (02) 2332-6531
> ☆Shilin: (02) 2839-1473
> ☆Tienmu: (02) 8523-1572
> ☻ Business hours:
> *11:00 a.m. ~ 10:00 p.m. (Tue. ~ Fri.)*
> *10:30 a.m. ~ 10:30 p.m. (Sat. ~ Sun.)*
> *Closed on Monday*

26. Who might go to Mama's House?

   A. David, a vegetable lover, who hates fatty foods.

   B. Sandy, who loves sugar and sweets.

   C. Harry, a meat eater, who can't live without beef.

   D. Beth, who thinks chicken is the most delicious meat.

27. Mr. and Mrs. Potter visited Mama's House with Harry, their 5-year-old son, on Friday night. Mrs. Potter had a coupon from the Daily Times for their meal. How much did they have to pay altogether?

A. $900.

B. $850.

C. $1,000.

D. $1,150.

28. What is NOT true about Mama's House?

A. It is open six days a week.

B. There are three spots in Taipei.

C. You can eat as much as you like.

D. You don't have to pay for your child if he or she is under 12.

■ **Questions 29-31**

May 12, 2013

Dear Susan,

I haven't seen you since Dragon Boat Festival. How's school in Taichung? I'm fine here in Taipei now, but we are moving to Kaohsiung next month.

I pack things in boxes every day. It's tiring. But I find many interesting things. Do you still remember my doll, Dora? It was a gift from my grandmother in Tainan. Her head is big. She has long hair and two big eyes. There is a butterfly on her skirt. She was our daughter when we played house. You were her father and I was her mother. It was a wonderful time. Now, we go to different schools and live in different cities. I really miss you.

I'm sending you the doll. I think you will be happy to have it. I hope we'll always be friends.

Love,
Tammy

29. Where is Tammy?

    A. In Taichung.

    B. In Kaohsiung.

    C. In Tainan.

    D. In Taipei.

30. What is probably true about Susan and Tammy?

    A. Tammy is going to visit Susan on Dragon Boast Festival.

    B. Their grandmother lives in Tainan.

    C. They used to go to the same school.

    D. Susan gave the doll to Tammy when she moved to Taichung.

31. Why does Tammy write to Susan?

    A. To ask her not to move.

    B. To tell her she wants to give her the doll.

    C. To ask her to look for the doll.

    D. To talk about their daughter.

■ Questions 32-35

Emma bought a new shirt at the store yesterday. Although she really likes it, she is going to have to take it back. When she put it on, a hole ripped in the bottom of the shirt. Emma realized that the shirt was of poor quality. Emma doesn't like to complain, but she is angry because she feels like the shirt was a waste of money. Emma has decided that she will go back to the store and demand a refund. She won't put up with any excuses from the sales staff about getting her money back, and she is sure that she will not recommend this store to any of her friends.

32. Why is Emma going to go back to the store?

    A. She wants to return a shirt that is of poor quality.

    B. She wants to buy another shirt at the store.

    C. She wants to exchange the shirt for a larger size.

    D. The shirt Emma bought is too long.

33. According to the passage, which statement is TRUE?

    A. Emma often complains to store managers.

    B. There was a hole in the shirt before Emma put it on.

    C. Emma thinks she wasted money on the shirt.

    D. The shirt Emma bought was very cheap.

34. What will Emma do if the clerk tries to make any excuses?

    A. She will accept it and spend more money there.

    B. She will tell her friends to buy shirts at the store.

    C. She will not get angry.

    D. She will not stand for it.

35. What does Emma want the store to do?

    A. Return her money.

    B. Allow her to get a new shirt.

    C. Apologize to her and fix the hole.

    D. Offer her some free shirts.

全民英檢初級聽力測驗
第四回 模擬試題答案紙

准考證號碼：521-17-00123　　　　考生姓名：_____

注意事項：

1. 限用 2B 鉛筆作答，否則不予計分。

2. 劃記要粗黑、清晰、不可出格，擦拭要清潔，若劃記過輕或汙損不清，不為機器所接受，考生自行負責。

3. 作答樣例：正確方式　錯誤方式

聽 力 測 驗

#					#			
1	A	B	C		26	A	B	C
2	A	B	C		27	A	B	C
3	A	B	C		28	A	B	C
4	A	B	C		29	A	B	C
5	A	B	C		30	A	B	C
6	A	B	C					
7	A	B	C					
8	A	B	C					
9	A	B	C					
10	A	B	C					
11	A	B	C					
12	A	B	C					
13	A	B	C					
14	A	B	C					
15	A	B	C					
16	A	B	C					
17	A	B	C					
18	A	B	C					
19	A	B	C					
20	A	B	C					
21	A	B	C					
22	A	B	C					
23	A	B	C					
24	A	B	C					
25	A	B	C					

全民英檢初級聽力測驗
第四回模擬試題

一、聽力測驗

本測驗分四個部份,全部都是單選題,共 30 題,作答時間約 20 分鐘。作答說明為中文,印在試題冊上並經由光碟放音機播出。

第一部份:看圖辨義　🎧 Tracks 91~95

共 5 題,每題請聽光碟放音機播出的題目和三個英語句子之後,選出與所看到的圖畫最相符的答案。每題只播出一遍。

■ **Question 1**

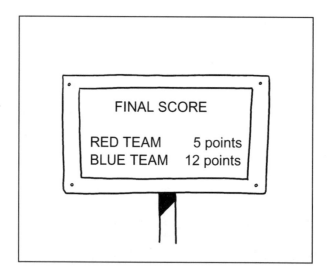

■ **Question 2**

■ Question 3

■ Question 4

■ Question 5

第二部份：問答　🎧 Tracks 96~105

共 10 題，每題請聽光碟放音機播出的英語句子，再從試題冊上三個回答中，選出一個最適合的答案。每題只播出一遍。

6. A. No, I don't. I like to grow vegetables.

   B. No, I prefer to take a bath.

   C. Yes, I like to take my dog for a walk.

7. A. Vivian is a good artist.

   B. That will taste good.

   C. Now she has green paint.

8. A. The bathrooms are dirty.

   B. The fitting room is over there on the left.

   C. The new pants you just bought look good.

9. A. I play soccer every weekend. It's great!

   B. Yes, soccer is a very interesting game.

   C. The game ended in a tie.

10. A. I usually take the bus.

    B. It takes fifteen minutes.

    C. It costs thirty-five dollars to go there by train.

11. A. Could you tell her to call me back?

    B. Yes, she can speak English.

    C. Hold on. I'll get her for you.

12. A. Please wait behind the white line.

    B. It will take us a long time to get our tickets.

    C. I can draw a line for you.

13. A. OK. We can cook it tomorrow.

    B. Yes, I can help you clean up tomorrow.

    C. Sure. We'll talk about it tomorrow.

14. A. Sure. Then we'll know which places to visit.

    B. Don't you have enough clothes?

    C. Yes, we need a tour guide.

15. A. How could you say that?

    B. Yes, Dad is coming home soon.

    C. Yeah, what should we do to celebrate it?

共 10 題，每題請聽光碟放音機播出一段對話和一個相關的問題後，再從試題冊上三個選項中，選出一個最適合的答案。每段對話和問題播出一遍。

16. A. Their boss.

 B. Their neighbor.

 C. Their son.

17. A. She doesn't like cakes.

 B. She wasn't expecting a cake.

 C. She forgot to order a cake for Mr. Harrison.

18. A. A sandwich and a Coke.

 B. French fries, a Coke, and a piece of cake.

 C. Fried chicken and a piece of cake.

19. A. Peter's former classmate.

 B. Peter's language teacher.

 C. Peter's former student from France.

20. A. Rent a DVD.

 B. Buy movie tickets.

 C. Pick up some seafood.

21. A. She's going camping with her family.

 B. She's learning about her family history.

 C. She's studying about plants and trees.

22. A. The taxi is downstairs.

 B. The man should put on a sweater.

 C. The man might be getting sick.

23. A. It was free.

 B. It was on sale.

 C. It was a gift from his parents.

24. A. He met her once before.

 B. He used to work with her.

 C. He doesn't know her.

25. A. The woman's trip.

 B. The man's holiday plans.

 C. Their vacation in Kenting.

第四部份：短文聽解　🎧 Tracks 116~120

共 5 題，每題有三個圖片選項。請聽光碟放音機播出的題目，並選出一個最適合的圖片。每題播出一遍。

■ Question 26

A	B	C

■ Question 27

A	B	C

■ **Question 28**

A	B	C
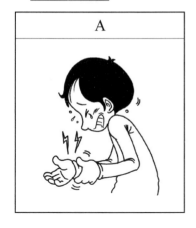		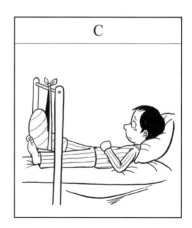

■ **Question 29**

A	B	C
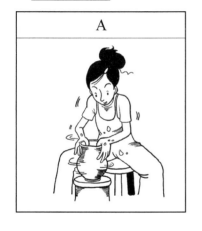		

■ **Question 30**

A	B	C

全民英檢閱讀能力測驗
第四回 模擬試題答案紙

准考證號碼：521-17-00123　　　　　考生姓名：＿＿＿＿＿＿＿＿＿＿＿＿＿

注意事項：

1. 限用 2B 鉛筆作答，否則不予計分。

2. 劃記要粗黑、清晰、不可出格，擦拭要清潔，若劃記過輕或汙損不清，不為機器所接受，考生自行負責。

3. 作答樣例：正確方式　錯誤方式

閱讀能力測驗

	A B C D		A B C D
1	□ □ □ □	26	□ □ □ □
2	□ □ □ □	27	□ □ □ □
3	□ □ □ □	28	□ □ □ □
4	□ □ □ □	29	□ □ □ □
5	□ □ □ □	30	□ □ □ □
6	□ □ □ □	31	□ □ □ □
7	□ □ □ □	32	□ □ □ □
8	□ □ □ □	33	□ □ □ □
9	□ □ □ □	34	□ □ □ □
10	□ □ □ □	35	□ □ □ □
11	□ □ □ □		
12	□ □ □ □		
13	□ □ □ □		
14	□ □ □ □		
15	□ □ □ □		
16	□ □ □ □		
17	□ □ □ □		
18	□ □ □ □		
19	□ □ □ □		
20	□ □ □ □		
21	□ □ □ □		
22	□ □ □ □		
23	□ □ □ □		
24	□ □ □ □		
25	□ □ □ □		

全民英檢初級閱讀能力測驗
第四回模擬試題

二、閱讀能力測驗

本測驗分三部份，全部都是單選題，共 35 題，作答時間 35 分鐘。

第一部份：詞彙和結構

共 15 題，每個題目裡有一個空格。請從四個選項中選出一個最適合題意的字或詞作答。

1. Billy is too ____ to ask any questions in class. He always asks his sister for help after school.

   A. shy
   B. brave
   C. polite
   D. talkative

2. My grandmother is starting to learn how to use a computer, and she just got an e-mail ____.

   A. garage
   B. object
   C. address
   D. block

3. Have you ____ the new movie playing at the theater downtown?

   A. tried
   B. gone
   C. looked
   D. seen

4. Mr. Brown loves traveling. He has ____ England, Canada, Egypt, and Brazil, and he is in Japan right now.

   A. been to
   B. had to
   C. gone to
   D. went to

5. The spicy food Mike ____ at the restaurant yesterday is giving him a very bad stomachache now.

   A. is eating
   B. will eat
   C. eat
   D. ate

6. Catherine ____, but he lost it in just one day.

   A. to Henry lent her book

   B. for Henry to lend her book

   C. lent her book to Henry

   D. lent her book from Henry

7. During the summertime, my cat likes to ____ on the floor to keep himself cool.

   A. lying   B. laid

   C. lay   D. lie

8. One of Sandy's dreams ____ around the world before she turns 35 years old.

   A. are traveling   B. is to travel

   C. will travel   D. travels

9. All of the students went on the field trip ____ for Bill, who came down with the flu today.

   A. in addition   B. as well

   C. including   D. except

10. Kevin really ____ his father. He always turns to his father for help when in trouble.

    A. makes up for   B. looks up to

    C. puts up with   D. hangs up on

11. You need to click on the button in order ____ to the music on this stereo.

    A. listening   B. that listens

    C. to listen   D. will listen

12. _____ money is more difficult than I realized.

    A. Save

    B. Saving

    C. That saves

    D. By saving

13. Roger would like to try _____ like rock climbing or skydiving.

    A. excited something

    B. something excited

    C. exciting something

    D. something exciting

14. Michael is about _____ to junior high school.

    A. go

    B. to go

    C. going

    D. goes

15. Bill walked so fast that I couldn't _____ up with him.

    A. catch

    B. run

    C. hold

    D. pick

第二部份：段落填空

共 10 題，包括二個段落，每個段落各含四到六個空格。每格均有四個選項，請依照文意選出最適合的答案。

■ Questions 16-20

Billy wants to play a practical joke on Mrs. Brown. He decides to wrap up a spider as a gift and __(16)__. Billy knows that Mrs. Brown is afraid __(17)__ spiders, and he thinks that it will be very funny. Mrs. Brown screams when she opens the gift, and she __(18)__ Billy to stand in the corner as a punishment. Now, the rest of Billy's class is worried that Mrs. Brown won't be their teacher __(19)__ . So, they decide to __(20)__ her a special party and buy her some flowers.

16. A. give her to it   B. give it to her

    C. to her give it   D. for her to give

17. A. of   B. in

    C. to   D. at

18. A. carries   B. invites

    C. orders   D. argues

19. A. anything   B. anywhere

    C. anyone   D. anymore

20. A. gather   B. throw

    C. make   D. create

■ Questions 21-25

Families are different around the world. In some countries, such as Taiwan, it is common for three __(21)__ to live in the same house. On the other hand, young people in the United States often __(22)__ away from home when they finish school. They try __(23)__ on their parents. __(24)__ they don't live at home, they are still close with their family. They __(25)__ their family a visit often. Parents often like the change, too. They feel like they have a new life and often begin new activities.

21. A. nations   B. stations

    C. generations   D. directions

22. A. leave   B. jump

    C. climb   D. move

23. A. not depend   B. to not depending

     C. not to depend   D. depending not

24. A. If   B. Before

     C. Ever since   D. Even though

25. A. call   B. pay

     C. drop   D. bring

第三部份：閱讀理解

共 10 題，包括數篇短文，每篇短文後面有三至四個相關問題。
請由四個選項中選出最適合的答案。

■ **Questions 26-28**

> ### Help Wanted
>
> **Looking for a new, exciting career in radio?**
>
> **106.7 FM is looking for a DJ to host a live on-air talk show.**
>
> - *Must have at least two years of experience in radio or television.*
> - *You must also have a fun personality and a strong speaking voice.*
>
> **Send your resume and a demo tape to Chad at**
> **fun1067@pmail.com.**

26. What is 106.7 FM looking for?

     A. Someone to hold a party.

     B. Someone to play music.

     C. Someone to read the news.

     D. Someone to host a radio show.

27. What must you have to apply for the job?

   A. At least two years of work experience.

   B. A good knowledge of music.

   C. To be able to speak quickly.

   D. A good education.

28. How do you apply for the job?

   A. Mail your demo tape to the station.

   B. Send a resume by e-mail.

   C. Call Chad at the station.

   D. Fill out a form at the station.

■ **Questions 29-31**

September 15, 2013

Dear Emma,

   I love to go to new places every summer. This summer I went to a water park with my mom, dad, and brother. We went on the first weekend in August. I got to ride many water rides. My favorite was the big water slide. My brother and my dad went on the ride, too. My mom was too scared to go on the ride. She just watched us and took pictures. At the end of the day, we ate hot dogs and watched the sun go down. I hope I can go back there soon. It was so much fun! How about you? Where did you go this summer?

Sincerely yours,
George

29. What is George's letter about?

    A. A place he goes every year.

    B. A place he wishes to go to.

    C. A place that his family owns.

    D. A place he visited in the summer.

30. What is George's favorite thing at the water park?

    A. The sunset.

    B. The large pool.

    C. The big slide.

    D. The food and drinks.

31. What does George say about his mother?

    A. She prepared hot dogs for everyone.

    B. She feared to go on the ride.

    C. She didn't like the water park.

    D. She couldn't go on the trip.

■ **Questions 32-35**

Ben went to visit Leah at the end of last summer. After seeing that Leah hadn't done anything all summer but watch TV, he was disappointed in her. He decided to plan some fun activities for the last week before school. First, they went to the Taipei Water Park, but it was closed. The next day, they went to the zoo with Leah's little sister, but she disappeared. They spent the whole day looking for her. Finally, they took a three-day trip to the beach. Just as they arrived, a typhoon hit. It ruined the entire trip. It seemed like everything went wrong!

32. Why was Ben disappointed in Leah?

    A. Leah didn't enjoy watching TV.

    B. Ben thought she didn't like him anymore.

    C. She hadn't done anything all summer.

    D. She didn't want to see Ben before school.

33. What happened to Leah's sister at the zoo?

    A. She fell down and got hurt.

    B. Ben and Leah could not find her.

    C. She had a great time at the zoo.

    D. Leah and Ben made her go home.

34. Which of the following is NOT true?

    A. Leah watched TV all summer.

    B. The story took place during the week before school began.

    C. The Water Park was not open.

    D. The typhoon struck before they went to the beach.

35. What is a good title for this story?

    A. What an Unlucky Week

    B. How to Prepare for a Typhoon

    C. Having Fun at the Water Park

    D. A Wonderful Trip to the Zoo

全民英檢初級聽力測驗
第五回 模擬試題答案紙

准考證號碼：521-17-00123　　　　　考生姓名：_____

注意事項：

1. 限用 2B 鉛筆作答，否則不予計分。

2. 劃記要粗黑、清晰、不可出格，擦拭要清潔，若劃記過輕或汙損不清，不為機器所接受，考生自行負責。

3. 作答樣例：正確方式　錯誤方式

聽 力 測 驗

1 A B C	26 A B C
2 A B C	27 A B C
3 A B C	28 A B C
4 A B C	29 A B C
5 A B C	30 A B C
6 A B C	
7 A B C	
8 A B C	
9 A B C	
10 A B C	
11 A B C	
12 A B C	
13 A B C	
14 A B C	
15 A B C	
16 A B C	
17 A B C	
18 A B C	
19 A B C	
20 A B C	
21 A B C	
22 A B C	
23 A B C	
24 A B C	
25 A B C	

全民英檢初級聽力測驗
第五回模擬試題

一、聽力測驗

本測驗分四個部份，全部都是單選題，共 30 題，作答時間約 20 分鐘。作答說明為中文，印在試題冊上並經由光碟放音機播出。

第一部份：看圖辨義　🎧 Tracks 121~125

共 5 題，每題請聽光碟放音機播出的題目和三個英語句子之後，選出與所看到的圖畫最相符的答案。每題只播出一遍。

■ **Question 1**

■ **Question 2**

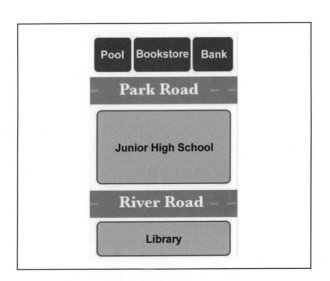

■ Question 3

■ Question 4

■ Question 5

第二部份：問答　　🎧 Tracks 126~135

共 10 題，每題請聽光碟放音機播出的英語句子，再從試題冊上三個回答中，選出一個最適合的答案。每題只播出一遍。

6. A. Walking is my favorite kind of exercise.

   B. I don't know, but it's time to take a break.

   C. We need to work hard and play hard.

7. A. I don't think I am. I just like to relax.

   B. You're right. I'm pretty busy.

   C. What? I'm not crazy!

8. A. Yes, I've been here once.

   B. Yes, I come here a lot.

   C. Yes, I wish I could come.

9. A. What happened? Is he sick?

   B. He must be very hungry.

   C. Are you feeling better now?

10. A. No, I don't have time right now.

    B. Yes, it's Friday today.

    C. Sure. It's 10:30.

11. A. That's terrible you dropped ice cream on the floor.

    B. Well, did you help clean up the floor?

    C. Why did you go to the second floor?

12. A. Good idea. We need more food.

    B. There's a drugstore on the corner.

    C. I think you have enough clothes.

13. A. She is talking to Mr. Lee.

    B. She is our new teacher.

    C. She is angry with me.

14. A. The package weighs two pounds.

    B. I will take the bus tomorrow.

    C. I will deliver it myself tomorrow.

15. A. I had to stay in bed for a week.

    B. They invited me back.

    C. It has been cold for the past month.

共 10 題，每題請聽光碟放音機播出一段對話和一個相關的問題後，再從試題冊上三個選項中，選出一個最適合的答案。每段對話和問題播出一遍。

16. A. In her left hand.

    B. At her home.

    C. At the restaurant.

17. A. No, she can't go out for dinner with them.

    B. Yes, but she is going to be a little late.

    C. She will change her plans and join them.

18. A. Only sofas.

    B. Everything but sofas.

    C. Many types of furniture.

19. A. The woman.

    B. The man.

    C. Both the man and woman.

20. A. He goes to work on foot.

    B. He usually has a meeting at 7:00.

    C. He does not live near his company.

21. A. It works really well.

    B. There's a problem with it.

    C. He spent a lot of money on it.

22. A. Do the dishes every day.

    B. Help his mother collect garbage.

    C. Wash the dishes and take out the garbage.

23. A. It is not nice to look at.

    B. She has a new one.

    C. The man broke it.

24. A. He already saw it, and it's quite interesting.

    B. He is too busy to see it.

    C. He doesn't think he would like it.

25. A. Because she forgot to bring her phone.

    B. Because he called the wrong number.

    C. Because her line is busy.

第四部份：短文聽解　🎧 Tracks 146~150

共 5 題，每題有三個圖片選項。請聽光碟放音機播出的題目，並選出一個最適合的圖片。每題播出一遍。

■ **Question 26**

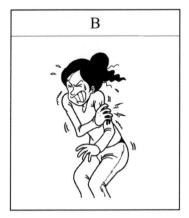

■ **Question 27**

■ Question 28

A	B	C
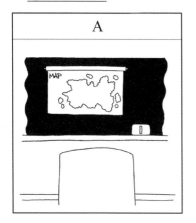		

■ Question 29

A	B	C
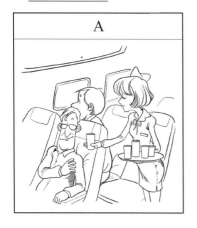	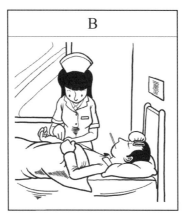	

■ Question 30

A	B	C

全民英檢閱讀能力測驗
第五回 模擬試題答案紙

准考證號碼：521-17-00123　　　　考生姓名：_____

注意事項：

1. 限用 2B 鉛筆作答，否則不予計分。

2. 劃記要粗黑、清晰、不可出格，擦拭要清潔，若劃記過輕或汙損不清，不為機器所接受，考生自行負責。

3. 作答樣例：正確方式　錯誤方式

閱 讀 能 力 測 驗

1	A B C D	26	A B C D
2	A B C D	27	A B C D
3	A B C D	28	A B C D
4	A B C D	29	A B C D
5	A B C D	30	A B C D
6	A B C D	31	A B C D
7	A B C D	32	A B C D
8	A B C D	33	A B C D
9	A B C D	34	A B C D
10	A B C D	35	A B C D
11	A B C D		
12	A B C D		
13	A B C D		
14	A B C D		
15	A B C D		
16	A B C D		
17	A B C D		
18	A B C D		
19	A B C D		
20	A B C D		
21	A B C D		
22	A B C D		
23	A B C D		
24	A B C D		
25	A B C D		

全民英檢初級閱讀能力測驗
第五回模擬試題

二、閱讀能力測驗

本測驗分三部份，全部都是單選題，共 35 題，作答時間 35 分鐘。

第一部份：詞彙和結構

共 15 題，每個題目裡有一個空格。請從四個選項中選出一個最適合題意的字或詞作答。

1. Mom is having a conversation with Aunt Molly _____ the phone.

   A. in   B. on

   C. to   D. by

2. The author's new novel is great. It is _____ as I expected.

   A. the most interesting   B. more interesting

   C. as interesting   D. so interesting

3. My grandfather fell down the _____ last night. Luckily, he didn't get hurt.

   A. faucets   B. stairs

   C. drawers   D. blankets

4. My brother likes to paint. He is a great _____.

   A. businessman   B. customer

   C. partner   D. artist

5. Jimmy doesn't like eating vegetables. He thinks they _____ terrible.

   A. act   B. spell

   C. taste   D. boil

6. It took six weeks for Mike's ____ leg to heal.

   A. breaking   B. break

   C. broke   D. broken

7. I'm lost. I don't know which way ____.

   A. gone   B. going

   C. to go   D. goes

8. I can't find my glasses, but I am sure they must be ____ in the room.

   A. where   B. somewhere

   C. everywhere   D. anywhere

9. Nobody knows what ____ in the future.

   A. happen   B. going to happen

   C. happening   D. will happen

10. The police are not sure ____ the man is the killer or not.

    A. why   B. what

    C. whether   D. however

11. I don't know if I should buy ____ sunglasses.

    A. a little   B. these

    C. this   D. a

12. My grandparents usually take a walk ____ the river after breakfast.

    A. in   B. over

    C. along   D. through

13. The rich man decided to give away his wealth and live ____.

    A. clearly   B. simply

    C. locally   D. recently

14. My neighbor's dog barked all night. He almost ____ me crazy!

    A. blew   B. chased

    C. shouted   D. drove

15. When you hold the baby, you must be ____.

    A. sudden   B. positive

    C. gentle   D. fair

第二部份：段落填空

共 10 題，包括二個段落，每個段落各含四到六個空格。每格均有四個選項，請依照文意選出最適合的答案。

■ Questions 16-20

It's true when they say that big things come in small packages. Just look at Taroko National Park. It is not big. It is not __(16)__ Taiwan's biggest national park. However, many people think it's the best __(17)__. It is popular with tourists from __(18)__ Taiwan and abroad. Since Taroko isn't big, you can see the best __(19)__ in one day. You can travel around it by tour bus, by car, or by scooter. You can even travel __(20)__ foot!

16. A. always   B. only

    C. sometimes   D. even

17. A. one   B. other

    C. ones   D. another

18. A. either   B. both

    C. not only   D. as well as

19. A. parts   B. piles

    C. plans   D. prices

20. A. with   B. by

    C. on   D. at

■ Questions 21-25

Debbie and Sue are friends from high school. Now, they are at __(21)__ ten-year class reunion. They are happy to know that they live near __(22)__ . Sue wants to contact Debbie soon. Debbie tells Sue that she can reach her at home or at her office. __(23)__ Debbie leaves, she tells Sue to get in touch with her soon. Sue tells Debbie that she __(24)__ out of town next week. __(25)__ , she will give her a call when she returns.

21. A. they're   B. theirs

    C. their   D. them

22. A. each one   B. one other

    C. another one   D. each other

23. A. Because   B. Before

    C. After   D. Although

24. A. was   B. would be

    C. went   D. will be

25. A. Therefore   B. Besides

    C. Already   D. Or

第三部份：閱讀理解

共 10 題，包括數篇短文，每篇短文後面有三至四個相關問題。
請由四個選項中選出最適合的答案。

■ Questions 26-28

Old Joe's Restaurant

99 Park Road

Open 24 hours, even on holidays!

Pizza	$2 / piece
Spaghetti	$6.49
Onion rings	$1.59
Soda or Coke	$1

Apple or Cherry Pie

Free with every meal!

26. When is Old Joe's Restaurant open?

   A. Only on holidays.

   B. All the time.

   C. Only on weekends.

   D. Every day except holidays.

27. What is the most expensive thing on the menu?

   A. The spaghetti.

   B. The pizza.

   C. The pie.

   D. The onion rings.

28. What do you get with every meal?

    A. A toy.

    B. Some fruit.

    C. A drink.

    D. Free dessert.

■ **Questions 29-31**

> August 19, 2013
>
> Dear Diary,
>
>   Today was not my day. First, I woke up late and didn't have time for breakfast. On my walk to school, it started raining, and I didn't have my umbrella, so I got wet. In math class, Mr. Jones gave us a surprise quiz. I just know I didn't do well.
>
>   But the worst thing happened at lunch. I was walking to my seat when I tripped and fell. My lunch landed on the floor. I was so sad that I cried. And I felt hungry all afternoon. At least I am home now. I can go to sleep and forget this awful, no good, very bad day.
>
> Anita

29. What kind of day did Anita have?

    A. A wonderful day.

    B. A terrible day.

    C. A lucky day.

    D. An interesting day.

R
初級英檢
全民閱讀
5

30. How did Anita get to school?

    A. She went to school on foot.

    B. She took the train.

    C. She rode her bike to school.

    D. She took the bus.

31. What happened to Anita at lunch?

    A. She felt sick.

    B. She didn't have a seat.

    C. She fell and dropped her lunch.

    D. She didn't have enough money.

■ Questions 32-35

Camping in Taiwan can be a lot different from camping in North America. One time, I decided to camp at Yang Ming Mountain with some friends. I brought my tent but was surprised to find that the place already had tents set up. We enjoyed a barbecue, and I suggested we build a fire before dark. But the people working at the campground said fires were not allowed. The most important part of camping was the same in Taiwan, though. I was able to enjoy some time in nature with some good friends.

32. What is the main idea of the passage?

    A. Camping in America is fun.

    B. There are great places to camp in Taiwan.

    C. It's always better to camp with friends.

    D. Camping in Taiwan is not the same as in the West.

33. How is camping in Taiwan different from camping in North America?

   A. Tents are set up in Taiwan.

   B. Most camp areas are in the mountains in Taiwan.

   C. People enjoy barbecues in Taiwan.

   D. Camping is not popular in Taiwan.

34. Why didn't the author build a campfire at the campground?

   A. She wanted to go to sleep.

   B. Workers at the campsite wouldn't let her.

   C. She didn't know how to.

   D. Other campers invited her to share their fire.

35. What does the author say is the same about camping in Taiwan and North America?

   A. She can go camping anywhere she wants.

   B. She can meet some new people.

   C. She can spend time outdoors with friends.

   D. She can take a hike.

R

全民英檢
初級閱讀

5

全民英檢初級聽力測驗
第六回 模擬試題答案紙

准考證號碼：521-17-00123　　　　考生姓名：＿＿＿＿＿＿＿＿＿＿＿

注意事項：

1. 限用 2B 鉛筆作答，否則不予計分。

2. 劃記要粗黑、清晰、不可出格，擦拭要清潔，若劃記過輕或汙損不清，不為機器所接受，考生自行負責。

3. 作答樣例：正確方式　錯誤方式

聽 力 測 驗

1	A B C		26	A B C
2	A B C		27	A B C
3	A B C		28	A B C
4	A B C		29	A B C
5	A B C		30	A B C
6	A B C			
7	A B C			
8	A B C			
9	A B C			
10	A B C			
11	A B C			
12	A B C			
13	A B C			
14	A B C			
15	A B C			
16	A B C			
17	A B C			
18	A B C			
19	A B C			
20	A B C			
21	A B C			
22	A B C			
23	A B C			
24	A B C			
25	A B C			

全民英檢初級聽力測驗
第六回模擬試題

一、聽力測驗

本測驗分四個部份，全部都是單選題，共 30 題，作答時間約 20 分鐘。作答說明為中文，印在試題冊上並經由光碟放音機播出。

第一部份：看圖辨義　🎧 Tracks 151~155

　　共 5 題，每題請聽光碟放音機播出的題目和三個英語句子之後，選出與所看到的圖畫最相符的答案。每題只播出一遍。

■ **Question 1**

■ **Question 2**

■ Question 3

■ Question 4

■ Question 5

第二部份：問答　🎧 Tracks 156~165

共 10 題，每題請聽光碟放音機播出的英語句子，再從試題冊上三個回答中，選出一個最適合的答案。每題只播出一遍。

6. A. Really? What did she do wrong?

   B. Yeah! She's really responsible.

   C. Great! She really needs the money.

7. A. It smells like chicken soup.

   B. It tastes like strawberries.

   C. It looks like chocolate.

8. A. It's OK. They sell food there.

   B. I thought you could read without it.

   C. They won't let you on without it.

9. A. No, he only has a son.

   B. Yes, he has two dogs.

   C. No, he takes the bus.

10. A. No, I haven't bought a ticket yet.

    B. So we're going to the movies tomorrow?

    C. Don't worry. We still have ten more minutes.

11. A. No, you have to do it now.

    B. Thanks for cleaning it up.

    C. Yes, I cleaned it.

12. A. By train.

    B. Near a park.

    C. Around 10:30 p.m.

13. A. I didn't talk to you.

    B. Sorry. I didn't mean it.

    C. I thought you were hungry.

14. A. Yes, we leave at 7:00 p.m.

    B. No, I haven't had a chance to read it.

    C. I gave it back already.

15. A. Did you give him any food today?

    B. Why? Will he bite me?

    C. I wish I had enough money to buy it.

共 10 題，每題請聽光碟放音機播出一段對話和一個相關的問題後，再從試題冊上三個選項中，選出一個最適合的答案。每段對話和問題播出一遍。

16. A. A letter in the mail.

    B. A letter on the computer.

    C. A birthday card.

17. A. She feels better.

    B. She still feels bad.

    C. She feels worse.

18. A. Run fast enough.

    B. Give the ball to others.

    C. Get enough points.

19. A. It is the wrong size.

    B. She doesn't like the color.

    C. She has too many dresses already.

20. A. He is writing a play.

    B. He got tickets for a play.

    C. He is acting in a play.

21. A. What they talk about in the meeting.

    B. Where they hold the meeting.

    C. Who is at the meeting.

22. A. In the basement.

    B. Next to the fence.

    C. Outside the yard.

23. A. She's pretty.

    B. She's tall.

    C. She's thin.

24. A. She is a customer.

    B. She is a waitress.

    C. She is the man's secretary.

25. A. A boring movie.

    B. A sad movie.

    C. A funny movie.

初級全民英檢聽力 L 6

第四部份：短文聽解　Tracks 176~180

共 5 題，每題有三個圖片選項。請聽光碟放音機播出的題目，並選出一個最適合的圖片。每題播出一遍。

■ **Question 26**

A	B	C
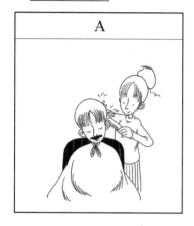	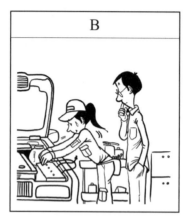	

■ **Question 27**

A	B	C
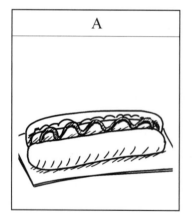	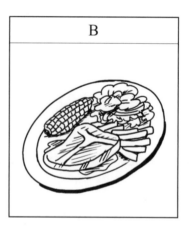	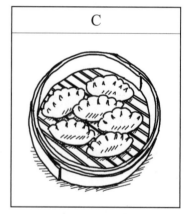

■ Question 28

A	B	C
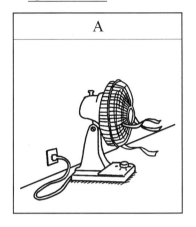		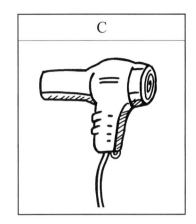

■ Question 29

A	B	C
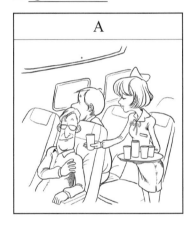		

■ Question 30

A	B	C

全民英檢閱讀能力測驗
第六回 模擬試題答案紙

准考證號碼：521-17-00123　　　　　考生姓名：＿＿＿＿＿＿＿＿＿＿＿＿

注意事項：

1. 限用 2B 鉛筆作答，否則不予計分。

2. 劃記要粗黑、清晰、不可出格，擦拭要清潔，若劃記過輕或汙損不清，不為機器所接受，考生自行負責。

3. 作答樣例：正確方式　錯誤方式

閱 讀 能 力 測 驗

#						#				
1	A	B	C	D		26	A	B	C	D
2	A	B	C	D		27	A	B	C	D
3	A	B	C	D		28	A	B	C	D
4	A	B	C	D		29	A	B	C	D
5	A	B	C	D		30	A	B	C	D
6	A	B	C	D		31	A	B	C	D
7	A	B	C	D		32	A	B	C	D
8	A	B	C	D		33	A	B	C	D
9	A	B	C	D		34	A	B	C	D
10	A	B	C	D		35	A	B	C	D
11	A	B	C	D						
12	A	B	C	D						
13	A	B	C	D						
14	A	B	C	D						
15	A	B	C	D						
16	A	B	C	D						
17	A	B	C	D						
18	A	B	C	D						
19	A	B	C	D						
20	A	B	C	D						
21	A	B	C	D						
22	A	B	C	D						
23	A	B	C	D						
24	A	B	C	D						
25	A	B	C	D						

全民英檢初級閱讀能力測驗
第六回模擬試題

二、閱讀能力測驗

本測驗分三部份，全部都是單選題，共 35 題，作答時間 35 分鐘。

第一部份：詞彙和結構

共 15 題，每個題目裡有一個空格。請從四個選項中選出一個最適合題意的字或詞作答。

1. The snake was still _____ even after it was run over by the car.

    A. alive   B. basic

    C. legal   D. instant

2. Johnny, it's ten o'clock. It's time for you _____ to bed.

    A. went   B. to go

    C. going   D. will go

3. The good thing about traveling is _____ you can leave your worries at home.

    A. so   B. after

    C. that   D. whether

4. Geography is my _____ subject. I like it best.

    A. private   B. painful

    C. funny   D. favorite

5. Remember to turn _____ the light when you leave the room.

    A. around   B. over

    C. off   D. in

6. There are usually traffic _____ on this busy road during rush hour.

    A. jams   B. crowds

    C. errors   D. bases

7. Yellow diamonds are _____. That's why they're so expensive.

    A. ordinary   B. plenty

    C. usual   D. rare

8. Mother's Day is on the _____ Sunday of May.

    A. two   B. second

    C. double   D. twice

9. The son of your brother or sister is your _____.

    A. niece   B. cousin

    C. nephew   D. grandson

10. When summer comes, the beach is always _____ of people on weekends.

    A. able   B. full

    C. huge   D. sure

11. The power failure in this area _____ the typhoon.

    A. was caused   B. caused by

    C. was caused by   D. has caused in

12. Amy was sad because she didn't receive _____ gifts on her birthday.

    A. all   B. few

    C. some   D. any

13. You cannot _____ your car in the middle of the street.

    A. park   B. pick

    C. pull   D. push

14. People in Taiwan are _____. They are always happy to help others.

    A. dizzy   B. noisy

    C. lonely   D. friendly

15. You have to pay a tip for the waiter's _____ at this restaurant.

    A. system   B. service

    C. solution   D. sample

第二部份：段落填空

共 10 題，包括二個段落，每個段落各含四到六個空格。每格均有四個選項，請依照文意選出最適合的答案。

■ Questions 16-20

    There once lived an old dog. When he was young, he was loved by his owner __(16)__ because he was the greatest hunter. But when he got old, he __(17)__ weak and slow.

    One day, the old dog and his owner __(18)__ in the forest when they saw a wild pig. The dog began to chase it. Finally, he caught the pig __(19)__ the ear. Unfortunately, __(20)__ his teeth were weak, the pig easily pulled away. The dog was worried that his owner would be angry.

16. A. very   B. lot

    C. very much   D. so many

17. A. changed   B. became

    C. started   D. made

18. A. were walking   B. would walk

    C. have walked   D. was walking

19. A. for   B. over

    C. by   D. at

20. A. if   B. although

    C. before   D. since

■ Questions 21-25

Daniel is reading a book about English names. He is interested __(21)__ changing his name. He thinks the name "Daniel" is __(22)__. In Taiwan, people get to choose their own English names. Daniel __(23)__ his name for himself when he started to learn English two years ago. In other words, "Daniel" is not his __(24)__ name. Daniel's friends think it's great that he can choose any name. Daniel's friend, Skip, wants him to __(25)__ his name in the book. He jokes that "Skip" must mean "super handsome"!

21. A. at   B. in

    C. by   D. on

22. A. bored   B. excited

    C. boring   D. exciting

23. A. selected   B. filled

    C. counted   D. ordered

24. A. family   B. new

    C. right   D. real

25. A. look at   B. look up

    C. look after   D. look down

第三部份：閱讀理解

共 10 題，包括數篇短文，每篇短文後面有三至四個相關問題。
請由四個選項中選出最適合的答案。

■ Questions 26-28

> ### *Attention*
>
> *Cougars have been seen in this mountain area for the past few weeks. Cougars usually eat small animals, but if they can't find them, they'll eat larger animals. So, keep children and pets close to you, or they could become a cougar's food!*
>
> If you see a cougar, follow these rules:
>
> ☻ Pick up small children first.
> ☻ Face the animal and walk backward slowly—NEVER run.
> ☻ Don't take your eyes off the animal.
> ☻ Shout or throw stones at the animal—it may get scared and run away.

26. What would be a cougar's first choice for food?

　A. A tall, heavy man.

　B. A bear.

　C. An elephant.

　D. A rabbit.

27. What shouldn't you do if you see a cougar?

    A. Turn around and run quickly.

    B. Shout loudly.

    C. Keep the cougar in sight.

    D. Throw small rocks at it.

28. What is the main purpose of this notice?

    A. To welcome people to this mountain area.

    B. To encourage people to hike in this mountain area.

    C. To warn people of danger in this mountain area.

    D. To give people directions to this mountain area.

■ **Questions 29-32**

To: wendy@bbc.com.tw
From: lucylin@coolnet.com
Sub: Trip to Spain
Sent: December 20, 2013

Dear Wendy,

How's your summer going?
I'm sad that I don't see you at the office anymore. I'm studying Spanish here in Taiwan since I am going to visit you in Spain during the Chinese New Year. What's it like there? Do you like your classes? When we meet up there, we can have dinner. You choose the restaurant, and I'll pay. Make sure that you choose somewhere with nice Spanish food.

I'll stay at a hotel near your school. I'll arrive on January 29, but it will be late at night. So, you can give me a call the next day. Oh, I got a new cell phone! My new number is 0911-234-567.

See you soon.

                                                     Lucy

29. Why does Lucy write to Wendy?

   A. She hopes Wendy to give her new number to her.

   B. She wants to get together with Wendy.

   C. She hopes to pick the restaurant for their dinner.

   D. She wants Wendy to teach her Spanish.

30. How do Lucy and Wendy know each other?

   A. They went to the same school.

   B. They are teacher and student.

   C. They worked together.

   D. They met each other in Spain.

31. How does Lucy get in touch with Wendy?

   A. She calls her on her cell phone.

   B. She sends her a postcard.

   C. She visits her school.

   D. She sends her an e-mail.

32. What do we know from this letter?

   A. Lucy will treat Wendy to dinner.

   B. Wendy will call Lucy on January 29.

   C. Wendy will return to Taiwan this Chinese New Year.

   D. Lucy wants to stay with Wendy when she visits Spain.

■ Questions 33-35

David likes to ride his bike to school. He thinks it is the best way to get to school. He can avoid all the cars and get to school early. David doesn't like the pollution in his city, though. It makes him hard to breathe when he rides his bike. Sometimes drivers don't watch out for bike riders. David tries to tell all of his friends to be careful when they drive. If they don't watch for bike riders, they might cause a lot of trouble!

33. Why is David able to get to school early?

    A. His friends drive him every day.

    B. His scooter is really fast.

    C. He lives close to his school.

    D. He doesn't have to worry about traffic.

34. What doesn't David like about riding to school?

    A. It makes him tired.

    B. Air pollution is a problem.

    C. Other people drive too fast.

    D. There is a lot of traffic.

35. Which of the following is TRUE?

    A. Pollution is a problem for David's friends.

    B. Most of David's friends are careful drivers.

    C. Drivers sometimes don't pay attention to bike riders.

    D. David always rides his bike carelessly.

全民英檢初級

聽力錄音稿

一、聽力測驗

本測驗分四個部份，全部都是單選題，共 30 題，作答時間約 20 分鐘。作答說明為中文，印在試題冊上並經由光碟放音機播出。

第一部份：看圖辨義

共 5 題，每題請聽光碟放音機播出的題目和三個英語句子之後，選出與所看到的圖畫最相符的答案。每題只播出一遍。

1. What are the men in the picture doing?

   A. They are having a fight.

   B. They are shaking hands.

   C. They are stealing money.

2. Where are the books?

   A. They are on the desk.

   B. They are against the wall.

   C. They are between the clock and the calendar.

3. What is true about Jack's schedule?

   A. He has a lot of free time.

   B. He is available on Wednesday.

   C. He is busy every day.

4. Where is Fluffy?

   A. In the man's arms.

   B. On the desk.

   C. Under the table.

5. What is true about the woman?

   A. She is riding a scooter.

   B. She is wearing a hat.

   C. She is running a race.

第二部份：問答

共 10 題，每題請聽光碟放音機播出的英語句子，再從試題冊上三個回答中，選出一個最適合的答案。每題只播出一遍。

6. What instrument do you want to learn how to play?

7. What do you think you will be when you grow up?

8. Can I ask you for some advice?

9. Does that steak come with a baked potato?

10. John did a wonderful job on his math test.

11. Do you have a minute for me?

12. Do you like to cook?

13. You should put a lock on your bike.

14. Bernice has made plans for summer vacation.

15. What do you like to do in your free time?

第三部份：簡短對話

共 10 題，每題請聽光碟放音機播出一段對話和一個相關的問題後，再從試題冊上三個選項中，選出一個最適合的答案。每段對話和問題播出一遍。

16. M: Where is Jack?
    W: He said he was going to the library.
    M: I didn't see him there.
    W: I can't believe he told me a lie!
    Q: What did Jack do?

17. M: Kathy, why are you in a hurry?
    W: I have to rush to the hospital.
    M: Why?
    W: My brother got into a car accident and was sent to the hospital.
    M: That's too bad. Do you need me to give you a ride?
    W: That will be great.
    Q: What will happen next?

18. W: Food and drinks are not allowed in the computer classroom.
    M: Oh, I'm sorry. It won't happen again.
    Q: What does the teacher mean?

19. M: My daughter wants a smartphone.
    W: Are you going to buy her one?
    M: I guess so. All her friends have one.
    W: Yes, they are very popular at the moment.
    M: I should get one for my wife and myself, too.
    Q: How many smartphones will the man probably buy?

20. M: Hi, Brenda. How was the movie?
    W: Great! Have you seen it? It's about a princess and a monster.
    M: I haven't yet, but I want to.
    W: It was so sad at the end that I had tears in my eyes.
    Q: What might happen to the princess and the monster at the end of the movie?

21. W: Is the supermarket far from here?
    M: No, it's just around the corner.
    W: Do you need me to get you anything?
    M: Yes, please pick up some milk for me.
    Q: Where is the supermarket?

22. M: I don't know why most people in the office don't like me.
    W: I think it's because you tell them what to do.
    M: But I'm just asking them to do their jobs while the boss is not in the office.
    W: You should stop doing that. You're not the boss after all.
    M: I think you should get back to your work, too.
    Q: Is the man the woman's boss?

23. M: Christmas is next week.
    W: I know! I'm quite excited.
    M: Me, too. What do you plan to do?
    W: I plan to take a two-week vacation. What about you?
    Q: How does the man feel about Christmas?

24. W: Why doesn't your son like going to school?
    M: He says that his classmates pick on him every day.
    Q: What may happen to the man's son at school?

25. W: Is it really cold outside?
    M: Yes, it's only 10°C today.
    W: Well, I have to go to the library.
    M: You should put on your coat. Here, take these, too. They can help keep your hands warm.
    W: Thanks, Dad. That's just what I need.
    Q: What does the man probably give his daughter?

第四部份：短文聽解

共 5 題，每題有三個圖片選項。請聽光碟放音機播出的題目，並選出一個最適合的圖片。每題播出一遍。

26. Please look at the following three pictures.

    David left a note for his son, Jack.

    What is wrong with Jack's mother?

    Please try to be nice to your mother today. She's been feeling very stressed because of her job. You know how she gets headaches when she's stressed out. So don't argue with her today. Let's be nice and help her calm down.

27. Please look at the following three pictures.

    Listen to the following short talk.

    What job does Ellen have?

    What do you think about Ellen? I'm thinking about making her in charge of the staff here. She always takes good care of the customers. She never brings the wrong dish to the wrong table. She seems smart and friendly, and she gets along with us bosses, too.

28. Please look at the following three pictures.

    Vincent is calling his friend.

    What kind of weather is Vincent in?

    Hi, Eric. It's Vincent. Let's go get some ice cream. I know I'm supposed to be on a diet, but I don't care. It's too hot. I need to eat something cold. After that, let's go find a place with air-conditioning. I absolutely cannot stand this heat anymore.

29. Please look at the following three pictures.

    Listen to the teacher talking to his students.

    What class is the teacher teaching?

    This area on the map here is called the Middle East. As you can see, it's between Europe and Asia. It is a land with a long, rich history. Does anybody know the names of any countries there? What are they?

30. Please look at the following three pictures.

    Listen to the following short talk.

    What job does the woman have?

    Who wouldn't want my job? I get paid just for wearing beautiful clothes and looking good in pictures. I get to meet famous people all the time, too. The only thing I don't like is having to diet all the time to stay skinny. No job is perfect, I guess.

一、聽力測驗

本測驗分四個部份，全部都是單選題，共 30 題，作答時間約 20 分鐘。作答說明為中文，印在試題冊上並經由光碟放音機播出。

第一部份：看圖辨義

共 5 題，每題請聽光碟放音機播出的題目和三個英語句子之後，選出與所看到的圖畫最相符的答案。每題只播出一遍。

1. How much does it cost to go from Taichung to Tainan?

   A. NT$130.

   B. NT$170.

   C. NT$530.

2. What is wrong with the man?

   A. He broke his arm.

   B. His back is in pain.

   C. He has a bad cold.

3. What is the girl trying to do?

   A. Chase the ball.

   B. Rent a ball.

   C. Catch the ball.

4. When does Sally usually get up?

   A. At 6:45.

   B. At 9:35.

   C. At 6:15.

5. How's the weather?

   A. It's cold and snowy.

   B. It's windy and rainy.

   C. It's hot and sunny.

第二部份：問答

共 10 題，每題請聽光碟放音機播出的英語句子，再從試題冊上三個回答中，選出一個最適合的答案。每題只播出一遍。

6. My parents know that I cheated on the test.

7. So, what were the results of your test?

8. How do you usually go to school?

9. Who does your uncle look like?

10. Why are you being so sneaky?

11. This computer was a waste of money.

12. Why does Bob look unhappy?

13. We would like to check in.

14. Excuse me. Is this seat taken?

15. Welcome. Have you booked a table, sir?

第三部份：簡短對話

共 10 題，每題請聽光碟放音機播出一段對話和一個相關的問題後，再從試題冊上三個選項中，選出一個最適合的答案。每段對話和問題播出一遍。

16. W: Christmas will be here soon. I'm so excited!

    M: Me, too. I love Christmas.

    W: I'm going to put my stocking up.

    M: I'll do that, too!

    Q: When is this conversation probably taking place?

17. M: May I help you?

    W: Yes! What's the price of the black shirt?

    M: It's $3,500.

    W: Oh! That's pretty expensive. I wonder if there is something cheaper.

    M: Well, here's a nice one for $990. I think it'll look great on you.

    Q: Where are the speakers?

18. M: I like this sofa. It's so comfortable.

    W: Yes, it's really nice.

    M: We should buy it.

    W: There isn't space for it in our apartment.

    Q: What's wrong with the sofa?

19. W: Are you ready to go?

    M: Yes. Do you know how to get there?

    W: Sure. I have a map.

    M: Great. Lead the way.

    Q: Who is going to go first?

20. W: Jenny's teacher called.

    M: What has she done now?

    W: She copied Allen's homework.

    M: We need to have a talk with her.

    Q: What did Jenny do?

21. M: Are you hungry, Lisa?

    W: Sure, Tim. Why?

    M: I got a couple of hamburgers. Want one?

    W: Yeah. Thanks!

    Q: How many hamburgers did Tim get?

22. M: Hi! I'd like to buy a new cell phone.

    W: OK, sir. Do you see any here you like?

    M: Is that one on sale?

    W: The black one? Let me check.

    Q: What does the man want?

23. W: Where are you, Marvin?

    M: I'm in the living room.

    W: Why don't you come with me for a walk?

    M: No, I'm busy surfing the Internet.

    W: Well, it's time for you to take a break.

    Q: What is the man doing?

24. M: How was your interview?

    W: The one I had yesterday?

    M: Yes. How did you do?

    W: I'm confident I got the job.

    Q: How did the woman do at the interview?

25. W: It's time to get up, Johnny.

    M: What time is it, Mom?

    W: It's a quarter to eight.

    M: Oh, no! I'm late for school.

    Q: What time is it?

第四部份：短文聽解

共 5 題，每題有三個圖片選項。請聽光碟放音機播出的題目，並選出一個最適合的圖片。每題播出一遍。

26. Please look at the following three pictures.

    Listen to the following short talk.

    What happened to the couple?

    Honey, you should stop the car. I smell smoke. I think it's coming from the engine. It may be getting too hot. We need to take a look and see what's going on under the hood. It may not be dangerous now, but it could be if we don't fix it soon.

27. Please look at the following three pictures.

    Listen to the following short talk.

    Who is the officer speaking to?

    Hello, sir. Do you know why I stopped you? You were going way too fast, and you rode through the red light. I'm going to have to write you a ticket. It's a good thing you're wearing a helmet, or you would have had to pay even more. Please ride more carefully next time.

28. Please look at the following three pictures.

    Listen to the following advertisement.

    What problem is it talking about?

    Do you feel older than you really are? Lower back pain is more common than you think. We can help you fix it. Put this pad on your lower back, and within an hour, you'll be getting around as if nothing was bothering you. Be yourself again!

29. Please look at the following three pictures.

    Listen to the following short talk.

    Who is the girl talking about?

    I'm so glad that man saved me. I woke up because of all the smoke in my room. My door felt hot, so I knew there was fire on the other side. I was so scared. But all of a sudden, the man broke down the door and carried me outside. I would be dead if it weren't for him.

30. Please look at the following three pictures.

    Gary is leaving a voice mail message.

    What kind of weather is Gary in?

    Hi, Anna. It's Gary. I don't think we should go hiking today. If we went now, it could be dangerous. I saw the wind blow down a tree earlier, and I don't want one to fall on us. Tomorrow should be less windy, so let's try to go then.

一、聽力測驗

本測驗分四個部份，全部都是單選題，共 30 題，作答時間約 20 分鐘。作答說明為中文，印在試題冊上並經由光碟放音機播出。

第一部份：看圖辨義

共 5 題，每題請聽光碟放音機播出的題目和三個英語句子之後，選出與所看到的圖畫最相符的答案。每題只播出一遍。

1. What is the boy doing?

   A. He is skiing.

   B. He is surfing the Internet.

   C. He is riding a skateboard.

2. What do we know about David's clothing business?

   A. It earns more than NT$4,000 a week.

   B. It makes less than NT$2,000 each month.

   C. It sells about 1,000 pieces of clothing every day.

3. What is true about the picture?

   A. The girl is hiding a ball from the boy.

   B. The girl and the boy are throwing away the ball.

   C. The boy is giving the girl a ball.

4. Which destination has the package with the longest stay?

   A. Japan.

   B. NT$17,500.

   C. 2 nights and 3 days.

5. What is true about the picture?

   A. The man is crying for help.

   B. The woman is running away.

   C. The man is robbing the woman of her bag.

第二部份：問答

共 10 題，每題請聽光碟放音機播出的英語句子，再從試題冊上三個回答中，選出一個最適合的答案。每題只播出一遍。

6. If you don't have a library card, you can't check out any books.

7. So, how big is your house?

8. I'm going to buy you a T-shirt. What is your favorite color?

9. What is the price of this table?

10. Excuse me, how do I get to a bank near here?

11. Are you going to the grocery store this afternoon?

12. How often do you play basketball?

13. Did you send Joe an e-mail?

14. I feel worse today.

15. Who is the author of this book?

第三部份：簡短對話

共 10 題，每題請聽光碟放音機播出一段對話和一個相關的問題後，再從試題冊上三個選項中，選出一個最適合的答案。每段對話和問題播出一遍。

16.M: The movie starts at 5:00 p.m.

    W: Oh, no! We are really running late.

    M: Take it easy. I don't like the first part of the movie anyway.

    Q: Why is the woman unhappy?

17.W: Our boss wants to know why you are late.

    M: Oh, no! It is going to be a long day.

    Q: What is the man saying?

18.M: What do you do on weekends?

    W: I love to go to the bookstore.

    M: Really?

    W: Yes, I could spend all day there.

    Q: What does the woman like to do?

19.W: Let's go to the movies tonight.

    M: Sure. Do you want me to pick you up?

    W: Great! How about 6:00 p.m.? We can have dinner on the way to the theater.

    M: No problem.

    Q: When will the speakers have dinner?

20.M: The cake is delicious.

    W: Then have some more.

    M: Where did you buy it? At the bakery around the corner?

    W: No, my mother baked it for me.

    Q: Where did the woman get the cake?

21.M: New York is a great city.

    W: We should go this winter.

    M: Maybe we should wait until summer.

    W: No, New York has too many visitors then.

    Q: What happens in New York in the summer?

22.W: Hey, Paul. Long time no see!

    M: Hello, Cindy. It's great to see you again.

    W: Do you have any time to chat tonight?

    M: No, but we can get together at lunch time tomorrow.

    W: OK. See you then.

    Q: When will the speakers meet?

23.W: Watching TV is really boring.

    M: So, what do you feel like doing then?

    W: Let's go shopping at the new department store.

    Q: What does the woman say about watching TV?

24.M: Did you buy that ring?

    W: No, it used to be my grandmother's.

    M: It's very beautiful.

    W: Yes, it's precious to me.

    Q: How did the woman get the ring?

25.M: I want to thank you by cooking you a meal.

    W: That is very nice of you.

    M: Do you like to eat steak?

    W: Of course. Steak is delicious!

    Q: What will the man cook for the woman?

第四部份：短文聽解

共 5 題，每題有三個圖片選項。請聽光碟放音機播出的題目，並選出一個最適合的圖片。每題播出一遍。

26. Please look at the following three pictures.

    Listen to the following news report.

    What job does the woman have?

    This is Barbara Waller reporting from the site of an apartment fire that started about half an hour ago. I have just learned that firefighters have rescued a father and two children and are now working on putting out the flames. I should be able to interview the fire chief later and will report back when I get more updates. Back to you, Ted.

27. Please look at the following three pictures.

    Listen to the following short talk.

    What kind of exercise does Duncan do?

    Wow! Look at Duncan over there. He's so strong. I don't understand how he lifts those huge weights. They're heavier than I am! He'll definitely win the competition. I've never seen arms that are as big as his. No wonder people are scared of him.

28. Please look at the following three pictures.

    Listen to the following short talk.

    What is Julia's hobby?

    Have you tried the cake yet? Julia made it. It's so good. I don't know how she finds time to cook such good food. She cooks even when she's tired from work. It's great to have a friend like her around. We always get to eat good food!

29. Please look at the following three pictures.

    Listen to the following short talk.

    What kind of activity does the boy enjoy?

    I don't like most sports, but I love being in the pool. I like the feeling of floating in the water and how all noises go away once my head is underwater. I also like how this exercises both my arms and legs. With more practice, I'll be the fastest on my team someday.

30. Please look at the following three pictures.

    Listen to the following commercial.

    Who works at this business?

    We're having a special this weekend. Come into our salon any time Saturday or Sunday, and our talented stylists will wash, cut, and style your hair for 30 percent off. Look like a million bucks without spending a million bucks!

一、聽力測驗

本測驗分四個部份，全部都是單選題，共 30 題，作答時間約 20 分鐘。作答說明為中文，印在試題冊上並經由光碟放音機播出。

第一部份：看圖辨義

共 5 題，每題請聽光碟放音機播出的題目和三個英語句子之後，選出與所看到的圖畫最相符的答案。每題只播出一遍。

1. What does the picture tell us?

   A. The red team has won by five points.

   B. The blue team has lost by twelve points.

   C. The blue team beat the red team by seven points.

2. Where are the people?

   A. They are planting trees in the garden.

   B. They are hiking in the forest.

   C. They are watching a movie in the theater.

3. What kind of club are the students in?

   A. A dance club.

   B. A drama club.

   C. A chess club.

4. How much do the pen and books cost?

   A. $50.

   B. $350.

   C. $300.

5. What is the boy doing?

   A. Listening to music.

   B. Acting in a play.

   C. Playing a game.

第二部份：問答

共 10 題，每題請聽光碟放音機播出的英語句子，再從試題冊上三個回答中，選出一個最適合的答案。每題只播出一遍。

6. Do you like to take a shower in the morning?

7. Vivian mixed blue and yellow paint.

8. Where can I try on this shirt?

9. How did the soccer game go? Who won?

10. How long does it take by train?

11. Hello, may I speak to Ms. Brown, please?

12. Oh, no! The lines are so long.

13. I'm in a rush. Let's discuss this tomorrow.

14. Should we buy a travel guide before we go to Hong Kong?

15. Dad's birthday is coming up.

第三部份：簡短對話

共 10 題，每題請聽光碟放音機播出一段對話和一個相關的問題後，再從試題冊上三個選項中，選出一個最適合的答案。每段對話和問題播出一遍。

16. W: I'm worried about Jeremy.
    M: What's wrong? Isn't he in his bedroom?
    W: He is. But he never studies, and he plays video games all night.
    M: OK. I'll talk to him about it right away.
    W: Maybe I should call his teacher, too.
    Q: Who are the speakers talking about?

17. M: Hello. May I speak to Ms. Smith, please?
    W: This is she speaking.
    M: This is Maria's Bakery. Can we deliver a birthday cake to you this morning?
    W: A cake? Are you sure? I didn't order a cake.
    M: Well, it is a gift from Mr. Harrison.
    W: Oh, I see. Please have it delivered after 10:30 a.m.
    Q: Why is the woman surprised?

18. M: I'd like a sandwich, and my friend would like fried chicken, please.
    W: Will that be all?
    M: I'd also like a Coke, and my friend would like a piece of cake for dessert.
    W: Both of your orders will be ready soon.
    Q: What does the man's friend order?

19. M: Peter speaks French very well.
    W: Yes, he studied it in high school.
    M: He must have been a hardworking student.
    W: Yes. Actually, he's one of the best students I've ever taught.
    Q: Who is the man probably talking to?

20. W: Are you still coming over for dinner tonight?
    M: Yeah, I'll be over in an hour.
    W: Is there anything that you don't eat?
    M: I don't like seafood. By the way, do you want me to rent a DVD before I come over?
    W: That will be great!
    Q: What will the man stop to do on his way to the woman's place?

21. M: Hi, Mandy. What are you doing?
    W: I am studying my family tree.
    M: That must be very interesting.
    W: Yes. Actually, I just found out that my great-grandfather was once a general.
    Q: What is the woman doing?

22. M: I don't feel very well.
    W: Maybe you're coming down with a cold.
    M: I think I'll go home and rest.
    Q: What is the woman saying?

23. M: Do you like my new cell phone?
    W: Yes, it's nice. Was it expensive?
    M: Not really. I got it for fifty percent off.
    W: Really? Where did you buy it?
    Q: What does the man say about the cell phone?

24. W: That woman is looking at you.
    M: What woman?
    W: The one in the pink dress.
    M: She's a stranger to me. I don't remember seeing her before.
    Q: What does the man say about the woman in the pink dress?

25. M: The five-day holiday is coming up.
    W: What are you going to do?
    M: I think I'll just watch TV.
    W: You shouldn't waste time like that.
    M: Well, maybe I will go on a trip to Kenting.
    Q: What are the people discussing?

第四部份：短文聽解

共 5 題，每題有三個圖片選項。請聽光碟放音機播出的題目，並選出一個最適合的圖片。每題播出一遍。

26. Please look at the following three pictures.

Tiffany's mother is talking to her neighbor.

What is Tiffany learning to do?

I'm so proud of Tiffany. She's growing up so fast. I took off her training wheels, and she learned how to ride on two wheels in just one afternoon! She kept falling in the beginning, but I made sure she wore a helmet so she wouldn't get hurt. It's exciting how quickly she's learning.

27. Please look at the following three pictures.

Listen to the following short talk.

What activity does the couple enjoy?

Harry and I are busy most mornings. We like to go outside and exercise together. We're not the most athletic. We don't run that fast. But while we jog, we like to talk about what's happening in our lives. It's really a fun way to exercise.

28. Please look at the following three pictures.

Listen to the following message for Paul.

What is wrong with Tony?

Hello, Paul. It's Tony. Thanks for coming to visit me. I'm usually pretty bored in here because I can't really move around. Sometimes I read or watch TV, but usually I just lie here and think. I really like getting visitors. It helps me forget that I'm stuck in this room.

29. Please look at the following three pictures.

Listen to the following short talk.

What does Pam like to do?

Ever since Pam was a kid, she has loved reading so much. Before she went to school, she would read. After class, she would read her textbooks, and then read more of her favorite novels. She even keeps a pile of books next to her bed so she can read before she falls asleep.

30. Please look at the following three pictures.

Listen to the following short talk.

What class is the boy in?

When you're done using that, may I borrow it? I need it to make my sculpture. I think it will really make the face look good. I think I already did a good job making the body. What are you making? It looks so beautiful. Do you know what color you'll paint it later?

一、聽力測驗

本測驗分四個部份，全部都是單選題，共 30 題，作答時間約 20 分鐘。作答說明為中文，印在試題冊上並經由光碟放音機播出。

第一部份：看圖辨義

共 5 題，每題請聽光碟放音機播出的題目和三個英語句子之後，選出與所看到的圖畫最相符的答案。每題只播出一遍。

1. What is the boy doing?

   A. Crossing the street.

   B. Entering a store.

   C. Chasing the dog.

2. Where is the bookstore?

   A. Inside the junior high school.

   B. Next to the bank.

   C. Across from the library.

3. If Sam leaves home at 9:00 p.m., which show will he be able to see?

   A. The 7:00 p.m. one.

   B. The 8:50 p.m. one.

   C. The 10:15 p.m. one.

4. What is true about the picture?

   A. The phone is ringing.

   B. It is noon.

   C. There is a computer.

5. How many people are there in the classroom?

   A. The boy feels bored.

   B. He is studying hard in his room.

   C. There is one boy in the classroom.

第二部份：問答

共 10 題，每題請聽光碟放音機播出的英語句子，再從試題冊上三個回答中，選出一個最適合的答案。每題只播出一遍。

6. How long have we been walking? I am so tired.

7. Why are you so lazy?

8. Do you eat in this restaurant often?

9. Kevin is in the hospital.

10. Excuse me, sir. Do you have the time?

11. My mother was angry because I got mud on the floor.

12. I have to buy groceries tonight.

13. Who is that tall, beautiful woman in pink?

14. When will you send me that important package?

15. What happened when you got a bad cold last month?

第三部份：簡短對話

共 10 題，每題請聽光碟放音機播出一段對話和一個相關的問題後，再從試題冊上三個選項中，選出一個最適合的答案。每段對話和問題播出一遍。

16.M: I really enjoyed the meal at that restaurant.
　　W: Me, too. Oh, no.
　　M: What's the problem?
　　W: I think I may have left my purse there.
　　Q: Where is the woman's purse?

17.M: Why don't you come and eat dinner with us?
　　W: Thanks for the invitation, but I already have plans tonight.
　　M: Come on!
　　W: Maybe next time.
　　Q: Is the woman going to join them?

18.M: So, what does your father do?
　　W: He owns a furniture shop downtown.
　　M: Oh? Does he sell sofas?
　　W: He sells all kinds of furniture.
　　Q: What does the woman's father sell?

19.W: Hey, where are you going?
　　M: I have to mail my mom a package.
　　W: I can do that on my way to the supermarket if you want.
　　M: Thanks. I appreciate it.
　　Q: Who is going to mail the package?

20.W: Why does it take you an hour to get to work?
　　M: I live far away from my office.
　　W: What time do you have to get up every morning?
　　M: I usually get up at 6:30 and leave home at 7: 00.
　　Q: Why does the man have to get up early?

21.M: I bought this cell phone yesterday.
　　W: Good for you.
　　M: Well, something is wrong with it.
　　W: Are you sure? You should take it back then.
　　Q: What does the man say about his cell phone?

22.M: Mom, can you give me one hundred dollars?
　　W: Forget it!
　　M: Please! I will help do the dishes tomorrow.
　　W: OK. But you have to take out the garbage, too.
　　Q: What does the boy have to do to get the money?

23.M: What are you doing with the table?
　　W: I'm throwing it away.
　　M: What? Why are you doing that?
　　W: Because it is really ugly.
　　M: Why don't you just give it to me? Mine broke yesterday.
　　Q: Why is the woman throwing out the table?

24.W: My favorite actor's new movie is playing now.
　　M: Sorry, but I'm not interested.
　　W: Come on! I think you would like it.
　　M: Uh, I doubt it.
　　Q: What does the man say about the movie?

25.M: Hello, I'd like to speak to Betty.
　　W: There's no one by that name here.
　　M: Is this 2577-2324?
　　W: No, this is 2577-2327.
　　M: Oops! I'm so sorry.
　　Q: Why can't the man speak to Betty?

第四部份：短文聽解

共 5 題，每題有三個圖片選項。請聽光碟放音機播出的題目，並選出一個最適合的圖片。每題播出一遍。

26. Please look at the following three pictures.

Lucy left a message on Mark's answering machine.

What is wrong with Katie?

Hi, Mark. This is Lucy. I'm sorry, but I can't go to the movies with you tonight. I have to stay home to take care of my sister, Katie. She was climbing a tree, and she fell. A branch scratched her arm pretty badly. I hope you can find someone else to go with you. Bye!

27. Please look at the following three pictures.

Listen to the following news story.

What is the speaker talking about?

An old shipwreck was found on the ocean floor yesterday by a local woman who was out diving for fun. She decided to go to a spot in the ocean she had never been before and swam toward a large group of fish. When she got closer, she saw that they were swimming near a sunken ship.

28. Please look at the following three pictures.

Listen to the following message for Tina.

What class is Ted talking about?

Hi, Tina. It's Ted. I didn't see you in class yesterday. Do you want to see my notes? The lecture was pretty difficult. It was about all the different parts of the brain. Our test will be about which parts of the brain control certain parts of the body. Good luck with your studying.

29. Please look at the following three pictures.

Listen to the following short talk.

Who is the speaker talking about?

That's too bad you had a bad flight. My flight was great. It was really long, but the service was excellent. I never went thirsty because the attendant kept giving us drinks. Also, she was very polite and helped me whenever I asked.

30. Please look at the following three pictures.

Listen to the following short talk.

Where is the man?

Hi, I have a few things I'd like to take care of. First, I would like to deposit this check. Also, I'd like to take out $100 in cash. Lastly, I just came back from vacation, so I have some extra foreign money I'd like to exchange.

一、聽力測驗

本測驗分四個部份，全部都是單選題，共 30 題，作答時間約 20 分鐘。作答說明為中文，印在試題冊上並經由光碟放音機播出。

第一部份：看圖辨義

共 5 題，每題請聽光碟放音機播出的題目和三個英語句子之後，選出與所看到的圖畫最相符的答案。每題只播出一遍。

1. What can we say about the man?

   A. He can hardly put up with the woman.

   B. He is talking loudly to the woman.

   C. He is having a nice chat with the woman.

2. Where is the money?

   A. In the boy's pocket.

   B. On the ground.

   C. In the sky.

3. What is the man doing?

   A. Dialing a number.

   B. Buying a phone.

   C. Hanging up.

4. What is true about the woman?

   A. She is in a shop.

   B. She is at a meeting.

   C. She is on a date.

5. What is true about the boy?

   A. He is telling a lie.

   B. He is wearing glasses.

   C. He is eating a cookie.

第二部份：問答

共 10 題，每題請聽光碟放音機播出的英語句子，再從試題冊上三個回答中，選出一個最適合的答案。每題只播出一遍。

6. Jane made a big mistake at work today.

7. What does the red one taste like?

8. Oh, no! I forgot my ticket at home!

9. Does Robert keep a pet?

10. If we don't leave now, we'll be late!

11. Can I clean my room later on, Mom?

12. What time did you get home last night?

13. Hey! Why did you push me?

14. Did you book our train tickets?

15. Be careful! You shouldn't touch that dog.

第三部份：簡短對話

共 10 題，每題請聽光碟放音機播出一段對話和一個相關的問題後，再從試題冊上三個選項中，選出一個最適合的答案。每段對話和問題播出一遍。

16. M: Maggie, are you coming to my birthday party?
    W: What party? I wasn't invited.
    M: Sure you were. I e-mailed you.
    W: Oh, I never check my e-mail.
    Q: What did the man send Maggie?

17. M: I heard you were sick last week.
    W: Yeah, I had a bad cold.
    M: How are you now?
    W: I've recovered. Thanks.
    Q: How does the woman feel now?

18. M: I heard Danny is good at soccer.
    W: Yes, but he doesn't pass enough.
    M: You should tell him that.
    W: I already have.
    Q: What doesn't Danny do?

19. M: Hello! May I help you?
    W: Yes, I'd like to return this dress, please.
    M: Sure. What seems to be the problem?
    W: It was a gift. It doesn't fit me.
    Q: Why does the woman return the dress?

20. M: Yeah! I am so excited!
    W: Why are you so happy?
    M: I got a role in the school play!
    W: Wow, that's great! Congratulations, Andrew!
    Q: Why is Andrew so happy?

21. W: Hey Simon, are you going to the meeting?
    M: No, Amy. I have to see the dentist.
    W: Well, you may miss something important.
    M: Will you tell me what is discussed?
    Q: What does Simon ask Amy to tell him?

22. W: Ben wants to go for a bike ride.
    M: That's a good idea. Will you go with him?
    W: I want to, but our bikes aren't in the basement.
    M: Oh, look in the yard beside the fence.
    Q: Where will the woman likely find the bikes?

23. W: Who's that girl over there?
    M: Oh, that's Melissa. She is our new neighbor.
    W: She is so slender.
    M: Yes, she is. She is also tall and beautiful.
    Q: What does the woman say about Melissa?

24. W: What would you like to order, sir?
    M: Do you have any spaghetti?
    W: Sorry. We are all out.
    M: OK. I'll have pizza instead.
    Q: Who is the woman?

25. M: That was a great movie.
    W: I know! Thanks for the ticket.
    M: Anytime. I laughed so hard.
    W: Me, too.
    Q: What kind of movie did the man and woman watch?

第四部份：短文聽解

共 5 題，每題有三個圖片選項。請聽光碟放音機播出的題目，並選出一個最適合的圖片。每題播出一遍。

26. Please look at the following three pictures.

Listen to the following short talk.

Where is the man?

My doctor prescribed me this medicine. Please hurry up and give it to me. I'm feeling absolutely terrible. It's tiring for me just to stand up right now. I just want to go home, take some pills, and fall asleep.

27. Please look at the following three pictures.

Listen to the following short talk.

What will the boy have for lunch?

I don't feel like having a big meal today, so that's why I'm having this. I love eating it with lots of mustard and a little ketchup. That's it. I don't need any other toppings, like pickles or onions. Best of all, I can just eat it with my hands.

28. Please look at the following three pictures.

Listen to the following message for Tom.

What is broken?

Hi, Tom. This is Nick. The thing that keeps me cool in my apartment is broken. It's been so hot recently, and I don't have an air-conditioner. Now is the worst time for it to stop working. I think I'm going to melt at home. Can I go to your place now? Thanks.

29. Please look at the following three pictures.

Listen to the following short talk.

What did Mary and her friend do yesterday?

I had a great time with my friend yesterday. The main actor is so handsome! The story wasn't great, but I didn't care. My friend didn't seem to have such a good time, though. He didn't like the actors or the story!

30. Please look at the following three pictures.

Susan is leaving a message on Mark's answering machine.

What happened to Bill?

Hi, Mark. Do you know what happened to Bill? This morning, I was outside playing when he rode his bike in front of me. Then he must have hit a rock or something, and he fell flat on his face. He's at home right now because he doesn't want anybody to see him.

聽力 第一回模擬試題

第一部份 看圖辨義		第二部份 問答		第三部份 簡短對話		第四部份 短文聽解	
音軌	內容	音軌	內容	音軌	內容	音軌	內容
1	說明及 Q1	6	說明及 Q6	16	說明及 Q16	26	說明及 Q26
2	Q2	7	Q7	17	Q17	27	Q27
3	Q3	8	Q8	18	Q18	28	Q28
4	Q4	9	Q9	19	Q19	29	Q29
5	Q5	10	Q10	20	Q20	30	Q30
		11	Q11	21	Q21		
		12	Q12	22	Q22		
		13	Q13	23	Q23		
		14	Q14	24	Q24		
		15	Q15	25	Q25		

聽力 第二回模擬試題

第一部份 看圖辨義		第二部份 問答		第三部份 簡短對話		第四部份 短文聽解	
音軌	內容	音軌	內容	音軌	內容	音軌	內容
31	說明及 Q1	36	說明及 Q6	46	說明及 Q16	56	說明及 Q26
32	Q2	37	Q7	47	Q17	57	Q27
33	Q3	38	Q8	48	Q18	58	Q28
34	Q4	39	Q9	49	Q19	59	Q29
35	Q5	40	Q10	50	Q20	60	Q30
		41	Q11	51	Q21		
		42	Q12	52	Q22		
		43	Q13	53	Q23		
		44	Q14	54	Q24		
		45	Q15	55	Q25		

聽力 第三回模擬試題

第一部份 看圖辨義		第二部份 問答		第三部份 簡短對話		第四部份 短文聽解	
音軌	內容	音軌	內容	音軌	內容	音軌	內容
61	說明及 Q1	66	說明及 Q6	76	說明及 Q16	86	說明及 Q26
62	Q2	67	Q7	77	Q17	87	Q27
63	Q3	68	Q8	78	Q18	88	Q28
64	Q4	69	Q9	79	Q19	89	Q29
65	Q5	70	Q10	80	Q20	90	Q30
		71	Q11	81	Q21		
		72	Q12	82	Q22		
		73	Q13	83	Q23		
		74	Q14	84	Q24		
		75	Q15	85	Q25		

聽力 第四回模擬試題

第一部份 看圖辨義		第二部份 問答		第三部份 簡短對話		第四部份 短文聽解	
音軌	內容	音軌	內容	音軌	內容	音軌	內容
91	說明及 Q1	96	說明及 Q6	106	說明及 Q16	116	說明及 Q26
92	Q2	97	Q7	107	Q17	117	Q27
93	Q3	98	Q8	108	Q18	118	Q28
94	Q4	99	Q9	109	Q19	119	Q29
95	Q5	100	Q10	110	Q20	120	Q30
		101	Q11	111	Q21		
		102	Q12	112	Q22		
		103	Q13	113	Q23		
		104	Q14	114	Q24		
		105	Q15	115	Q25		

聽力 第五回模擬試題

第一部份 看圖辨義		第二部份 問答		第三部份 簡短對話		第四部份 短文聽解	
音軌	內容	音軌	內容	音軌	內容	音軌	內容
121	說明及 Q1	126	說明及 Q6	136	說明及 Q16	146	說明及 Q26
122	Q2	127	Q7	137	Q17	147	Q27
123	Q3	128	Q8	138	Q18	148	Q28
124	Q4	129	Q9	139	Q19	149	Q29
125	Q5	130	Q10	140	Q20	150	Q30
		131	Q11	141	Q21		
		132	Q12	142	Q22		
		133	Q13	143	Q23		
		134	Q14	144	Q24		
		135	Q15	145	Q25		

聽力 第六回模擬試題

第一部份 看圖辨義		第二部份 問答		第三部份 簡短對話		第四部份 短文聽解	
音軌	內容	音軌	內容	音軌	內容	音軌	內容
151	說明及 Q1	156	說明及 Q6	166	說明及 Q16	176	說明及 Q26
152	Q2	157	Q7	167	Q17	177	Q27
153	Q3	158	Q8	168	Q18	178	Q28
154	Q4	159	Q9	169	Q19	179	Q29
155	Q5	160	Q10	170	Q20	180	Q30
		161	Q11	171	Q21		
		162	Q12	172	Q22		
		163	Q13	173	Q23		
		164	Q14	174	Q24		
		165	Q15	175	Q25		

《全民英檢初級全真模考 + 詳解（擬真版 1）》讀者回函卡

謝謝您購買全民英檢初級全真模考 + 詳解（擬真版 1）產品

如果您願意，請您詳細填寫下列資料，免貼郵票寄回 LiveABC 即可
獲贈《CNN 互動英語》、《Live 互動英語》、《每日一句週報》電子學習
報 3 個月期（價值：900 元）及 LiveABC 不定期提供的最新出版資訊。

姓名　　　　　　　　**性別** □男 □女

出生日期　年　月　日

　　　　聯絡電話

住址

E-mail

學歷
□國中以下　　□國中　　□高中
□大專及大學　□研究所

職業
□學生　　　　□資訊業　　□工　　　□商
□服務業　　　□軍警公教
□其他 _____　　□自由業及專業

您從何處得知本書？

□書店　　　□網站
□電子型錄　□他人推薦
□雜誌
□其他 _____

您以何種方式購得此書？

□一般書店　□連鎖書店
□網路　　　□郵局劃撥
□其他 _____

您覺得本書的價格？

	偏低	合理	偏高
書名	□	□	□
封面	□	□	□
內容	□	□	□
編排	□	□	□
紙張	□	□	□

您對本書的評價

	書名	封面	內容	編排	紙張
很滿意	□	□	□	□	□
還不錯	□	□	□	□	□
普通	□	□	□	□	□
不滿意	□	□	□	□	□
很後悔	□	□	□	□	□

您希望我們製作哪些學習主題？

您對我們的建議：

縣　市

市區鄉鎮

村里路街

段

鄰巷

號

樓

室

１０５

台北市松山區八德路三段
32號
12樓

英語數位學習第一品牌

GEPT 完全命中

全民英檢 初級 聽力閱讀
全真模考✚詳解

擬真版 **1** 解析本 　　　*GEPT Mock Tests*

GEPT 完全命中

全民英檢 初級 聽力閱讀
全真模考✛詳解

擬真版 1 解析本　*GEPT Mock Tests*

發 行 人　鄭俊琪

社　　長　阮德恩

總 編 輯　陳豫弘

責 任 編 輯　林芸儀

英 文 編 輯　Jerome Villegas

封 面 設 計　羅靜琪

美 術 編 輯　羅靜琪

出 版 發 行　希伯崙股份有限公司

　　　　　　105 台北市松山區八德路三段 32 號 12 樓

　　　　　　劃撥：939-5400

　　　　　　電話：(02)2578-7838

　　　　　　傳真：(02)2578-5800

　　　　　　電子郵件：Service@LiveABC.com

法 律 顧 問　朋博法律事務所

印　　刷　禹利電子分色有限公司

出 版 日 期　2014 年 7 月 初版一刷

　　　　　　2018 年 10 月 初版四刷

目 錄

~ 第一回 模擬試題解答 ~

聽力 Listening

第一部份 看圖辨義	第二部份 問答		第三部份 簡短對話		第四部份 短文聽解
1. B	6. A	11. A	16. B	21. C	26. B
2. A	7. C	12. A	17. B	22. B	27. B
3. B	8. B	13. B	18. C	23. C	28. B
4. C	9. B	14. A	19. C	24. A	29. C
5. A	10. C	15. A	20. A	25. C	30. B

閱讀 Reading

第一部份 詞彙和結構			第二部份 段落填空		第三部份 閱讀理解	
1. C	6. D	11. A	16. B	21. A	26. A	31. A
2. A	7. B	12. A	17. A	22. C	27. B	32. A
3. C	8. D	13. C	18. C	23. B	28. D	33. C
4. D	9. C	14. A	19. C	24. A	29. B	34. B
5. C	10. D	15. C	20. D	25. D	30. C	35. D

第一回
聽力模擬試題解析

一、聽力測驗

本測驗分四個部份，全部都是單選題，共 30 題，作答時間約 20 分鐘。作答說明為中文，印在試題冊上並經由光碟放音機播出。

第一部份：看圖辨義

共 5 題，每題請聽光碟放音機播出的題目和三個英語句子之後，選出與所看到的圖畫最相符的答案。每題只播出一遍。

 1. What are the men in the picture doing?
   A. They are having a fight.
   B. They are shaking hands.
   C. They are stealing money.

Answer: B

本題測驗疑問詞 what 引導的疑問句，用 "What is someone doing?" 來詢問「某人正在做什麼？」。
從圖片判斷，可知答案為 B，shake hands：握手。

例：Don't shake hands with Tim. He never washes his hands. (不要跟 Tim 握手。他從不洗手。)

重要字彙

fight：(n. & v.) 爭吵、打架，**have a fight：**發生爭吵／打架　　　　　**steal：(v.)** 偷

 2. Where are the books?
   A. They are on the desk.
   B. They are against the wall.
   C. They are between the clock and the calendar.

Answer: A

本題用 "Where are...?" 來詢問「……在哪裡？」，測驗重點為表位置的說法。根據圖片，可知答案為 A，on the desk：在桌子上。
B. against the wall：靠在牆上
C. between the clock and the calendar：在時鐘和日曆中間

 3. What is true about Jack's schedule?

    A. He has a lot of free time.

    B. He is available on Wednesday.

    C. He is busy every day.

Answer: B

重要關鍵

本題測驗重點為 schedule：(n.) 時間表，busy：(adj.) 忙碌的，以及 free：(adj.) 有空的。題目問「關於 Jack 的時間表，何者為是？」，由圖片中可以看出，Jack 除了星期三有空以外，每天都很忙碌，故答案為 B，available：(adj.) 有空的。

例：Are you available this Saturday? (你這個星期六有空嗎？)

 4. Where is Fluffy?

    A. In the man's arms.

    B. On the desk.

    C. Under the table.

Answer: C

重要關鍵

本題測驗疑問詞 where 引導的疑問句，用 "Where is...?" 來詢問「……在哪裡？」。圖中的 Fluffy 正在桌子底下，故答案選 C。

 5. What is true about the woman?

    A. She is riding a scooter.

    B. She is wearing a hat.

    C. She is running a race.

Answer: A

重要關鍵

本題測驗「關於圖片中的女子，何者為是？」，由圖片中可以看出，這名女子正騎著一輛機車，故答案選 A，scooter (n.) 機車，ride a scooter：騎機車。

 重要字彙

wear：(v.) 穿、戴　　　　　　　　　　　　　**race：(n.) 比賽，run a race：賽跑**

第二部份：問答

共 10 題，每題請聽光碟放音機播出的英語句子，再從試題冊上三個回答中，選出一個最適合的答案。
每題只播出一遍。

6. What instrument do you want to learn how to play?
A. I want to take violin lessons.
B. I like to listen to music when I have free time.
C. My uncle owns a music store.

Answer: A

重要關鍵

instrument：(n.) 樂器，本題測驗重點為 what instrument：何種樂器，故答案選 A，take violin lessons：
上小提琴課，violin：(n.) 小提琴。

7. What do you think you will be when you grow up?
A. I sometimes help my mom grow vegetables.
B. I know. I'm the shortest in the class.
C. I think I want to be an animal doctor.

Answer: C

重要關鍵

本題測驗重點為 grow up：成長、長大。題目句意為「你認為你長大後會成為什麼？」，因此答案選 C，
animal doctor (動物醫生)，補充：vet：(n.) 獸醫。

重要字彙

vegetable：(n.) 蔬菜、青菜，grow vegetables：種菜

8. Can I ask you for some advice?
A. Yeah, please do me a favor.
B. Sure. What's the problem?
C. That's OK. I don't like rice.

Answer: B

重要關鍵

本題測驗重點為 advice：(n.) 忠告、建議，ask someone for advice：向某人徵詢忠告、建議。題目問
「我可以徵詢你的建議嗎？」，故答案選 B「當然，是什麼問題呢？」。

 重要字彙

favor : (n.) 恩惠，**do someone a favor** : 幫某人一個忙

例：**Would you please do me a favor? (** 可以請你幫我一個忙嗎？ **)**

---

9. Does that steak come with a baked potato?

    A. Yes, you can either have steak or a baked potato.

    B. Yes, you can get a baked potato with it.

    C. No, I asked for French fries.

Answer: B

 重要關鍵

本題測驗重點為 come with... : (主餐之外) 附有……菜。

例：Today's special comes with a plate of salad. (今日特餐附有一盤沙拉。)

故知答案應選 B。

 重要字彙

steak : (n.) 牛排

baked potato : 烤馬鈴薯，**bake** : (v.) 烘、烤

例：**It took me 40 minutes to bake the cookies. (** 我花了四十分鐘烤餅乾。**)**

French fries : (n.) 薯條

---

10. John did a wonderful job on his math test.

    A. Really? I thought John liked math class.

    B. That's true. John needs to study more.

    C. I know. John is very good at math.

Answer: C

 重要關鍵

本題測驗重點為 wonderful : (adj.) 很棒的。C 選項中的 be good at... (擅長於……) 與 do a wonderful job (表現極好) 相呼應，故答案為 C。

---

11. Do you have a minute for me?

    A. Sorry, I'm really busy right now.

    B. Sure. It's a quarter past nine.

    C. Yes, the meeting will take more than ten minutes.

Answer: A

重要關鍵

本題測驗重點為 "Do you have a minute for me?"，表示「你現在有空嗎？」或「能耽誤你一點時間嗎？」，其中 for me 可省略。

例：Do you have a minute (for me)? I need some advice. (你現在有空嗎？我需要一些建議。)

故答案為 A 「很抱歉，我現在忙翻了。」。

重要字彙

quarter : (n.) 一刻鐘、十五分鐘
例：a quarter past nine : 九點十五分，a quarter to nine : 八點四十五分

---

12. Do you like to cook?
　　 A. Yes, cooking is one of my favorite activities.
　　 B. Yes, that restaurant has delicious food.
　　 C. Yes, I love to eat birthday cake on my birthday.

Answer: A

重要關鍵

題目問「你喜不喜歡烹飪？」，選項 A 說「烹飪是我最喜歡的活動之一。」，用來回答本題最為適當，故答案為 A。

重要字彙

favorite : (adj.) 最喜愛的　　　　　　　　　　　　delicious : (adj.) 美味的

---

13. You should put a lock on your bike.
　　 A. Sorry, I have other plans.
　　 B. Yes, I don't want it to get stolen.
　　 C. No, I go to school by bus.

Answer: B

重要關鍵

本題測驗重點為 lock : (n.) 鎖。題目說「你應該在你的腳踏車上加把鎖。」，因此答案選 B「對啊，我不想它被偷。」。get stolen : 被偷，steal : (v.) 偷，動詞三態為 steal, stole, stolen。

重要片語

by bus : 搭公車

 14. Bernice has made plans for summer vacation.

    A. Really? What is she going to do?

    B. Yes, she just left for the party.

    C. Oh? I didn't know she likes summer.

Answer: A

 重要關鍵

本題測驗重點為 make plans for... : 為……做計劃。

例 : I'm making plans for my father's birthday party next Friday.

    (我正在為我父親下星期五的生日派對做計劃。)

因此答案選 A「她打算要做什麼？」。

 重要片語

leave for... : 出發前往……

例 : **I'll leave for Jackie's house soon. (我馬上就要出發去 Jackie 家了。)**

 15. What do you like to do in your free time?

    A. I usually go swimming or hiking.

    B. I will never shop there again.

    C. I am seldom late for school.

Answer: A

重要關鍵

本題測驗重點為 in your free time : 在空閒時間。題目問「你在空閒時間時喜歡做什麼？」，選項 A 指出兩項休閒活動，故為正確答案。go + V-ing 表「從事某活動」。

例 : go swimming (去游泳)，go hiking (去健行)，go shopping (去逛街)，go jogging (去慢跑)，go camping (去露營)。

第三部份：簡短對話

共 10 題，每題請聽光碟放音機播出一段對話和一個相關的問題後，再從試題冊上三個選項中，選出一個最適合的答案。每段對話和問題播出一遍。

16. M: Where is Jack?

W: He said he was going to the library.

M: I didn't see him there.

W: I can't believe he told me a lie!

Q: What did Jack do?

    A. Played a joke on the woman.

    B. Said something that isn't true.

    C. Stole something from the woman.

Answer: B

重要關鍵

tell a lie 是動詞片語「說謊」的意思，因此女生說 "I can't believe he told me a lie!" 是「我不敢相信他對我說謊！」之意，故答案選 B。

選項 A：play a joke 是「開玩笑」的意思；選項 C：steal 是動詞「偷；竊取」，整句為「從女子那裡偷走某物。」之意。

17. M: Kathy, why are you in a hurry?

W: I have to rush to the hospital.

M: Why?

W: My brother got into a car accident and was sent to the hospital.

M: That's too bad. Do you need me to give you a ride?

W: That will be great.

Q: What will happen next?

    A. The woman will send her brother to the hospital.

    B. The man will drive the woman to the hospital.

    C. The woman will meet the man at the hospital.

Answer: B

重要關鍵

本題測驗重點為 give someone a ride：載某人一程。

例：Can you give me a ride to the airport? (你可以載我去機場嗎？)

對話中男子問女子是否需要載她一程，女子回答說 "That will be great." (那就太好了。)，可知接下來男子會載女子去醫院，故答案為 B。

重要片語

in a hurry：匆忙的、趕時間   **rush to + 地方**：趕往某地

 18. W: Food and drinks are not allowed in the computer classroom.

　　M: Oh, I'm sorry. It won't happen again.

　　Q: What does the teacher mean?

　　　A. There are only a few computers in the classroom.

　　　B. You can learn how to cook on the Internet.

　　　C. Students must eat and drink outside of the classroom.

Answer: C

重要關鍵 💡

本題測驗重點為 be not allowed：不被允許。

例：Smoking is not allowed here. (此處禁止吸菸。)

選項 C 的 eat and drink 與題目中的 food and drinks (食物與飲料) 相呼應，故為正選。

重要字彙

the Internet : (n.) 網際網路

 19. M: My daughter wants a smartphone.

　　W: Are you going to buy her one?

　　M: I guess so. All her friends have one.

　　W: Yes, they are very popular at the moment.

　　M: I should get one for my wife and myself, too.

　　Q: How many smartphones will the man probably buy?

　　　A. One.

　　　B. Two.

　　　C. Three.

Answer: C

重要關鍵 💡

本題測驗重點有二：一為男子所說 "I guess so." (我想是吧。)，亦即他會買智慧型手機 (smartphone) 給他女兒；二為對話最後男子所說 "I should get one for my wife and myself, too." (我應該給我太太和自己也買一支。)，由此可知，他可能會買三支手機，故答案為 C。

重要字彙

popular : (adj.) 流行的

20. M: Hi, Brenda. How was the movie?

W: Great! Have you seen it? It's about a princess and a monster.

M: I haven't yet, but I want to.

W: It was so sad at the end that I had tears in my eyes.

Q: What might happen to the princess and the monster at the end of the movie?

    A. They could never see each other again.

    B. They lived happily ever after.

    C. They beat the bad guy and saved the world.

Answer: A

重要關鍵

男生問女生電影好不好看，女生回答 "It was so sad at the end that I had tears in my eyes."，tear 是名詞「眼淚」之意，因此整句的意思為「那部電影到最後好悲傷，悲傷到我都哭了。」由此可知，這部電影有個悲傷的結局，故答案選 A。

重要字彙

princess : (n.) 公主　　　　　　　　　　monster : (n.) 怪物、怪獸

beat : (v.) 擊敗，三態為 beat, beat, beaten　　bad guy : (n.) 壞人、壞蛋

重要片語

live happily ever after : 從此過著幸福快樂的生活

21. W: Is the supermarket far from here?

M: No, it's just around the corner.

W: Do you need me to get you anything?

M: Yes, please pick up some milk for me.

Q: Where is the supermarket?

    A. It is far away from where the woman lives.

    B. The woman should take a taxi.

    C. It is nearby.

Answer: C

重要關鍵

本題測驗重點為 around the corner : 在附近，故答案選 C，nearby : (adv.) 在附近。

重要片語

pick up... : 買……

例 : I'm going to pick up a newspaper from the store. (我要去商店買份報紙。)

far away from... : 離……很遠
take a taxi : 搭計程車
補充：take a train : 搭火車，take a plane : 搭飛機，take the MRT : 搭捷運

 22. M: I don't know why most people in the office don't like me.

W: I think it's because you tell them what to do.

M: But I'm just asking them to do their jobs while the boss is not in the office.

W: You should stop doing that. You're not the boss after all.

M: I think you should get back to your work, too.

Q: Is the man the woman's boss?

    A. No, the woman is the boss.

    B. No, the man is not the boss.

    C. Yes, the man is the boss.

Answer: B

 重要關鍵

從對話中女子說 "You're not the boss after all." (你畢竟不是老闆。) 可知，男子並不是老闆，故答案選 B。

 重要片語

after all : 畢竟、終究

例：Don't get mad at her. After all, she's just a kid. (別生她的氣。畢竟，她只是個小孩而已。)

 23. M: Christmas is next week.

W: I know! I'm quite excited.

M: Me, too. What do you plan to do?

W: I plan to take a two-week vacation. What about you?

Q: How does the man feel about Christmas?

    A. He's going to take a vacation.

    B. He doesn't care.

    C. He's very excited.

Answer: C

 重要關鍵

本題測驗重點為 Me, too. (我也是。)，用來回應別人自己也是如此。

例：Sam: The crowds are driving me crazy! (Sam: 這麼多人讓我快抓狂了！)

    Tom: Me, too! (Tom: 我也是！)

題目問「男子對於聖誕節感覺如何？」，在對話中，女子說自己對於下星期即將到來的聖誕節感到相當興奮 (quite excited)，男子回答說 "Me, too." (我也是。)，所以答案為 C。要去度兩個星期假的是對話中的女子，故 A 不予考慮。

24. W: Why doesn't your son like going to school?

M: He says that his classmates pick on him every day.

Q: What may happen to the man's son at school?

    A. His classmates make fun of him.

    B. He gets along well with his classmates.

    C. All of his classmates want to play with him.

Answer: A

重要關鍵 💡

本題測驗重點為 pick on someone：(口) 找某人的碴、找某人的麻煩。

例：Stop picking on me. (別再找我麻煩了。)

故答案選 A，make fun of...：取笑……。

例：They made fun of his funny voice. (他們拿他的怪嗓音來取笑他。)

重要片語 ✏️

get along well with someone：與某人相處得很好

例：**Mary gets along well with her neighbors. (Mary 和她鄰居都處得很好。)**

 25. W: Is it really cold outside?

M: Yes, it's only 10℃ today.

W: Well, I have to go to the library.

M: You should put on your coat. Here, take these, too. They can help keep your hands warm.

W: Thanks, Dad. That's just what I need.

Q: What does the man probably give his daughter?

    A. A pair of pants.

    B. A pair of socks.

    C. A pair of gloves.

Answer: C

 重要關鍵 💡

題目問「男子可能給他女兒何物？」，本題測驗重點為 help keep your hands warm (幫助妳的雙手保暖)，由此可知，答案應是「手套」，故選 C，a pair of gloves：一副手套。A 選項的 a pair of pants 是「一條褲子」，B 選項的 a pair of socks 則是「一雙襪子」。

第四部份：短文聽解

共 5 題，每題有三個圖片選項。請聽光碟放音機播出的題目，並選出一個最適合的圖片。每題播出一遍。

 26. Please look at the following three pictures.

David left a note for his son, Jack. What is wrong with Jack's mother?

Please try to be nice to your mother today. She's been feeling very stressed because of her job. You know how she gets headaches when she's stressed out. So don't argue with her today. Let's be nice and help her calm down.

A	B	C
	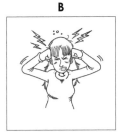	

Answer: **B**

 重要關鍵

今天請試著對媽媽好一點。她因為工作承受很大的壓力。你知道當她飽受壓力時，總是頭痛。所以今天不要跟她爭論任何事。讓我們對她好一點，並幫助她平靜下來。
由此可知，媽媽頭痛。

 重要字彙

stressed：(adj.) 有壓力的，be stressed out：飽受壓力的
headache：(n.) 頭痛
argue：(v.) 爭論

重要片語

calm down：平靜／冷靜下來

 27. Please look at the following three pictures.

Listen to the following short talk. What job does Ellen have?

What do you think about Ellen? I'm thinking about making her in charge of the staff here. She always takes good care of the customers. She never brings the wrong dish to the wrong table. She seems smart and friendly, and she gets along with us bosses, too.

A　　　　　　B　　　　　　C

Answer: B

你覺得 Ellen 如何？我想讓她負責管理這裡的員工。她總是把顧客服務得很好。她從來沒把菜送錯桌過。她似乎很聰明也很親切，而且她跟我們這些老闆也處得很好。

由此可知，Ellen 的職業是女服務生。

重要字彙

staff : (n.) 職員、員工　　　　　　　　　　　　　**customer** : (n.) 顧客
friendly : (adj.) 親切的、友善的

重要片語

in charge of... : 負責 (管理)……
get along with someone : 和某人處得來、相處融洽

 28. Please look at the following three pictures.

Vincent is calling his friend. What kind of weather is Vincent in?

Hi, Eric. It's Vincent. Let's go get some ice cream. I know I'm supposed to be on a diet, but I don't care. It's too hot. I need to eat something cold. After that, let's go find a place with air-conditioning. I absolutely cannot stand this heat anymore.

 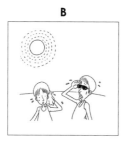 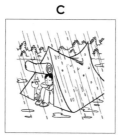

A　　　　　　B　　　　　　C

Answer: B

重要關鍵

嗨，Eric。我是 Vincent。我們去吃冰淇淋吧！我知道我應該在節食，但是我不在乎。因為真的太熱了，我需要吃點冰涼的東西。吃完之後，我們去找個有冷氣的地方。我絕對再也無法忍受這種高溫了。

由此可知，男子講的是天氣太熱。

 重要字彙

diet : (n.) 節食、規定的飲食，be on a diet : 節食　　air-conditioning : (n.) 空調

absolutely : (adv.) 絕對地　　stand : (v.) 忍受

heat : (n.) 高溫

---

29. Please look at the following three pictures.

Listen to the teacher talking to his students. What class is the teacher teaching?

This area on the map here is called the Middle East. As you can see, it's between Europe and Asia. It is a land with a long, rich history. Does anybody know the names of any countries there? What are they?

A　　　　　　B　　　　　　C

Answer: C

重要關鍵

地圖上的這塊區域我們稱之為中東。就像你所看到的，它在歐洲跟亞洲的中間。這是一塊具有悠久以及豐富歷史的土地。有誰知道那裡任何一個國家的名字嗎？它們是什麼？

由此可知，老師在上地理課。

重要字彙

map : (n.) 地圖

Middle East : 中東，middle : (adj.) 中間的

history : (n.) 歷史

30. Please look at the following three pictures.

Listen to the following short talk. What job does the woman have?

Who wouldn't want my job? I get paid just for wearing beautiful clothes and looking good in pictures. I get to meet famous people all the time, too. The only thing I don't like is having to diet all the time to stay skinny. No job is perfect, I guess.

A	B	C
		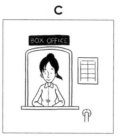

Answer: B

誰會不想要我的工作？我只需要穿著漂亮衣服在照片上看起來美美的，就可以拿到薪水。我也常常有機會見到名人。唯一我不喜歡的事就是我必須時時控制飲食來保持苗條。我想，沒有工作是完美的。

由此可知，女子的職業是模特兒。

重要字彙

famous : (adj.) 有名的
diet : (v.) 節食
skinny : (adj.) 瘦的

all the time : 一直

第一回

閱讀模擬試題解析

二、閱讀能力測驗

本測驗分三部份,全部都是單選題,共 35 題,作答時間 35 分鐘。

第一部份:詞彙和結構

共 15 題,每個題目裡有一個空格。請從四個選項中選出一個最適合題意的字或詞作答。

1. I want to give my girlfriend a _____. I'm going to send her roses on her birthday.

    A. future   B. control   C. surprise   D. knowledge

Answer: C

重要關鍵

A. future:(n.) 未來、將來

例:Don't dream about the future. Think about the present. (不要夢想未來,想想現在。)

B. control:(n.) 控制

C. surprise:(n.) 驚喜、驚訝

例:I have a surprise for you. (我要給妳一個驚喜。)

D. knowledge:(n.) 知識

空格後的句意是「我要在她生日那天送她玫瑰花。」,所以是想給他女朋友一個「驚喜」,故答案為 C。

2. I am _____ a dress to wear to my sister's wedding.

    A. looking for   B. putting off   C. giving up   D. running over

Answer: A

重要關鍵

A. look for...:尋找……

例:Owen spent two hours looking for his glasses last night.
    (Owen 昨天晚上花了兩個小時找他的眼鏡。)

B. put off...:將……延期

例:The meeting will be put off until next week. (會議將延到下星期。)

C. give up...:放棄……、戒除……

例:The doctor told my father to give up smoking. (醫生叫我爸爸要戒菸。)

D. run over...:輾過……

例:The car almost ran over that cat. (那輛車差點就輾過那隻貓。)

根據上下文語意,故答案選 A。

3. Wendy was upset because she studied very hard but still did _____ on her final exams.

    A. shortly   B. hardly   C. poorly   D. generally

Answer: C

重要關鍵

A. shortly：(adv.) 立刻、馬上

B. hardly：(adv.) 幾乎不

C. poorly：(adv.) 很差地、差勁地

do poorly on + 考試：考試考得差

例：Ned did poorly on his math exam. (Ned 的數學考得很差。)

do well on + 考試：考試考得好

例：Gina did well on her mid-term. (Gina 的期中考考得很好。)

D. generally：(adv.) 通常、一般而言

本題測驗重點為〝do poorly on + 考試〞，故答案選 C。

---

4. Jill had a great time at the class reunion _____ she saw many high school friends.

    A. if   B. so   C. therefore   D. because

Answer: D

重要關鍵

本題測驗表「因果」關係的副詞連接詞。空格前後為兩個句子，可知空格需要副詞連接詞來連接兩句，選項 C，therefore (因此) 為副詞，故不選。空格後的句子說「她見到許多高中朋友」，表示「因」，空格前的句子「Jill 在同學會上很愉快」則為「果」，故知答案應選 D，because (因為)。if (如果) 及 so (所以) 置入後不合語意，故 A、B 不選。

重要字彙

reunion：(n.) 重聚、團聚

例：class reunion (同學會)、family reunion (家族聚會)

---

5. This _____ shows what my grandparents looked like when they were young.

    A. menu   B. voice   C. photo   D. idea

Answer: C

重要關鍵

A. menu：(n.) 菜單

B. voice：(n.) 聲音

C. photo：(n.) 照片、相片

例：Can you take a photo of my brother and me? (可以幫我和我哥照一張相嗎？)

D. idea：(n.) 主意、想法

例：My idea gained the support of my friends. (我的想法獲得朋友們的支持。)

能讓人知道我祖父母年輕時長什麼樣子的是「照片」，所以答案為 C。

---

6. It's going to rain. You had better _____ an umbrella.

    A. brought   B. been bringing   C. to bring   D. bring

Answer: D

重要關鍵

"Someone had better + 原形動詞" 是用來建議「（某人）最好……」的句型，had better 後必須接原形動詞。

例：That cup is dirty. You had better wash it. (那個杯子很髒。你最好洗一下。)

由此可知，答案為 D。

---

7. Tammy is very generous; she always _____ her toys with her friends.

    A. hangs   B. shares   C. checks   D. accepts

Answer: B

重要關鍵

A. hang：(v.) 懸掛

例：Where should I hang my coat? (我要把外套掛在哪裡？)

B. share：(v.) 分享，share something with someone：和某人分享某物

例：Nadia shared the soup with Anna. (Nadia 和 Anna 一起喝那碗湯。)

C. check：(v.) 檢查

例：The dentist checked my teeth. (牙醫檢查我的牙齒。)

D. accept：(v.) 接受

例：Why didn't you accept Tom's present? (你為什麼不接受 Tom 的禮物？)

根據用法及上下文語意，故答案選 B。

重要字彙

generous：(adj.) 慷慨的、大方的

8. Let's go to Taipei 101 and watch the fireworks, _____?

    A. do we   B. don't you   C. will you   D. shall we

Answer: D

重要關鍵

本題測驗重點為附加問句：前句若是「肯定句」，附加問句用「否定」，前句若是「否定句」，附加問句用「肯定」，主詞則為與前句主詞相對應的人稱代名詞 (he, she, they, you, we...)，而附加問句的動詞則須視前句中的動詞而定。

例：Kevin is a student, isn't he? (Kevin 是學生，不是嗎？)

    Sherry can't speak Chinese, can she? (Sherry 不會說中文，對嗎？)

    The apple pie tasted good, didn't it? (那蘋果派很好吃，對不對？)

以原形動詞起首的祈使句，附加問句固定用 will you。

例：Turn off the radio, will you? (把收音機關掉，好嗎？)

以 Let's 開頭的句子，附加問句固定用 shall we。

例：Let's take a break, shall we? (我們休息一下，好不好？)

    Let's go, shall we? (我們走吧，好不好？)

比較：Let us go, will you? (讓我們走，好不好？)

＊ 本句的 Let us 視為以原形動詞起首的祈使句，因此附加問句用 will you。

根據上述，本題答案應選 D。

重要字彙

firework：(n.) 煙火 (作此義時，常用複數形)

9. It's so dark in the room that I can't see _____. Could you please turn on the light for me?

    A. thing   B. something   C. anything   D. nothing

Answer: C

重要關鍵

A. thing：(n.) 事情、事物，為可數名詞。

例：Dean likes to debate things with his parents. (Dean 喜歡和他父母爭論事情。)

B. something：(n.) 某事、某物，通常使用於肯定句中。

例：I have something for you. (我有東西要給你。)

C. anything：(n.) 任何事物，通常使用於否定句及疑問句中。

例：Do you have anything to tell me? (你有什麼事情要告訴我嗎？)

D. nothing：(n.) 無事、無物，因 nothing 本身已經具有否定意味，因此通常不可再與否定詞 (如 not, no 等)並用，以避免形成雙重否定。

例：I have nothing to tell you. (我沒有事情要告訴你。)

根據用法及上下文語意，可知答案為 C。

 重要片語

turn on the light：打開電燈　　　　　　　　　　　　　**turn off the light**：關掉電燈

---

10. Can you give me some advice about _____ for my vacation?

    A. I should go where　　　B. to where I go　　　C. where should I go　　　D. where to go

Answer: D

重要關鍵

本題測驗疑問詞引導的名詞片語。名詞片語的形成方式為「疑問詞 (what, where, when, how 等) + 不定詞片語 (to V)」，名詞片語與名詞子句一樣，在句子中可作主詞、及物動詞或介系詞的受詞。

例：Where to hold the meeting is not decided yet. (在哪裡開會尚未決定。)

　　He doesn't know how to handle the problem. (他不知道如何處理這個問題。)

空格前有介系詞 about，故知答案應選 D。選項 A 及 選項 C 若改為名詞子句 where I should go 則亦可選。

重要字彙

advice：(n.) 建議，為不可數名詞，**a piece of advice**：一項建議，**give someone advice about...**：給某人關於……的建議。

例：**Please give me some advice about making good use of time. (請給我一些善用時間的建議。)**

---

11. _____ about shopping at the new mall this Friday?

    A. What　　　　　　B. Why　　　　　　C. When　　　　　　D. Whether

Answer: A

重要關鍵

本題測驗 What about + V-ing? (我們……如何？)，用來表建議。

例：What about eating beef noodles tonight? (我們今晚吃牛肉麵如何？)

所以答案選 A。

重要字彙

mall：(n.) 購物中心

12. I tried to ignore the people who were talking _____ on the bus.

    A. loudly   B. bravely   C. silently   D. easily

Answer: A

重要關鍵

A. loudly：(adv.) 大聲地

例：Stop talking so loudly. The baby is sleeping. (講話別這麼大聲。小寶寶正在睡覺。)

B. bravely：(adv.) 勇敢地

例：Bob faces his illness bravely. (Bob 勇敢面對病魔。)

C. silently：(adv.) 沉默地、寂靜地

例：Mr. Smith stood there silently. (Smith 先生靜靜地站在那兒。)

D. easily：(adv.) 容易地

例：Jill solved the problem easily. (Jill 輕而易舉地就解決了這個問題。)

根據上下文語意，故答案選 A。

重要字彙

ignore：(v.) 忽略、無視

13. We decided to hire Adam, _____ can speak both English and Japanese.

    A. that   B. which   C. who   D. whose

Answer: C

重要關鍵

本題測驗重點為關係代名詞的用法。

關係代名詞兼有代名詞和連接詞的功能，用來代替前面的名詞 (即先行詞)，和連接後面的子句。代替「人」時用 who / that，所有格則為 whose，which / that 則用來代替「物」，而且 that 之前不可有逗點。

例：The girl who / that has long hair is very friendly. (那個留長頭髮的女孩很友善。)

    I don't like Frank, who often tells lies. (我不喜歡 Frank，他經常說謊。)

    The girl standing over there is Mary, whose mother is my teacher.

    (站在那裡的女生是 Mary，她的母親是我的老師。)

    The necklace which / that is made of gold is beautiful. (那條金子做的項鍊很漂亮。)

空格前的先行詞是表「人」的 Adam，後面有動詞，而且空格前有逗點，故答案應選 C。

重要字彙

hire：(v.) 僱用

14. I am still waiting for a response to the e-mail I _____ Helen two weeks ago.

A. sent   B. send   C. have sent   D. were sending

Answer: A

重要關鍵

本題測驗重點為 ago 與時態的關係。ago（之前）是副詞，使用時，之前需加上一段時間（如 two weeks，five days 等），表「若干時間之前」的意思，而且句中動詞須用過去簡單式。

例：Allie moved to Taichung two years ago. (Allie 兩年前搬到臺中。)

由此可知，本題答案應選 A。

send：(v.) 寄出、寄送，動詞三態為 send, sent, sent

例：Ryan sent a postcard to me from Spain. (Ryan 從西班牙寄了一張明信片給我。)

重要字彙

response：(n.) 回答、回覆

15. It was _____ to leave the window open when you knew rain was coming.

A. generous   B. patient   C. foolish   D. humble

Answer: C

重要關鍵

A. generous：(adj.) 慷慨的、大方的

例：Jim is not a rich man, but he is very generous. (Jim 不是個有錢人，但他很慷慨。)

B. patient：(adj.) 有耐心的

例：Mr. Lee is the most patient teacher in the school. (李老師是學校裡最有耐心的老師。)

C. foolish：(adj.) 愚蠢的

例：It was foolish of you to spend money like that. (你像那樣子花錢真是愚蠢。)

D. humble：(adj.) 謙虛的

例：Jack is always humble about his success. (對於自己的成功，Jack 總是非常謙虛。)

根據上下文語意，故答案選 C。

第二部份：段落填空

共 10 題，包括二個段落，每個段落各含四到六個空格。每格均有四個選項，請依照文意選出最適合的答案。

Questions 16-20

Bill has a new skateboard. His friends think it is really cool. They all want to ride it, but Bill does not want to share. __(16)__, he lets Jim ride it. However, Bill tells him he cannot ride it __(17)__ more than ten minutes. Jim loves the skateboard. He imagines __(18)__ one, too. Jim thinks about having a new skateboard __(19)__ that he becomes careless and falls to the ground. He knows that is not very smart. Jim is lucky that he __(20)__ break his leg or Bill's new skateboard.

16. A. Whenever	B. Finally	C. Next	D. Although
			Answer: B

A. whenever：(conj.) 每當、每次，後面要接子句。

B. finally：(adv.) 最後、終於

C. next：(adv.) 接下來

D. although：(conj.) 雖然，後面要接子句。

空格後為逗點，whenever 與 although 為副詞連接詞，因此 A、D 不予考慮。

空格前的句子說「Bill 不肯讓別人一起玩」，空格後又說「他讓 Jim 玩」，因此本題答案選 B. Finally 來承接語意。

17. A. for	B. by	C. until	D. during
			Answer: A

本題測驗重點為介系詞 for，用來表示「一段時間」。

例：Linda is going to New York for ten days. (Linda 要去紐約十天。)

因此本題答案選 A。

18. A. to buy	B. bought	C. buying	D. buys
			Answer: C

本題測驗重點為動詞 imagine 的用法。imagine：(v.) 想像、幻想，後面只能接動名詞作受詞，而不能接不定詞。

例：Lily often imagines marrying a prince when she grows up. (Lily 經常想像長大後嫁給王子。)

故答案選 C。

19. A. very　　　　　B. enough　　　　　C. so much　　　　　D. too much

本題測試重點為 "so...that..." 的用法。

so + adj. / adv. + that 子句：如此……以致於……

例：The food was so spicy that Larry couldn't eat it. (食物太辣了，以致於 Larry 吃不下去。)

　　Jill loved James so much that she cried all day when he left her.

　　(Jill 如此深愛 James，以致於 James 離開她時，她哭了一整天。)

由此可知，本題答案要選 C。

20. A. can't　　　　　B. won't　　　　　C. hasn't　　　　　D. doesn't

本篇短文皆以現在簡單式陳述，且空格後為原形動詞 break，B 為未來式，C 為完成式，因此均不予考慮。can't 及 doesn't 兩者皆可填入空格，但根據上下文語意，故選 D。

重要字彙

skateboard：(n.) 滑板
share：(v.) 分享
lucky：(adj.) 幸運的

more than：超過……、多於……
例：More than 200 doctors work in this hospital. (有超過兩百位醫生在這間醫院上班。)

Questions 21-25

Mr. Smith is chatting with his students. He is wondering __(21)__ they would like to be when they grow up. One of his students, Barry, says that he hopes __(22)__ a lot of money when he is older. He wants to be a successful businessman. Mr. Smith __(23)__ Barry that it can be a challenging and stressful job. Barry knows that it won't be easy, but he __(24)__ watching his father for many years, and his father assures him that it is a very rewarding profession. __(25)__, Barry will do his best to make this dream come true.

21. A. what   B. why   C. how   D. where

Answer: A

 重要關鍵

wonder：(v.) 納悶、想知道，後面常接名詞子句當受詞。

例：I wonder what her name is.（我在想她叫什麼名字。）

  I wonder whether you like her.（我想知道你是否喜歡她。）

what, why, how 及 where 均可引導名詞子句做前面動詞 wondering 的受詞，但只有 what 為疑問代名詞，可在後面句子中原形 be 動詞後做主詞補語，故答案為 A。

22. A. earning   B. will earn   C. to earn   D. earns

Answer: C

 重要關鍵

本題測驗重點為 hope to + 原形動詞：希望 / 想要……。

例：Jonathan hopes to study abroad. (Jonathan 想要出國唸書。)

由此可知，本題答案選 C。

23. A. had reminded B. reminds C. will remind D. was reminding

Answer: B

重要關鍵

本篇短文皆以現在簡單式陳述，故選 B，使時態一致。

remind：(v.) 提醒，remind someone + that 子句：提醒某人……

例：Sandy reminds her boss that he has a meeting in an hour.

  (Sandy 提醒她老闆一個小時後要開會。)

remind 也可以表示「使想起」，remind A of B：使 A 想起 B。

例：The song reminded me of my high school days.（這首歌讓我想到高中時代。）

24. A. has been   B. was   C. is   D. can be

Answer: A

重要關鍵

英文句中若有時間副詞片詞 "for + 一段時間"（有若干時間之久）出現時，被修飾的動詞多用完成式或完成進行式。

例：Vanessa has been working as a secretary for ten years.

  (Vanessa 已經當秘書十年了。)

由此可知，答案應選 A。本句文意為「Barry 耳濡目染父親經商多年」。

25. A. Since   B. After   C. Although   D. Therefore

Answer: D

重要關鍵

A. since：(adv.) 從那時起、自此之後，主要子句的動詞經常是完成式或完成進行式，since 可置於句尾或句中，完成式助動詞 have, has, had 之後。

例：I met Emily in high school, and we have been good friends since.

（我在高中時就認識 Emily，從那時起我們就是好朋友。）

B. after：(adv.) 之後，修飾過去式的主要子句。

例：Larry quit his job. Soon after, he moved to Paris. (Larry 辭去工作。不久之後，他便搬去巴黎。)

C. although：(conj.) 雖然，之後接主詞和動詞，形成副詞子句修飾主要子句。

例：Although we're late, we still caught the train. (雖然我們晚到，但還是趕上那班火車。)

D. therefore：(adv.) 因此

例：Nancy is getting married. Therefore, we should have a party.

（Nancy 要結婚了，所以我們該辦場派對。）

根據上述用法及語意，故答案選 D。

重要字彙

chat：(v. & n.) 閒談、聊天

例：I chatted with my sister about the film. (我跟我姊姊閒聊著那部電影。)

challenging：(adj.) 有挑戰性的

stressful：(adj.) 令人有壓力的

例：Being a president is pretty stressful. (當總統相當有壓力。)

assure：(v.) 向……保證，assure someone that... : 向某人保證……

assure someone of something : 向某人保證某事物

例：The tour guide assured me of the safety to travel there. (導遊向我保證去那兒旅遊的安全性。)

rewarding：(adj.) 有報酬的，reward : (v.) 獎賞

例：They will reward the winner with a trip to London. (他們將獎賞優勝者到倫敦旅行。)

profession：(n.) (尤指受過良好教育或專門訓練者，如律師、醫生、教師的) 職業

例：She intends to make teaching her profession. (她打算以教書為業。)

重要片語

do someone's best to V : 盡某人所能……

come true : 成真、實現

第三部份：閱讀理解

共 10 題，包括數篇短文，每篇短文後面有三至四個相關問題。請由四個選項中選出最適合的答案。

Questions 26-28

> # Love of Drama Acting Class
>
> **Do you want to be an actor / actress? Love of Drama acting classes can teach you how to be a success in the movie business. Let your friends and family see you in the end of summer show!**
>
> ☻ *Morning Classes: Tuesday and Thursday 9-12*
>
> ☻ *Evening Classes: Monday-Friday 5-9*
>
> ☻ *Weekends: 8-12*

26. How many days a week can you go to a class held in the morning?

    A. Two.

    B. Three.

    C. Four.

    D. Five.

    Answer: A

27. What time of the day can you not go to class?

    A. Night time.

    B. Afternoon.

    C. Morning.

    D. Evening.

    Answer: B

28. What month might you be able to see the show?

    A. March.

    B. June.

    C. November.

    D. August.

    Answer: D

重要字彙

actor : (n.) 男演員　　　　　　　　　　　　　　　actress : (n.) 女演員

success : (n.) 成功的人或事物

Questions 29-31

> March 24, 2013
>
> Dear Wendy,
>
> 　　Hi, I'm Richard. We are in the same history class. I am tall with brown hair. I am not very smart, but I always try my best. Do you know who I am? I hope so!
>
> 　　Are you free this weekend? I am on the baseball team and we have a game. Maybe you can come and watch us. I think we will win. We have a good team.
>
> 　　I think you are smart and pretty. Will you be my friend? Maybe you can write back to me and tell me.
>
> 　　　　　　　　　　　　Sincerely yours,
> 　　　　　　　　　　　　Richard

29. How does Richard know Wendy?

　　A. They live next door to each other.

　　B. They are in the same class.

　　C. They are on a team together.

　　D. They play baseball together on weekends.

Answer: B

30. What is NOT true about Richard?

　　A. He is not very good at history.

　　B. He has brown hair.

　　C. He doesn't work hard.

　　D. He wants to be friends with Wendy.

Answer: C

31. What does Richard ask Wendy to do?

A. Watch him play baseball.

B. Help him with his homework.

C. Go on a date with him.

D. Play baseball with him.

Answer: A

重要字彙

smart : (adj.) 聰明的   team : (n.) 隊伍

重要片語

try someone's best : 盡某人所能、某人盡全力
例 : I'll try my best to help you out. (我會竭盡全力來幫助你。)

Questions 32-35

Most children look forward to celebrating Halloween, which takes place on the last day of October every year. Children love this special day because they are able to do many interesting activities which they can't normally do. They can go trick-or-treating, wear interesting and frightening costumes, and stay out late at night.

The most common tradition during Halloween is when children go out at night to knock on doors and ask for candy. While most girls like to dress up as Snow White or other Disney princesses, boys like to put on scary masks and frighten people. Besides dressing up in many different styles of clothing, children also like to play tricks on their friends to have a good Halloween. Even though Halloween is a time for fun, it is important for parents to take care of children and keep them safe.

32. Which of the following is NOT a Halloween tradition?

A. Give money to each other.

B. Trick-or-treat.

C. Wear costumes.

D. Play tricks on people.

Answer: A

33. Why do children enjoy Halloween so much?

A. They can have fun at Disneyland for free.

B. They don't need to go to school.

C. They can stay up late and eat candy.

D. They like to be scared at night.

Answer: C

34. According to the passage, what should parents do on Halloween night?

   A. Dress up in a costume and go trick-or-treating with their kids.

   B. Keep an eye on their children to make sure they are safe.

   C. Eat candy and watch TV with their children all night long.

   D. Put on a mask at night and scare the neighbors.

Answer: B

35. What might be a good title for this passage?

   A. What Parents and Children Can Do Together on Halloween

   B. Things Kids Shouldn't Do on Halloween

   C. How to Frighten People on Halloween

   D. Halloween Fun for Kids

Answer: D

重要字彙

celebrate : (v.) 慶祝

Halloween : (n.) 萬聖節 (10 月 31 日)，俗稱西洋鬼節

normally : (adv.) 正常地

trick-or-treat : (v.) 不給糖就搗蛋 (指萬聖節孩子們挨家逐戶要糖果等禮物，如不遂願便惡作劇一番的風俗)

frightening : (adj.) 嚇人的

costume : (n.) (指參加派對等的) 特殊服裝、戲服

common : (adj.) 常見的、一般的

tradition : (n.) 傳統

knock : (v.) 敲、打，**knock on doors** : 敲門

Snow White : (n.) 白雪公主

scary : (adj.) 嚇人的

mask : (n.) 面具

frighten : (v.) 使驚恐

例 : **The ghost movie frightened me.** (那部鬼片嚇壞我了。)

重要片語

look forward to + n. / V-ing : 期待……

例 : **I'm looking forward to the Christmas party.** (我期待耶誕派對的來臨。)

take place : 發生、舉行

例 : **When will the party take place?** (派對何時舉行？)

dress up as... : 打扮成……

例 : **Sherry dressed up as a vampire for the party.** (Sherry 在派對上打扮成吸血鬼。)

put on... : 穿上、戴上……，**put on masks** : 戴上面具

play tricks on... : 對……惡作劇、捉弄……

例：Many children like to play tricks on their playmates. (許多小孩子喜歡捉弄他們的玩伴。)

even though... : 即使、雖然……

例：Even though it rains, I will go out. (即使下雨，我還是會外出。)

take care of... : 照顧……

例：Mothers always take great care of their children. (媽媽總是無微不至地照顧小孩。)

stay up late : 不睡覺、熬夜

for free : 免費

keep an eye on... : 看照、注意……

~ 第二回 模擬試題解答 ~

聽力 Listening

第一部份 看圖辨義	第二部份 問答		第三部份 簡短對話		第四部份 短文聽解
1. B	6. B	11. A	16. C	21. B	26. C
2. A	7. C	12. B	17. B	22. A	27. B
3. C	8. B	13. C	18. A	23. C	28. A
4. A	9. A	14. A	19. B	24. A	29. C
5. B	10. C	15. C	20. C	25. B	30. B

閱讀 Reading

第一部份 詞彙和結構			第二部份 段落填空		第三部份 閱讀理解	
1. D	6. D	11. B	16. B	21. C	26. A	31. C
2. C	7. A	12. D	17. C	22. B	27. D	32. D
3. B	8. C	13. A	18. D	23. D	28. C	33. C
4. A	9. A	14. D	19. C	24. A	29. D	34. B
5. C	10. D	15. C	20. A	25. B	30. B	35. A

第二回
聽力模擬試題解析

一、聽力測驗

本測驗分四個部份，全部都是單選題，共 30 題，作答時間約 20 分鐘。作答說明為中文，印在試題冊上並經由光碟放音機播出。

第一部份：看圖辨義

共 5 題，每題請聽光碟放音機播出的題目和三個英語句子之後，選出與所看到的圖畫最相符的答案。
每題只播出一遍。

 1. How much does it cost to go from Taichung to Tainan?
   A. NT$130.
   B. NT$170.
   C. NT$530.

Answer: B

本題測驗疑問詞 how 引導的疑問句，用 "How much does it cost to go from A to B?" 來詢問「從 A 地到 B 地要多少錢？」。

例：How much does it cost to go from Taipei to Hsinchu by train? (從台北搭火車到新竹要多少錢？)
題目問「從台中到台南要多少錢？」，從圖片中可知，從台中 (Taichung) 到台南 (Tainan) 的票價 (ticket price) 是台幣一百七十元，故答案為 B。

 2. What is wrong with the man?
   A. He broke his arm.
   B. His back is in pain.
   C. He has a bad cold.

Answer: A

本題測驗疑問詞 what 引導的疑問句，用 "What is wrong with someone?" 來詢問「某人怎麼了？/ 某人發生什麼事？」。

例：You look upset. What's wrong with you? (你看起來很不開心。怎麼了？)
從圖片看來，男子的手臂骨折了，故答案選 A。

in pain：在疼痛中、在痛苦中　　　　　　　　　　　　　**have a bad cold**：罹患重感冒

 3. What is the girl trying to do?

    A. Chase the ball.

    B. Rent a ball.

    C. Catch the ball.

Answer: C

 重要關鍵

本題用 "What is someone trying to do?" 來詢問「某人正試圖做什麼？」。

測驗重點是 catch：(v.) 接；捉，catch the ball：接球。

由圖片可知，女生正要接球，故選項 C 為正確答案。

重要字彙

chase：(v.) 追逐
                                                      rent：(v.) 租

 4. When does Sally usually get up?

    A. At 6:45.

    B. At 9:35.

    C. At 6:15.

Answer: A

 重要關鍵

本題是以疑問詞 when 起首的疑問句，聽到以 when 開頭的問題，就要注意圖片中任何與時間有關的訊息。

題目問「Sally 每天通常幾點起床？」，從圖片牆上的時鐘指著六點四十五分可知，答案應選 A。

重要片語

get up：起床

 5. How's the weather?

    A. It's cold and snowy.

    B. It's windy and rainy.

    C. It's hot and sunny.

Answer: B

 重要關鍵

本題測驗重點為 "How's the weather?"，用來問「天氣如何？」，同樣也可用 "What's the weather like?"。由圖片內容可看出在刮風 (windy) 和下雨 (rainy)，因此答案選 B。

第二部份：問答

共 10 題，每題請聽光碟放音機播出的英語句子，再從試題冊上三個回答中，選出一個最適合的答案。
每題只播出一遍。

6. My parents know that I cheated on the test.

A. I'm glad they could help you study.

B. They must be really angry with you.

C. You must feel happy about that.

Answer: B

重要關鍵

本題是直述句，測驗重點為 cheat on the test：考試作弊。

例：I know you won't cheat on the test. I trust you. (我知道你考試不會作弊。我信任你。)

題目說「我父母知道我考試作弊了。」，由此推測，談話者的父母一定很生氣，故答案為 B，be angry
with someone：對某人生氣。

例：Tammy was angry with her son because he didn't do his homework.
(Tammy 對她兒子很生氣，因為他沒有做功課。)

7. So, what were the results of your test?

A. I really studied a lot.

B. Our teacher is helping us prepare.

C. Great! I'm glad I did so well.

Answer: C

重要關鍵

本題測驗重點為 result：(n.) 成績、結果。

例：What was the result of your driving test? (你考駕照的結果如何？)

題目問「你考試的成績如何？」，因此用 "Great! I'm glad I did so well." (很棒！我很開心自己考得這麼
好。) 來回答最適當，故選 C。

重要字彙

study : (v.) 學習

help : (v.) 幫助，help 後面可省略不定詞 to 而直接接動詞。

例：She helped me cook the dinner. (她幫我煮晚餐。)

prepare : (v.) 準備

 8. How do you usually go to school?

    A. I don't have to go to school on weekends.

    B. I ride my bike to school.

    C. I am never late for school.

Answer: B

 重要關鍵

本題用疑問詞 how 來詢問搭乘何種交通工具，"How does someone (usually) go to...?" 表示「某人 (通常) 怎麼去……？」。

例：Andy: How does your father go to work? (Andy: 妳爸爸怎麼去上班？)

    Beth: He goes to work by car. (Beth: 他開車上班。)

題目問「你通常怎麼去上學？」，因此答案選 B「我騎腳踏車上學。」。

 重要片語

on weekends：每逢週末，on the weekend：在週末，weekend：(n.) 週末

be late for school / work：上學 / 上班遲到

9. Who does your uncle look like?

    A. He looks like my grandfather.

    B. He always looks happy.

    C. I think he likes Michelle.

Answer: A

重要關鍵

本題測驗重點為 look like...：看起來像……。

例：Billy doesn't look like his brother. (Billy 和他哥哥長得不像。)

題目問「你的叔叔長得像誰？」，最適當的回應為 "He looks like my grandfather." (他長得像我爺爺。)，故答案選 A。

10. Why are you being so sneaky?

    A. I just heard a funny joke.

    B. I haven't slept much recently.

    C. I was trying to surprise you.

Answer: C

 重要關鍵

本題測驗重點為 sneaky：(adj.) 鬼鬼祟祟的。

題目問「你為什麼鬼鬼祟祟的？」，故答案選 C "I was trying to surprise you." (我想要嚇你一跳。)，

surprise : (v.) 使驚訝、使嚇一跳

例 : It surprised me to see you there. (在那裡看到你令我吃驚。)

重要字彙

funny : (adj.) 好笑的，a funny joke : 好笑的笑話　　　　　**recently : (adv.) 最近、近來**

11. This computer was a waste of money.
    A. I agree. It doesn't work well, and it was so expensive.
    B. I can't believe it only cost NT$5,000.
    C. Yeah, I'm so glad we got it.

Answer: A

重要關鍵

本題是直述句，測驗重點為 waste : (n.) 浪費。

例 : What a waste of money! (真浪費錢！)

題目說「這部電腦真是浪費錢。」，用選項 A "I agree. It doesn't work well." (我同意。它運作得不是很好。) 來回應最適當，故為正確答案，work : (v.) 運作。

例 : The elevator is not working. (電梯壞了。)

12. Why does Bob look unhappy?
    A. He is going to get a pay raise.
    B. His report was rejected by the boss again.
    C. He just won first place in the talent show.

Answer: B

重要關鍵

本題測驗重點為 unhappy : (adj.) 不高興的，以及 reject : (v.) 拒絕、駁回。

例 : I was rejected by the company. (那家公司沒錄取我。)

題目問「Bob 為什麼看起來不高興？」，故答案選 B "His report was rejected by the boss again."
(他的報告又被老闆退回了。)，report : (n.) 報告，boss : (n.) 老闆；主管。

A「他要加薪了。」以及 C「他在才藝比賽中得到第一名。」都是值得高興的事，故均不可選。

重要字彙

raise : (n.) 增加，a pay raise : 加薪
first place : (n.) 第一名，win first place : 得第一名
talent show : (n.) 才藝表演

 13. We would like to check in.

    A. Your total is NT$999.

    B. We hope to see you again.

    C. Sure. What's your name, please?

Answer: C

 重要關鍵

本題是直述句,測驗重點為 check in:辦理入住登記。

例:You have to check in to get your room key. (你得辦理入住登記才能拿到房間鑰匙。)

題目說「我們想辦理入住登記。」,因此答案選 C「好的,請問您尊姓大名?」。

A「總共是九百九十九元。」應是告訴顧客所購買的物品總價,total:(n.) 總額、總數。

B「期待您下次再度光臨。」應是客人要退房離開時,飯店人員所說的話。

重要片語

would like to V:想要……

例:I would like to go home early today. (我今天想早點回家。)

 14. Excuse me. Is this seat taken?

    A. No, it's not. You can have it.

    B. Could I have a seat in the back, please?

    C. Yes, this way, please.

Answer: A

重要關鍵

本題測驗重點為 seat:(n.) 座位。

例:This seat is taken. (這個位子有人坐了。)

題目問「請問一下。這個位子有人坐嗎?」,故答案選 A「沒有,這個位子沒人坐。你可以坐。」。

 15. Welcome. Have you booked a table, sir?

    A. Yes, I'd like to pay cash.

    B. No, I'm single.

    C. Yes, it's under the name of Larry Chen.

Answer: C

本題測驗重點為 book：(v.) 預訂，book a table：訂位。

例：I booked a table for six at the new buffet.（我在那家新開的自助餐廳訂了六個人的位子。）

題目問「歡迎光臨。請問先生有訂位嗎？」，為了確認訂位，需要提供姓名，故以選項 C 為最適合的回應，under the name of + 名字：登記在某人的名下。

cash：(n.) 現金，pay cash：付現　　　　　　　　　　　　　　　**single：(adj.) 單身的**

第三部份：簡短對話

共 10 題，每題請聽光碟放音機播出一段對話和一個相關的問題後，再從試題冊上三個選項中，選出一個最適合的答案。每段對話和問題播出一遍。

16. W: Christmas will be here soon. I'm so excited!

M: Me, too. I love Christmas.

W: I'm going to put my stocking up.

M: I'll do that, too!

Q: When is this conversation probably taking place?

A. At 12:25 p.m.

B. In January.

C. On December 23.

Answer: C

題目問「這段對話可能是在什麼時候發生的？」，關鍵句在女子一開頭所說 "Christmas will be here soon."（聖誕節就快到了。），聖誕節的日期是十二月二十五日，由此可知，本題答案應選 C「在十二月二十三日。」而非 B「在一月份。」。A「在下午十二點二十五分。」則答非所問。

excited：(adj.) 感到興奮的　　　　　　　　　　　　　　　**stocking：(n.) 長襪**

put...up / put up...：懸掛……　　　　　　　　　　　　　　　**take place：發生**

 17. M: May I help you?

W: Yes! What's the price of the black shirt?

M: It's $3,500.

W: Oh! That's pretty expensive. I wonder if there is something cheaper.

M: Well, here's a nice one for $990. I think it'll look great on you.

Q: Where are the speakers?

A. At a gym.

B. At a clothing store.

C. At a supermarket.

Answer: B

重要關鍵

題目問「談話者在哪裡？」，從對話中的 black shirt (黑色襯衫) 可知，他們在服飾店，故答案選 B。

 18. M: I like this sofa. It's so comfortable.

W: Yes, it's really nice.

M: We should buy it.

W: There isn't space for it in our apartment.

Q: What's wrong with the sofa?

A. It's too big.

B. It's too expensive.

C. It's the wrong color.

Answer: A

重要關鍵

本題測驗重點為 space，是「空間」的意思。

例：There's not much empty space in this building. (這棟大樓裡的可用空間不多。)

"There isn't space for it in our apartment." 即表示「我們的公寓沒有它的空間。」，也就是

"It's too big." (它太大了。)，故本題答案為 A。

重要字彙

comfortable：(adj.) 舒適的

19. W: Are you ready to go?

M: Yes. Do you know how to get there?

W: Sure. I have a map.

M: Great. Lead the way.

Q: Who is going to go first?

    A. The man.

    B. The woman.

    C. They will go together.

Answer: B

本題測驗重點為 lead，是動詞「帶領」的意思，lead the way 即「帶路」之意。

例：A: Do you want me to show you where the drugstore is? (A：你需要我帶你去藥局嗎？)

    B: That would be great. Lead the way. (B：那太好了，帶路吧。)

題目問「誰會先走？」，對話中女生有地圖，因此男生回答 "Great. Lead the way."（太好了，妳來帶路。），意為男生要女生「先走」，故選 B。

20. W: Jenny's teacher called.

M: What has she done now?

W: She copied Allen's homework.

M: We need to have a talk with her.

Q: What did Jenny do?

    A. She gave Allen her homework.

    B. She did Allen's homework for him.

    C. She looked at Allen's homework and wrote the same.

Answer: C

本題測驗重點為動詞 copy，是「抄寫；複製」的意思。女子在對話中說 "She copied Allen's homework."（Jenny 抄 Allen 的回家作業。），因此答案選 C「她看 Allen 的作業然後寫一樣的東西。」。選項 A 意為「將她的作業給 Allen。」；選項 B 意為「她幫 Allen 寫作業。」

 21. M: Are you hungry, Lisa?

W: Sure, Tim. Why?

M: I got a couple of hamburgers. Want one?

W: Yeah. Thanks!

Q: How many hamburgers did Tim get?

A. One.

B. Two or three.

C. None.

Answer: B

 重要關鍵

本題測驗重點為 a couple of... : 一些⋯⋯、幾個⋯⋯。

例 : John was a couple of hours late. (John 遲到好幾個小時。)

題目問「Tim 有幾個漢堡?」,故答案為 B「兩個或三個。」。

重要字彙

hamburger : (n.) 漢堡

 22. M: Hi! I'd like to buy a new cell phone.

W: OK, sir. Do you see any here you like?

M: Is that one on sale?

W: The black one? Let me check.

Q: What does the man want?

A. A lower-priced phone.

B. A colorful phone.

C. A smaller phone.

Answer: A

 重要關鍵

本題測驗重點為 on sale : 特價中、減價出售。

例 : These gloves and scarves are on sale. (這些手套和圍巾在特價。)

題目問「男子想要什麼?」,關鍵句在男子所說 "Is that one on sale?"(那支有在特價嗎?),可知他想要比較便宜的價格 (lower price),故答案選 A。

重要字彙

colorful : (adj.) 彩色的、鮮豔的

23. W: Where are you, Marvin?

M: I'm in the living room.

W: Why don't you come with me for a walk?

M: No, I'm busy surfing the Internet.

W: Well, it's time for you to take a break.

Q: What is the man doing?

    A. Taking a break.

    B. Cleaning the living room.

    C. Using the computer.

Answer: C

本題測驗重點為 surf the Internet：瀏覽網頁、上網。

例：It is my habit to surf the Internet when I go home.（回家後上網是我的習慣。）

題目問「男子正在做什麼？」關鍵句在男子所說 "I'm busy surfing the Internet"（我正忙著上網），所以他正在使用電腦，故答案為 C。

take a break：休息一下

例：After working the whole morning, Kathy needed to take a break.

   （工作了一整個早上後，Kathy 需要休息一下。）

24. M: How was your interview?

W: The one I had yesterday?

M: Yes. How did you do?

W: I'm confident I got the job.

Q: How did the woman do at the interview?

    A. She did well.

    B. She did poorly.

    C. She doesn't know.

Answer: A

本題測驗重點為 confident：(adj.) 有信心的。

例：When you have a job interview, you have to look confident.（面試時要看起來有自信。）

題目問「女子在面試中表現如何？」，關鍵在女子所說 "I'm confident I got the job."（我有信心我得到那份工作。），可見她在面試中表現得很好 (do well)，故答案選 A。

 重要字彙

interview : (n.) 面試   poorly : (adv.) 差勁地

🎧 25. W: It's time to get up, Johnny.

M: What time is it, Mom?

W: It's a quarter to eight.

M: Oh, no! I'm late for school.

Q: What time is it?

    A. It's after eight.

    B. It's before eight.

    C. It's eight.

Answer: B

 重要關鍵

本題測驗時間的說法。quarter : (n.) 一刻鐘、十五分鐘,如 a quarter to twelve 表示差十五分十二點,也就是「十一點四十五分」,而「十一點十五分」則可以說 a quarter past eleven。

對話中女子回答 "It's a quarter to eight." ,意思是「現在差十五分八點。」,也就是「現在七點四十五分。」,所以答案選 B "It's before eight." ,即「現在還沒八點。」。

 重要片語

get up : 起床

第四部份:短文聽解

共 5 題,每題有三個圖片選項。請聽光碟放音機播出的題目,並選出一個最適合的圖片。每題播出一遍。

🎧 26. Please look at the following three pictures.

Listen to the following short talk. What happened to the couple?

Honey, you should stop the car. I smell smoke. I think it's coming from the engine. It may be getting too hot. We need to take a look and see what's going on under the hood. It may not be dangerous now, but it could be if we don't fix it soon.

A	B	C
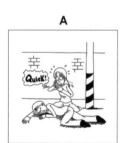		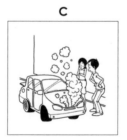

Answer: C

重要關鍵

親愛的，你應該把車停下來。我聞到煙味。我想應該是來自於引擎。有可能是太熱了。我們需要看一下引擎蓋底下怎麼了。現在可能不危險，但如果我們不盡快修理的話，可能就會危險了。

由此可知，這對夫婦的車子冒煙了。

重要字彙

smoke：(n.) 煙　　　　　　　　　　　　　engine：(n.) 引擎
hood：(n.) 汽車車蓋　　　　　　　　　　fix：(v.) 修理

27. Please look at the following three pictures.

Listen to the following short talk. Who is the officer speaking to?

Hello, sir. Do you know why I stopped you? You were going way too fast, and you rode through the red light. I'm going to have to write you a ticket. It's a good thing you're wearing a helmet, or you would have had to pay even more. Please ride more carefully next time.

A　　　　　　　　　　B　　　　　　　　　　C

Answer: B

重要關鍵

你好，先生。你知道為什麼我叫你停下來嗎？你騎太快，而且闖紅燈。我不得不開你一張罰單。幸好你有戴安全帽，不然你會被罰更多。下一次請小心騎車。

由此可知，警察在跟機車騎士說話。

重要字彙

ticket：(n.) 罰單
helmet：(n.) 安全帽
carefully：(adv.) 小心地

28. Please look at the following three pictures.

Listen to the following advertisement. What problem is it talking about?

Do you feel older than you really are? Lower back pain is more common than you think. We can help you fix it. Put this pad on your lower back, and within an hour, you'll be getting around as if nothing was bothering you. Be yourself again!

A 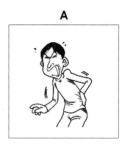   B 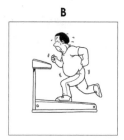   C

Answer: A

 重要關鍵

你覺得自己比實際年齡老嗎?腰痛比你想得還要常見。我們可以幫你治好它。把這個墊子放在你的腰部,一小時內,你就可以四處走,彷彿沒有毛病在困擾你。再度做回你自己吧!

由此可知,廣告說的問題是腰痛。

重要字彙

lower back : (n.) 腰部   common : (adj.) 常見的

fix : (v.) 治療、醫治;修理   pad : (n.) 墊子

bother : (v.) 困擾

重要片語

get around : 四處走動   as if... : 彷彿 / 好像……

29. Please look at the following three pictures.

Listen to the following short talk. Who is the girl talking about?

I'm so glad that man saved me. I woke up because of all the smoke in my room. My door felt hot, so I knew there was fire on the other side. I was so scared. But all of a sudden, the man broke down the door and carried me outside. I would be dead if it weren't for him.

A    B 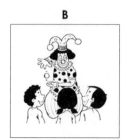   C

Answer: C

我真慶幸那個男子救了我。我因為房間滿是煙霧而醒來。我感覺門很燙，所以我知道門的另一邊失火了。我好害怕，但突然間，那男子破門而入把我帶到外面。如果不是他，我就會死掉。

由此可知，女孩講的是消防員。

scared : (adj.) 害怕的、嚇壞的

all of a sudden : 突然地

🎧 30. Please look at the following three pictures.

Gary is leaving a voice mail message. What kind of weather is Gary in?

Hi, Anna. It's Gary. I don't think we should go hiking today. If we went now, it could be dangerous. I saw the wind blow down a tree earlier, and I don't want one to fall on us. Tomorrow should be less windy, so let's try to go then.

A	B	C

Answer: B

嗨，Anna。我是 Gary。我覺得我們今天不能去健行。如果我們現在出去，可能會很危險。稍早前我看到風把一棵樹吹倒，我不想也有樹倒在我們身上。明天風應該會比較小，我們到時候再去吧！

由此可知，現在的天氣是刮風。

windy : (adj.) 風大的、刮風的

go hiking : 去健行　　　　　　　　　　　　　**blow down... :** 吹倒……

第二回
閱讀模擬試題解析

二、閱讀能力測驗

本測驗分三部份，全部都是單選題，共 35 題，作答時間 35 分鐘。

第一部份：詞彙和結構

共 15 題，每個題目裡有一個空格。請從四個選項中選出一個最適合題意的字或詞作答。

---

1. I like Tim's ____. He always tells the truth.

　　A. humor　　　　　　B. respect　　　　　　C. courage　　　　　　D. honesty

Answer: D

A.　humor：(n.) 幽默

例：I don't understand Paul's humor. (我不懂 Paul 的幽默。)

B. respect：(n.) 尊敬

例：Sammy has a lot of respect for his mother. (Sammy 非常尊敬她的母親。)

C. courage：(n.) 勇氣

例：Peter has a lot of courage. (Peter 很有勇氣。)

D. honesty：(n.) 誠實

例：Honesty is the best policy. (誠實為上策。──諺語)

本題空格後面有 tells the truth (說實話)，可知答案應選 D。

---

2. Jeremy won the race, so his father was very ____ of him.

　　A. nervous　　　　　　B. selfish　　　　　　C. proud　　　　　　D. bright

Answer: C

A.　nervous：(adj.) 緊張的

例：Exams make Teddy very nervous. (考試讓 Teddy 很緊張。)

B. selfish：(adj.) 自私的

例：Lucy has few friends because she is very selfish. (因為 Lucy 很自私，所以她沒什麼朋友。)

C. proud：(adj.) 驕傲的，be proud of...：為⋯⋯感到驕傲、以⋯⋯為榮

例：Mrs. Lin is very proud of her successful son. (林太太非常以她成功的兒子為榮。)

D. bright：(adj.) 明亮的、光明的

例：The moon looks so bright tonight. (今晚的月亮看起來好亮。)

根據上下文語意及用法，故答案選 C。

3. The shoes were of poor _____. The bottoms fell off the first day I wore them.

　　A. diet　　　　　　B. quality　　　　　　C. health　　　　　　D. price

Answer: B

重要關鍵

A. diet：(n.) (控制體重的) 飲食，poor diet：不良的飲食

B. quality：(n.) 品質，be of poor / high quality：品質很差 / 很好

例：The bag I bought online turned out to be of poor quality. (我在網路上買的那個包包結果品質很差。)

C. health：(n.) 健康，be in poor / good health：健康不佳 / 良好

D. price：(n.) 價格、價錢

空格後的句子說「我第一天穿鞋底就脫落了。」可知是「品質」不好，故答案選 B。

重要字彙

bottom：(n.) 底部

重要片語

fall off：掉落

4. Bill is so strong that he can _____ 100 kilograms.

　　A. lift　　　　　　B. cancel　　　　　　C. praise　　　　　　D. revise

Answer: A

重要關鍵

A. lift：(v.) 舉起、抬起

例：She lifted the box up. (她舉起了箱子。)

B. cancel：(v.) 取消

例：The baseball game was canceled because of the heavy rain. (棒球比賽因為下大雨而被取消了。)

C. praise：(v.) 稱讚、讚美

例：Everyone is praising Daniel's new book. (大家都對 Daniel 的新書讚譽有加。)

D. revise：(v.) 修訂、校訂

例：There is a lot in your report that needs to be revised. (你這份報告有許多地方有待修正。)

根據上下文語意，故答案選 A。

5. The restaurant is _____ here, so we should leave early or take a taxi.

    A. ahead of   B. in front of   C. far from   D. across from

Answer: C

重要關鍵

A. ahead of... : 在……之前

例 : Lisa made reservations ahead of time. (Lisa 提前訂位。)

B. in front of... : 在……前面

例 : Michelle is too shy to perform in front of her friends.

    (Michelle 太害羞，不敢在朋友面前表演。)

C. far from... : 離……很遠

例 : There's a night market not far from where I live. (離我住的不遠處有個夜市。)

D. across from... : 在……對面

例 : The coffee shop is across from our school. (那家咖啡廳在我們學校對面。)

空格後說應該要早點出發或搭計程車，故知答案應選 C。

---

6. Before you buy that carton of a dozen eggs, make sure _____ of them are broken.

    A. no   B. neither   C. either   D. none

Answer: D

重要關鍵

A. no : (adj.) 沒有 (之後接名詞)

例 : The little boy has no friends to talk to. (那個小男孩沒有朋友可以說話。)

B. neither : (pron.) (兩者之中) 無一、兩者皆不

例 : I know neither of those two people. (那兩個人我都不認識。)

C. either : (pron.) (兩者之中) 任何一個

例 : Watching either of the two movies is fine with me. (這兩部電影我看哪一部都可以。)

D. none : (pron.) (三者以上) 無一，none of 後可接可數或不可數名詞，若當主詞時，需注意其後動詞的用法 :

none of + 複數可數名詞 + 複數動詞

例 : None of these pens work. (這些筆沒一枝能用的。)

none of + 不可數名詞 + 單數動詞

例 : None of the trash smells bad. (那些垃圾聞起來都不會臭。)

空格後有 of them，故知空格內應置名詞或代名詞，A 項的 no 是形容詞，故不予考慮。

原題句中有 dozen eggs (一打蛋)，故知空格內應置 none，因此 D 項為正選。

重要字彙

carton : (n.) 紙盒

7. Lori's mother makes her _____ her teeth before she goes to bed every night.

A. brush
B. brushes
C. to brush
D. brushing

Answer: A

重要關鍵 💡

make 是使役動詞，加受詞後，其後須接原形動詞。

例：That sad song made me cry. (那首悲傷的歌讓我落淚。)

根據上述，所以答案選 A。

8. Someone's cell phone _____ on the bench in the park.

A. left
B. leaves
C. was left
D. is leaving

Answer: C

重要關鍵 💡

cell phone (手機) 是「物」，一定是「被」某人遺留在公園的板凳上，所以要用被動語態 "be + p.p."，故答案為 C。

9. Tony _____ to your birthday party if he has time tomorrow.

A. will go
B. has gone
C. goes
D. went

Answer: A

重要關鍵 💡

本題測試 if 引導的條件句與時態的關係，句中出現 if (如果) 引導的現在式副詞子句時 (稱為條件句)，主要子句應採未來式 (will / will not + 原形動詞)。

例：If it rains tomorrow, we will not go hiking. (如果明天下雨，我們就不會去健行。)

本句後面有條件句 "if he has time"，其中 has 是現在式動詞，故知之前的主要子句應採未來式，即空格內應填入 will go，因此 A 項為正選。

10. The knife is _____. You may cut yourself if you are not careful.

A. quick
B. useful
C. modern
D. sharp

Answer: D

A. quick：(adj.) 快速的

例：I took a quick look at the menu. (我很快地看了一下菜單。)

B. useful : (adj.) 有用的

例：A flashlight is very useful when you go camping. (手電筒在露營時非常管用。)

C. modern : (adj.) 現代的、現代化的

例：Modern people are often stressed out by their schoolwork or jobs.

(現代人常被課業或工作壓得喘不過氣來。)

D. sharp : (adj.) 尖銳的、銳利的

例：The floor was covered with sharp pieces of metal. (地上佈滿了尖銳的金屬。)

題目的後半段說「如果你不小心可能會割傷自己。」，因此刀子應該是「銳利的」，所以答案為 D。

---

11. Monica always keeps her mother's words _____.

    A. at head   B. in mind   C. to heart   D. by brain

Answer: B

重要關鍵

本題測驗重點為 keep...in mind：記住 / 牢記……。

例：Jimmy said he'd keep your suggestion in mind. (Jimmy 說他會記住你的建議。)

"keep...in mind" 為固定用法，因此答案選 B。

---

12. Jeremy and his friends played basketball _____ Saturday afternoon.

    A. in   B. at   C. for   D. on

Answer: D

重要關鍵

本題測驗重點為介系詞 on 與時間搭配的用法。介系詞 on 其後接特定的日子，像「日期」、「星期幾」或「節日」。

例：on June 15, on Monday(s), on my birthday, on Teacher's Day 等。此外，與「日期」、「星期幾」或「節日」並用的早上、下午或晚上，介系詞也要以「日期」、「星期幾」或「節日」為準，故亦須用 on。

例：A: When is the picnic? (A: 野餐在何時？)

    B: It's on Sunday morning. (B: 在星期天早上。)

由此可知，故答案為 D。

13. The clerk said we need to _____ of the hotel before twelve o'clock.

   A. check out   B. break up   C. run away   D. leave for

Answer: A

重要關鍵

A. check out of a / the hotel：辦理退房手續，check out：退房、結帳離開

例：Mr. Smith has checked out of the hotel this morning. (Smith 先生今早已經退房了。)

   Can I store my bags here for two hours after I check out?

   (退房後我可不可以把我的包包寄放在這裡兩小時？)

補充：check into a hotel = check in (at a / the hotel)：住進旅館、在旅館辦理住宿手續

B. break up：終止、破裂。後面常與介系詞 with 並用，形成 break up with...：與……分手。

例：It's a pity that Stan broke up with Cindy. (真可惜 Stan 和 Cindy 分手了。)

C. run away：跑走，與介系詞 from 並用，形成 run away from...：逃離……。

例：Jack often ran away from home when he was young. (Jack 年輕時經常逃家。)

D. leave for... : 出發前往……

例：Neil will leave for New Zealand tomorrow. (Neil 明天即將前往紐西蘭。)

本題測驗重點為「在旅館辦理退房手續」的用法，因此答案選 A。

14. I left a message for Fred, but he didn't _____.

   A. record   B. recover   C. repair   D. reply

Answer: D

重要關鍵

A. record：(v.) 記錄；錄製

例：Irene recorded a song for her friend. (Irene 錄了一首歌給她朋友。)

B. recover：(v.) 恢復、復原

例：Getting enough sleep will help you recover sooner. (睡眠充足有助你早日復原。)

C. repair：(v.) 修理

例：Albert is repairing his scooter. (Albert 正在修理他的機車。)

D. reply：(v.) 回答、答覆

例：He hasn't replied to my question. (他還沒回答我的問題。)

根據上下文語意，故答案選 D。

重要字彙

message：(n.) 留言、信息，leave a message (for someone)：留言 (給某人)

例：If I'm not home when you call, leave a message. (如果你打來時我不在家，就留言吧。)

15. Mr. Hanks fell _____ in his chair because he was so tired.

A. sleeps   B. sleeping   C. asleep   D. slept

Answer: C

本題測驗重點為 fall asleep：睡著，fall 的三態為 fall, fell, fallen，asleep：(adj.) 睡著的。

例：My cat fell asleep on the sofa.（我的貓在沙發上睡著了。）

故答案為 C。

第二部份：段落填空

共 10 題，包括二個段落，每個段落各含四到六個空格。每格均有四個選項，請依照文意選出最適合的答案。

Questions 16-20

Andy wants to ask the most beautiful girl in school, Monica, out on a date. He is shy, __(16)__ he asks his friend, Greg, to help him. Greg composes a beautiful love song and tells Andy to sing it under Monica's window. Monica thinks he is very sweet after __(17)__ the song. Next, Greg writes a love letter and asks Andy to sign his name at the bottom and __(18)__ it. Monica thinks the letter is beautiful and she decides to __(19)__ Andy. Andy is very happy and thanks Greg __(20)__ all his help.

16. A. or   B. so   C. therefore   D. however

Answer: B

空格前後為兩個子句，因此需要連接詞來連接兩句，therefore（因此）與 however（然而）為副詞，故 C、D 不予考慮。

本題測驗重點為附屬連接詞表示「前因後果」的用法。Andy 因為害羞，「所以」請 Greg 幫忙，因此須填入表示「結果」的連接詞 so，故答案為 B。

17. A. hear	B. hears	C. hearing	D. heard

Answer: C

本題測驗重點為 after 做介系詞的用法。after 除可做附屬連接詞,也可做介系詞,後面接名詞或動名詞做受詞。

例:I started studying after lunch. (吃完午餐後我開始讀書。)

After trying for 10 minutes, Dave finally got the car to start.

(試了十分鐘後,Dave 終於把車子發動了。)

由此可知,故答案選 C。

18. A. throw	B. lend	C. return	D. mail

Answer: D

A. throw : (v.) 丟

B. lend : (v.) 借出

C. return : (v.) 歸還

D. mail : (v.) 郵寄

由前半句知道 Greg 寫了一封 love letter (情書),因此可判斷,他請 Andy 將情書「寄出」給 Monica,故答案選 D,mail it = mail the letter : 寄信。

19. A. give up	B. point at	C. go out with	D. put up with

Answer: C

A. give up... : 放棄……

例:Danny gave up studying Chinese because it was too difficult. (Danny 放棄學中文,因為太難了。)

B. point at... : 指著……

例:It's rude to point at people. (指著人是很不禮貌的。)

C. go out with someone : 與某人外出

例:Now and then, Nick goes out with his coworkers. (Nick 有時會和同事出去。)

D. put up with someone : 忍受某人

例:Henry couldn't put up with his noisy neighbor anymore. (Henry 再也無法忍受他吵鬧的鄰居了。)

根據上下文語意,Monica 認為情書很美,故決定與 Andy 外出約會,因此答案選 C。

20. A. for	B. by	C. with	D. because

Answer: A

重要關鍵

本題測驗重點為 thank someone for... : 為……感謝某人。

例：Sandy thanked her friend for his timely help. (Sandy 感謝她朋友及時的幫忙。)

因此答案選 A。

重要字彙

shy : (adj.) 害羞的

compose : (v.) 作 (詩、曲)

例：He spent his spare time composing songs. (他用空餘時間作曲。)

sign : (v.) 簽名

例：He signed his name on the check. (他在支票上簽了名。)

bottom : (n.) 底部

例：Please read the sentence at the bottom of this page. (請唸此頁底部的那個句子。)

重要片語

ask someone out on a date : 約某人約會

例：Jack has been asking me out on a date. (Jack 一直約我出去約會。)

Questions 21-25

James is the best student in school. He is so __(21)__ that he gets an A in every class. He uses a computer database at his school to search __(22)__ information. He also likes to search the Internet. Reading nonfiction books __(23)__ him think of new ideas. He believes that there is always room for improvement. That is the reason __(24)__ he studies so hard. He wants to become a teacher __(25)__. He thinks education is one of the most important things in life.

21. A. silly	B. careless	C. intelligent	D. jealous

Answer: C

重要關鍵

A. silly : (adj.) 愚蠢的

B. careless : (adj.) 不小心的

C. intelligent : (adj.) 聰明的

D. jealous : (adj.) 忌妒的

根據上下文語意，答案應選 C，呼應前句 the best student 及後半句 gets an A in every class。

22. A. on	B. for	C. over	D. into

Answer: B

重要關鍵

本題測驗重點為 search for... : 尋找……。

例：He searched for work at various stores. (他在各家商店尋找工作。)

search for... 為固定用法，故選 B。

23. A. help	B. which help	C. and helping	D. helps

Answer: D

重要關鍵

本題測驗重點為動名詞作主詞的用法。動名詞作主詞時，視為第三人稱單數，須搭配單數動詞。

例：Getting up early is a good habit. (早起是個好習慣。)

　　Collecting stamps is Wendy's hobby. (集郵是 Wendy 的嗜好。)

根據上述，故選 D。

24. A. why	B. where	C. which	D. what

Answer: A

重要關鍵

本題測驗重點為關係副詞 why 的用法。

why 當關係副詞時，用以修飾先行詞 the reason (原因、理由)。

例：Tell me the reason why you were late. (告訴我你遲到的原因。)

空格前有先行詞 the reason，因此空格應填關係副詞 why，故答案為 A。

25. A. next time	B. one day	C. on time	D. the other day

Answer: B

重要關鍵

A. next time : 下一次

B. one day : 將來有一天

例：Joey hopes that he can meet the president one day. (Joey 希望有一天能見到總統。)

C. on time : 準時

D. the other day : 前些時候 (與過去式並用)

例：Sam got in a car accident the other day. (Sam 前幾天發生了車禍。)

根據上下文語意及用法，故知答案應選 B。

重要字彙

database : (n.) 資料庫

information : (n.) 資訊、消息 (不可數名詞)

nonfiction : (n.) 非小說類散文文學

improvement : (n.) 進步，room for improvement : 進步的空間

education : (n.) 教育

重要片語

search the Internet : 搜尋網路

第三部份：閱讀理解

共 10 題，包括數篇短文，每篇短文後面有三至四個相關問題。請由四個選項中選出最適合的答案。

Questions 26-28

Room for Rent in Shared Apartment

- *Close to campus, bus stop, parks, supermarket*
- *Own room + bath, share kitchen + living room*
- *Comes with bed, desk, chair; no closet*
- *NT$6,000 per month - Female student only*

Interested? Contact Ms. Sarah Chen today 6421-9824

---

26. What can you NOT find near the apartment?

    A. A theater.

    B. A place to relax.

    C. A school.

    D. A place to shop.

Answer: A

27. Who can rent the room?

    A. Anyone that is interested.

    B. Only men that are students.

    C. Anyone that is single.

    D. Only women that are students.

Answer: D

28. What is NOT included in the room?

    A. A bed.

    B. A chair.

    C. A closet.

    D. A desk.

Answer: C

 重要字彙

rent : (n. & v.) 出租、租用，for rent : 招租

shared : (adj.) 分享的、共用的，share : (v.) 分享、共用

apartment : (n.) 公寓

campus : (n.) 校園

supermarket : (n.) 超市

own : (adj.) 自己的

closet : (n.) 衣櫃

female : (adj.) 女性的，male : (adj.) 男性的

contact : (v.) 聯絡

single : (adj.) 單身的

include : (v.) 包含

重要片語

close to... : 靠近……

come with... : 附有……

例 : **All meals come with salad, drink, and dessert. (** 所有餐點均附有沙拉、飲料和甜點。**)**

Questions 29-31

> May 19, 2013
>
> Dear Annie,
>
>   My favorite season is spring. In spring, I can ride my bike in the park with my friends. I also like to play Frisbee with my dog there. In addition, the air always smells nice because of all of the flowers. I like the weather, too. It is always warm. Well, except when it rains.
>
>   Baseball starts in spring, too! I love baseball so much. Oh, and finally, I also like spring because my birthday is in spring. It's later this month, and it's coming soon!
>
>   How about you? What is your favorite season?
>
> Sincerely,
> Charlie

29. What is the main idea of this letter?

    A. Asking for help.

    B. Talking about his best friend.

    C. Making up a funny story.

    D. Talking about a season.

    Answer: D

30. What does Charlie do in the park?

    A. Play baseball.

    B. Ride his bike.

    C. Walk his dog.

    D. Enjoy the rain.

    Answer: B

31. What will Charlie do this month?

    A. Play Frisbee with his friends.

    B. Ride his bike to school.

    C. Celebrate his birthday.

    D. Visit Annie.

Answer: C

重要字彙

favorite：(adj.) 最喜歡的

Frisbee：(n.) 飛盤，**play Frisbee**：玩丟飛盤遊戲

except：(prep.) 除了……之外

celebrate：(v.) 慶祝

重要片語

in addition：而且、此外

例：**Bobby is friendly. In addition, he is very smart. (Bobby 人很和善，而且也很聰明。)**

because of...：因為……、由於……

Questions 32-35

    A bully is someone who uses their power to scare or hurt someone who is weaker. In school, "bullying" happens all the time, especially when there are no teachers or adults around.

    Usually, bullies are mean to kids that are a little different from everyone else. If you have ever been "bullied" in school, you are not alone. About half the kids you know have been bullied, too. If you need help, the best thing you can do is talk to an adult about what is happening to you.

32. What best describes a bully?

    A. He is a funny guy.

    B. He is a smart kid.

    C. He is a little strange.

    D. He is a mean person.

Answer: D

33. According to the passage, when does "bullying" usually happen?

    A. When no kids are around.

    B. When classes begin.

    C. When no grown-ups are around.

    D. When kids leave school.

Answer: C

34. How many kids have been bullied before?

    A. Less than ten percent of kids.

    B. Around fifty percent of kids.

    C. Only a few kids in a class.

    D. Almost every kid.

Answer: B

35. What can you do if you have been bullied?

    A. Tell your parents.

    B. Discuss it with your classmates.

    C. Ask a bigger kid to protect you.

    D. Talk to the person who is bullying you.

Answer: A

重要字彙

bully：(n.) 惡霸 & (v.) 霸凌

scare：(v.) 使恐懼、驚嚇

例：You scared me when you opened the door suddenly. (你突然開門嚇到了我。)

weak：(adj.) 弱的，weaker 是 weak 的比較級

bullying：(n.) 恃強凌弱的事件

adult：(n.) 成人

mean：(adj.) 惡毒的

describe：(v.) 描寫、形容

funny：(adj.) 幽默風趣的

smart：(adj.) 聰明的

strange：(adj.) 奇怪的

grown-up：(n.) 成年人

percent：(n.) 百分比

discuss：(v.) 討論

protect：(v.) 保護

重要片語

all the time：一直

例：He studies in the library all the time. (他總是在圖書館唸書。)

be different from... : 和……不同

the best thing (that) someone can do is (to) + 原形動詞：某人能做到最好的是……

~ 第三回 模擬試題解答 ~

聽力 Listening

第一部份 看圖辨義	第二部份 問答		第三部份 簡短對話		第四部份 短文聽解
1. C	6. C	11. C	16. B	21. B	26. C
2. B	7. B	12. A	17. C	22. C	27. B
3. C	8. A	13. B	18. B	23. B	28. C
4. A	9. C	14. A	19. C	24. C	29. B
5. C	10. A	15. B	20. A	25. B	30. A

閱讀 Reading

第一部份 詞彙和結構			第二部份 段落填空		第三部份 閱讀理解	
1. C	6. B	11. A	16. C	21. D	26. C	31. B
2. D	7. D	12. C	17. A	22. B	27. B	32. A
3. B	8. C	13. A	18. C	23. A	28. D	33. C
4. A	9. D	14. D	19. D	24. D	29. D	34. D
5. C	10. B	15. C	20. B	25. C	30. C	35. A

第三回
聽力模擬試題解析

一、聽力測驗

本測驗分四個部份，全部都是單選題，共 30 題，作答時間約 20 分鐘。作答說明為中文，印在試題冊上並經由光碟放音機播出。

第一部份：看圖辨義

共 5 題，每題請聽光碟放音機播出的題目和三個英語句子之後，選出與所看到的圖畫最相符的答案。每題只播出一遍。

1. What is the boy doing?
   A. He is skiing.
   B. He is surfing the Internet.
   C. He is riding a skateboard.

Answer: C

what 主要用來詢問事物、動作等，聽到 what 問句時，要注意圖片中包含的事物、動作或資訊。本題用 "What is someone doing?" 來詢問「某人正在做什麼？」。

本題測驗重點為 ride a skateboard：溜滑板，ride：(v.) 乘坐、搭乘，skateboard：(n.) 滑板，故答案為 C。

重要字彙

ski：(v.) 滑雪　　　　　　　　　　　　the Internet：(n.) 網際網路，surf the Internet：上網

2. What do we know about David's clothing business?
   A. It earns more than NT$4,000 a week.
   B. It makes less than NT$2,000 each month.
   C. It sells about 1,000 pieces of clothing every day.

Answer: B

本題測驗重點為「月份」。圖表中的 Jan.（一月）、Feb.（二月）、Mar.（三月）、Apr.（四月）、May（五月）等都是表月份，選項中只有 B 的敘述與月份 (month) 有關，故答案為 B。

 3. What is true about the picture?

　　A. The girl is hiding a ball from the boy.

　　B. The girl and the boy are throwing away the ball.

　　C. The boy is giving the girl a ball.

Answer: C

題目問「關於圖片，何者為是？」，由圖可看出，男孩把球交給另一個女孩，因此答案為 C。

重要字彙

hide：(v.) 躲、藏，三態為 hide, hid, hidden

hide A from B：將 A 藏起來避免被 B 發現

例：Billy hid his test sheet from his father. (Billy 把考卷藏起來避免被他爸爸發現。)

重要片語

throw away...：丟棄……

 4. Which destination has the package with the longest stay?

　　A. Japan.

　　B. NT$17,500.

　　C. 2 nights and 3 days.

Answer: A

Trip Packages

Destination	Length	Price
Korea	4 nights / 5 days	NT$17,500
Japan	7 nights / 8 days	NT$35,000
Hong Kong	2 nights / 3 days	NT$9,999

★ Packages include flight and hotel ★

以 which 所引導的問句，是在問選擇項目或指出某特定事物。本題測驗重點為 which place (哪一個地方)，選項中只有 A，Japan (日本) 為地方，故答案為 A。

重要字彙

package：(n.) 套裝行程

include：(v.) 包含

destination：(n.) 目的地

flight：(n.) 飛行、班機

5. What is true about the picture?

   A. The man is crying for help.

   B. The woman is running away.

   C. The man is robbing the woman of her bag.

Answer: C

本題測驗「關於圖片，何者為是？」，由圖片中可以看出，男子搶了女子的皮包後拔腿就跑，女子則大聲呼救，因此答案為 C，rob someone of something：搶劫某人某物。

例：The man robbed Mr. Lee of his gold watch. (這名男子搶了李先生的金錶。)

重要片語 📝

cry for help：呼救、求救　　　　　　　　　　　　**run away**：跑走

第二部份：問答

共 10 題，每題請聽光碟放音機播出的英語句子，再從試題冊上三個回答中，選出一個最適合的答案。
每題只播出一遍。

6. If you don't have a library card, you can't check out any books.

   A. Yes, I love reading books.

   B. No, I don't like to study in the library.

   C. Please tell me how to apply for a card.

Answer: C

本題測驗重點為 library card：圖書館借書證，check out books：將書借走。題目說「如果沒有圖書館借書證的話，你就不能借書」，因此選項 C 為適切的答案，how to apply for a card：如何申請借書證，apply for...：申請……。

例：If you want to apply for a credit card, please fill out this form.

　　(如果你想申請信用卡，請填寫這張表格。)

7. So, how big is your house?

    A. I just moved to a new house.

    B. My house is as big as John's house.

    C. My parents built our house.

Answer: B

 重要關鍵

本題測驗重點為 "How big is...?" ，表示「……有多大？」，題目問 "How big is your house?" (你家有多大？)，可知答案應選 B，as big as John's house (跟 John 的家一樣大)。

as + adj. / adv. + as + A：與 A 一樣……

例：Kathy is as beautiful as her sisters. (Kathy 和她的姊妹們一樣漂亮。)

補充：How + adj. 常用來詢問「有多……」，如：How old (年紀多大、幾歲)、How tall (有多高)、How long (有多久) 等。

例：How tall is your brother? (你哥哥多高？)

    How long does it take to go from here to Taipei? (從這裡到台北要多久？)

 重要字彙

move：(v.) 搬動、移動，move to a new house：搬新家

8. I'm going to buy you a T-shirt. What is your favorite color?

    A. I like blue the best.

    B. I'm a medium.

    C. I love ice cream very much.

Answer: A

 重要關鍵

題目意為「你最喜歡什麼顏色？」，因此只有 A「我最喜歡藍色。」符合句意。

B「我的尺寸是 M 號。」應是問服飾的尺寸，medium：(n. & adj.) 中號 (的)

C「我很喜歡冰淇淋。」應是詢問喜歡的食物。

9. What is the price of this table?

   A. It is made of wood.

   B. It is pretty small.

   C. It's NT$800.

Answer: C

price 是名詞，表示「價錢、價格」的意思，此題詢問「這張桌子多少錢？」，因此答案選 C「台幣八百元。」。
A「它是木製的。」應問桌子的材質。B「它相當小。」則應詢問桌子的大小。

10. Excuse me, how do I get to a bank near here?

   A. Just keep walking and you will see one on the right.

   B. Yes, I usually keep my money in the bank.

   C. The bank is open until 3:30 p.m.

Answer: A

本題測驗重點為 "How do someone get to...?"，表示「某人要如何到達……？」。

例：Excuse me, sir. I'm lost. How do I get to the train station?

   (先生，不好意思。我迷路了。請問要怎麼去火車站？)

由此可知，答案應選 A「一直走，你就會看到右手邊有一家。」。

keep + V-ing. : 保持、繼續……，on the right : 在右邊，on the left : 在左邊

例：Keep going straight and you'll see the bookstore on the left. (一直走，你就會在左手邊看到書局。)

11. Are you going to the grocery store this afternoon?

   A. Yes, it's faster to get there by bus.

   B. I have been to many stores before.

   C. No, but I will go next week.

Answer: C

本題測驗重點為 "Are you going to + 地方 ?"，用來詢問對方是否要去某地。

例：Are you going to the convenience store? (你要去便利商店嗎？)

由此可知，本題答案應選 C。

重要字彙

grocery store (n.) : 雜貨店

 12. How often do you play basketball?

    A. Twice a week.

    B. With my brother.

    C. In the park.

Answer: A

重要關鍵

題目的疑問詞是 How often (多久)，問的是做某事的頻率，答句常搭配頻率副詞如：sometimes, always, never 或 every day, once a week, twice a month 等時間副詞片語一起使用。

例：A: How often do you read the newspaper? (A: 你多常看報紙？)

    B: I read it every day. (B: 我每天都看。)

故 A 為正選。

 13. Did you send Joe an e-mail?

    A. Yes, Joe sent me a letter.

    B. No, I called him on the phone.

    C. Actually, Joe is my cousin.

Answer: B

重要關鍵

本題測驗重點為 send someone an e-mail：寄電子郵件給某人。題目問「你有寄電子郵件給 Joe 嗎？」故答案選 B「沒有，我是打電話給他。」，call someone on the phone：打電話給某人。

例：I was doing the dishes when you called me on the phone. (你打電話給我時，我正在洗碗。)

 重要字彙

letter：(n.) 信件，**send someone a letter**：寄信給某人　　　　**actually**：(adv.) 事實上

cousin：(n.) 表 (堂) 兄、弟、姊、妹

 14. I feel worse today.

    A. Then you should see a doctor.

    B. I'm glad that you feel better.

    C. Yes, it was raining hard this morning.

Answer: A

重要關鍵

本題測驗重點為 feel worse：感覺更差 / 更糟，worse 為 bad 的比較級，feel better 則是「感覺比較好」，better 為 good 的比較級。題目說「我今天感覺更糟了。」故知答案應選 A，see a doctor：看醫生。

15. Who is the author of this book?
   A. Arthur is my friend.
   B. Arthur Smith wrote it.
   C. It is a book on King Arthur.

Answer: B

本題測驗重點為 author：(n.) 作者、作家。題目問「誰是這本書的作者？」可知答案應選 B「Arthur Smith 寫的。」。C 選項的 "a book on..." 是「有關於……的書」之意。

第三部份：簡短對話

共 10 題，每題請聽光碟放音機播出一段對話和一個相關的問題後，再從試題冊上三個選項中，選出一個最適合的答案。每段對話和問題播出一遍。

16. M: The movie starts at 5:00 p.m.
   W: Oh, no! We are really running late.
   M: Take it easy. I don't like the first part of the movie anyway.
   Q: Why is the woman unhappy?
      A. She doesn't like to run.
      B. They won't be on time for the movie.
      C. She doesn't want to see the movie.

Answer: B

本題測驗重點為 be running late，意指「快要遲到、快來不及」，與「跑步」無關。B 選項中的 on time 意指「準時」，故選 B。

重要字彙

unhappy：(adj.) 不開心的

anyway：(adv.) 反正

take it easy：別急、慢慢來
例：Take it easy! We still have a lot of time. (別急！我們還有很多時間。)

17. W: Our boss wants to know why you are late.

M: Oh, no! It is going to be a long day.

Q: What is the man saying?

A. The man thinks he is taller than the boss.

B. The boss did not like his work.

C. He is going to have a hard day at work.

Answer: C

本題測驗重點為 a long day，意指「漫長、難熬的一天」。

例：You must be tired after such a long day. (經過這麼漫長的一天，你一定累了吧。)

選項中的 a hard day (難熬的一天) 與 a long day 意思相近，故選 C。

18. M: What do you do on weekends?

W: I love to go to the bookstore.

M: Really?

W: Yes, I could spend all day there.

Q: What does the woman like to do?

A. She likes to eat.

B. She likes to read.

C. She likes to exercise.

Answer: B

本題的關鍵句為對話中的 "I love to go to the bookstore." (我喜歡去書店。)，也就表示女子喜歡「看書」，所以答案為 B。

19. W: Let's go to the movies tonight.

M: Sure. Do you want me to pick you up?

W: Great! How about 6:00 p.m.? We can have dinner on the way to the theater.

M: No problem.

Q: When will the speakers have dinner?

A. At 6:00 p.m.

B. After the movie.

C. Before they see the movie.

Answer: C

重要關鍵

本題測驗重點為 on the way to + 地方:去某地的途中 / 路上。

例:On the way to work, David saw a terrible accident. (在上班途中,David 目睹一場嚴重的車禍。)

對話中女子說「我們可以在去電影院的路上吃晚餐」,可知他們會在看電影之前吃晚餐,故答案選 C。

 重要片語

pick someone up / pick up someone:接某人

例:I'll pick you up tonight at seven o'clock. (我今晚七點會去接你。)

 20. M: The cake is delicious.

W: Then have some more.

M: Where did you buy it? At the bakery around the corner?

W: No, my mother baked it for me.

Q: Where did the woman get the cake?

　　A. From her mother.

　　B. At the bakery.

　　C. She made it herself.

Answer: A

 重要關鍵

本題關鍵句為女子所說 "My mother baked it for me." (我媽媽幫我烤的。),bake:(v.) 烘、烤。

例:Karen baked a yummy chocolate cake. (Karen 烤了一個美味的巧克力蛋糕。)

題目問「女子的蛋糕是哪來的?」,故答案選 A。

重要字彙

bakery:(n.) 麵包店

 重要片語

around the corner:在 (轉角) 附近

例:There's a convenience store around the corner. (在轉角附近有家便利商店。)

21. M: New York is a great city.

W: We should go this winter.

M: Maybe we should wait until summer.

W: No, New York has too many visitors then.

Q: What happens in New York in the summer?

A. Everything closes early.

B. Too many people come to the city.

C. The weather is too hot.

Answer: B

本題關鍵句是最後一句「紐約那時會有太多觀光客。」，visitor : (n.) 觀光客、旅遊者，意即選項 B「有太多人去到那座城市。」。

22. W: Hey, Paul. Long time no see!

M: Hello, Cindy. It's great to see you again.

W: Do you have any time to chat tonight?

M: No, but we can get together at lunch time tomorrow.

W: OK. See you then.

Q: When will the speakers meet?

A. Tonight.

B. At lunch time today.

C. Tomorrow.

Answer: C

本題關鍵句是男子所說 "we can get together at lunch time tomorrow"，亦即「我們明天午餐時間可以聚一聚」，get together : 聚會、團聚。

例 : I got together with my old friends last night. (我昨晚和老朋友聚會。)

題目問「說話者何時會碰面？」，故答案為 C。

23. W: Watching TV is really boring.

M: So, what do you feel like doing then?

W: Let's go shopping at the new department store.

Q: What does the woman say about watching TV?

A. She really enjoys watching TV.

B. She feels bored when she watches TV.

C. She feels like buying a new TV.

Answer: B

本題測驗重點為 boring 和 bored。

boring : (adj.) 無聊的

例 : The baseball game is boring. (那場棒球賽很無聊。)

bored : (adj.) 感到無聊的

例 : Jim feels bored because he has nothing to do. (Jim 覺得很無聊,因為他無事可做。)

女子說「看電視很無聊。」故答案選 B。

feel like + V-ing : 想要……

例 : **He feels like going to a movie. (他想要去看電影。)**

go shopping : 去購物

24. M: Did you buy that ring?

W: No, it used to be my grandmother's.

M: It's very beautiful.

W: Yes, it's precious to me.

Q: How did the woman get the ring?

A. She bought it herself.

B. It's a present from her mother.

C. Her grandmother gave it to her.

Answer: C

本題測驗重點為 used to + 原形動詞 : 曾經……、過去時常……。

例 : Bonnie and I used to play basketball together. (Bonnie 和我過去時常一起打籃球。)

女子說戒指曾經是她祖母的,可知是她祖母送她的,因此答案選 C。

precious : (adj.) 貴重的、珍貴的　　　　　　　　　　　　　**present : (n.) 禮物**

 25. M: I want to thank you by cooking you a meal.

W: That is very nice of you.

M: Do you like to eat steak?

W: Of course. Steak is delicious!

Q: What will the man cook for the woman?

    A. Fish.

    B. Beef.

    C. Pork.

Answer: B

重要關鍵 💡

本題測驗重點是 steak：牛排，因此答案選 B，beef：(n.) 牛肉。

A. fish：(n.) 魚

C. pork：(n.) 豬肉

第四部份：短文聽解

共 5 題，每題有三個圖片選項。請聽光碟放音機播出的題目，並選出一個最適合的圖片。每題播出一遍。

 26. Please look at the following three pictures.

Listen to the following news report. What job does the woman have?

This is Barbara Waller reporting from the site of an apartment fire that started about half an hour ago. I have just learned that firefighters have rescued a father and two children and are now working on putting out the flames. I should be able to interview the fire chief later and will report back when I get more updates. Back to you, Ted.

A

B

C

Answer: C

重要關鍵 💡

我是 Barbara Waller，正從一棟半小時前發生火災的公寓現場為您做報導。我剛剛得知消息，有消防員救出了一位父親和兩個小孩，現在正在盡力撲滅火勢。稍後我應該可以訪問到消防隊長，當我有進一步消息時，會再為您報導。把現場交還給你，Ted。

由此可知，女子的職業是記者。

重要字彙

firefighter : (n.) 消防員

flame : (n.) 火焰

chief : (n.) 長官、首領

rescue : (v.) 解救

interview : (v.) 訪問、訪談

update : (n.) 最新的情況、最新的信息

重要片語

put out... : 熄滅 / 撲滅⋯⋯

27. Please look at the following three pictures.

Listen to the following short talk. What kind of exercise does Duncan do?

Wow! Look at Duncan over there. He's so strong. I don't understand how he lifts those huge weights. They're heavier than I am! He'll definitely win the competition. I've never seen arms that are as big as his. No wonder people are scared of him.

A 　　　B 　　　C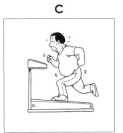

Answer: B

哇！你看 Duncan。他好壯，我不知道他怎麼舉得起那麼重的槓鈴。它們比我還要重耶！他肯定會贏得這次的比賽。我從來沒有見過比他更大更壯的手臂。難怪大家都很怕他。

由此可知，Duncan 做的運動是舉重。

重要字彙

lift : (v.) 舉起

competition : (n.) 競賽

definitely : (adv.) 肯定地

重要片語

no wonder : 難怪⋯⋯

be scared of... : 害怕⋯⋯

28. Please look at the following three pictures.

Listen to the following short talk. What is Julia's hobby?

Have you tried the cake yet? Julia made it. It's so good. I don't know how she finds time to cook such good food. She cooks even when she's tired from work. It's great to have a friend like her around. We always get to eat good food!

A   B   C

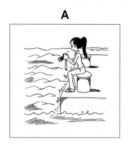  

Answer: C

 重要關鍵

你吃過蛋糕了嗎？是 Julia 做的。它很好吃。我不知道她哪來的時間做出如此美味的食物。就算她工作很累，她也會下廚。有她這樣的朋友真是太好了。我們可以常常吃到很棒的食物！

由此可知，Julia 的興趣是做菜。

29. Please look at the following three pictures.

Listen to the following short talk. What kind of activity does the boy enjoy?

I don't like most sports, but I love being in the pool. I like the feeling of floating in the water and how all noises go away once my head is underwater. I also like how this exercises both my arms and legs. With more practice, I'll be the fastest on my team someday.

A   B   C

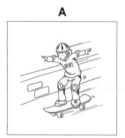 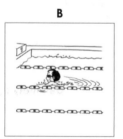 

Answer: B

重要關鍵

我不喜歡大部份的運動，但我喜歡在泳池裡。我喜歡那種漂在水中的感覺，而且只要我的頭進到水中，所有的噪音都會不見。我也很喜歡這種運動讓我的手臂和腿都有運動到。只要練習得夠多，總有一天我一定會變成隊裡最快的人。

由此可知，男孩喜歡游泳。

重要字彙

pool : (n.) 水池、游泳池

noise : (n.) 噪音

practice : (n.) 練習

float : (v.) 漂浮

underwater : (adv.) 在水中

someday : (adv.) 將來有一天

---

30. Please look at the following three pictures.

Listen to the following commercial. Who works at this business?

We're having a special this weekend. Come into our salon any time Saturday or Sunday, and our talented stylists will wash, cut, and style your hair for 30 percent off. Look like a million bucks without spending a million bucks!

A
B
C

Answer: A

重要關鍵

我們本週有個特惠活動。只要在週六或是週日的任何時間來我們沙龍，我們店裡才華洋溢的設計師會幫您洗髮、剪髮還有設計髮型，通通打七折。讓你不用花大錢就看起來神清氣爽。

由此可知，這個行業是髮型設計師。

重要字彙

commercial : (n.) 電視或廣播中的廣告

salon : (n.) 沙龍

stylist : (n.) 設計師

buck : (n.) 美金一塊錢 (= dollar)

special : (n.) 特惠活動、特價品

talented : (adj.) 有才華的

style : (v.) 設計

第三回
閱讀模擬試題解析

二、閱讀能力測驗

本測驗分三部份，全部都是單選題，共 35 題，作答時間 35 分鐘。

第一部份：詞彙和結構

共 15 題，每個題目裡有一個空格。請從四個選項中選出一個最適合題意的字或詞作答。

1. Jimmy will bring his teddy bear _____ on the camping trip.

    A. back   B. up   C. along   D. about

Answer: C

重要關鍵

A. bring...back / bring back... : 把……帶回來、送還……

例：Please bring back our ladder after you've used it. (用完梯子後，請拿回來還我們。)

B. bring...up / bring up... : 提起 / 談起……；扶養……

例：Benjamin's uncle brought him up. (Benjamin 是他舅舅撫養長大的。)

C. bring...along / bring along... : 帶著……一起

例：Don't forget to bring along your scarf. (別忘了帶圍巾。)

D. bring about... : 造成 / 導致……

例：The car accident brought about lots of changes in Pat's life.

    (那場車禍對 Pat 的生活造成很大的變化。)

根據前後語意，故答案選 C。

重要字彙

teddy bear : (n.) 玩具熊 (英國泰迪熊)

camping : (n.) 露營

例：He goes camping once a month. (他一個月露營一次。)

2. We usually go to the park to fly our kites on _____ days.

    A. helpful   B. funny   C. painful   D. windy

Answer: D

重要關鍵

A. helpful : (adj.) 有幫助的、幫得上忙的

例：This map is very helpful. (這張地圖很管用。)

B. funny : (adj.) 好笑的、滑稽的

例：a funny story (好笑的故事)

C. painful : (adj.) 疼痛的、痛苦的

例：It's painful to me to listen to rock music. (聽搖滾樂對我來說是很痛苦的。)

D. windy : (adj.) 風大的、多風的

例：It's very windy outside. (外面風很大。)

fly a kite 意思是「放風箏」，因此應該是在「風大的」日子去放風箏，所以答案為 D。

3. Sabrina bought a _____ of Jay because he's her favorite singer.

    A. plant   B. poster   C. planet   D. prize

Answer: B

重要關鍵

A. plant : (n.) 植物

例：My mother is watering the plants in the garden. (我媽媽正在花園裡澆花。)

B. poster : (n.) 海報

C. planet : (n.) 行星

D. prize : (n.) 獎品、獎賞

例：They won the prize worth $ 3,000. (他們獲得價值三千元的獎品。)

根據前後語意，Sabrina 是買了她最喜歡的歌手海報，故答案選 B。

4. Whenever John talks, he has trouble _____ his audience interested.

    A. keeping   B. to keep   C. keeps   D. kept

Answer: A

重要關鍵

本題測驗重點為 "have trouble + V-ing" 的固定用法，表示「做……有困難」。

例：Tim has trouble communicating with his father. (Tim 跟他父親溝通有困難。)

根據上述，故知答案應選 A。

重要字彙

audience : (n.) 觀眾、聽眾   interested : (adj.) 感興趣的

5. It is better to buy fruit and vegetables in _____.

    A. year   B. period   C. season   D. month

Answer: C

重要關鍵

本題測驗重點為 in season 的固定用法。

in season：正值盛產季，反之則是 out of season：不在盛產季、不合季節的。

例：Watermelons are in season in the summer. (西瓜在夏季是盛產期。)

     It's hard to find cherries now. They're out of season. (現在很難看到櫻桃；它們已過了時令。)

故本題答案選 C。

6. I'm going to _____ a DVD. What kind of movie do you want to see?

    A. beat   B. rent   C. greet   D. treat

Answer: B

重要關鍵

A. beat：(v.) 打、擊

B. rent：(v.) 出租、租用

例：I rented the apartment from an old lady. (我向一位老太太租了這棟公寓。)

C. greet：(v.) 迎接；問候

例：Brad greeted his guests at the door. (Brad 在門口迎接他的客人。)

D. treat：(v.) 對待

例：Ricky treats Andrew like his brother. (Ricky 把 Andrew 當親兄弟般對待。)

空格後說「你想看哪一種電影？」，故知答案為 B。

7. I'm very thirsty. _____ you get me a glass of water?

    A. Whether   B. Should   C. Must   D. Could

Answer: D

重要關鍵

本題測驗重點為助動詞的用法。

whether 表示「是否」，為連接詞，無法引導疑問句，故不予考慮。

should 表示「應該」，must 表示「必須」，could 表示「能夠、可以」，只有過去式助動詞 could 使用在問句中時，可表示客氣、婉轉的語氣。

例：Could you show me how to use this machine? (你能教我如何使用這台機器嗎？)

本句是在請求對方做某事，故答案選 D。

8. Edward pressed the button to _____ the computer.

    A. look into   B. break into   C. turn on   D. call on

Answer: C

重要關鍵

A. look into... : 調查……

例 : The police are looking into the case. (警方正在調查這起案件。)

B. break into... : 闖入……

例 : Someone broke into Ted's house last night. (昨晚 Ted 家被闖空門了。)

C. turn on... : 打開電視、收音機、電燈等電器的電源

例 : turn on the TV (打開電視)、turn on the radio (打開收音機)、turn on the light (開燈) 等，「關掉……」則為 turn off...。

D. call on... : 拜訪……

例 : David will call on an old friend tomorrow. (David 明天要去拜訪一位老朋友。)

根據前後語意，故知答案選 C，turn on the computer : 開電腦。

重要字彙

press : (v.) 按、壓   **button : (n.) 按鈕**

---

9. The new teacher is smart as _____ as handsome.

    A. good   B. many   C. long   D. well

Answer: D

重要關鍵

A. A is as good as B. : A 和 B 一樣好

例 : This movie is as good as that one. (這部電影和那部一樣好。)

B. as many as + 複數名詞 : 與……一樣多、多達……

例 : There are as many as 100 people at the party. (那場派對上的人有一百名之多。)

C. A is as long as B. : A 和 B 一樣長

例 : Johnny's arms are as long as his father's. (Johnny 的手臂和他爸爸的一樣長。)

D. A as well as B : A 以及 B，為對等連接詞，可用以連接詞性或時態相同的字詞。

例 : Jim likes to play sports as well as read books. (Jim 喜歡運動以及看書。)

空格前後為兩個詞性相同的形容詞，根據上述，故知答案選 D。

重要字彙

smart : (adj.) 聰明的   **handsome : (adj.) 英俊的**

10. Helen has two brothers. One is a pianist, and _____ is a lawyer.

    A. other   B. the other   C. the others   D. another

Answer: B

重要關鍵

本題測試重點為代名詞 "one...the other..." 的用法：

one...the other... : 一個……另一個……，用於限定的兩者。

例 : Mr. Liu has two daughters. One is a doctor, and the other is a teacher.

    (劉先生有兩個女兒。一個是醫生，另一個是老師。)

one...another...the other... : 一個……一個……另一個……，用於限定的三者。

例 : John has three sisters. One is good at dancing, another sings well, and the other is a famous

    writer. (John 有三個姊妹。一個擅長跳舞，一個歌唱得很棒，還有一個是知名的作家。)

題目第一句說 "Helen has two brothers."，可知是限定的兩者，空格前已有 one，因此空格內須填 the
other，故選 B。

重要字彙

pianist : (n.) 鋼琴家   **lawyer** : (n.) 律師

11. _____ if you are angry, you should never hit anyone.

    A. Even   B. Yet   C. Still   D. Once

Answer: A

重要關鍵

本題測驗重點為 "even if..." 的用法。even if... : 即使……，為從屬連接詞，引導副詞子句，修飾主要子句。

例 : Even if it rains tomorrow, Sam will go fishing. (即使明天下雨，Sam 還是會去釣魚。)

even if 是固定用法，故選 A。

12. _____ students in Cindy's class wear glasses.

    A. Every   B. A lot   C. Several   D. Much

Answer: C

重要關鍵

本題測驗重點為表示數量的形容詞。

A. every : 每一個，後面要接單數名詞。

例 : every room (每個房間)

B. a lot 不可用來修飾名詞，要用 a lot of 或 lots of：許多的。

例：a lot of people (許多人)、a lot of water (許多水) 等。

C. several：好幾個，後面接複數名詞。

例：several friends (好幾個朋友)

D. much：許多，用來修飾不可數名詞，而且用於否定句或疑問句中，而不用於肯定句中，肯定句應使用 a lot of 或 lots of。

例：The man doesn't have much money. (那名男子沒什麼錢。)

空格後的 students 為複數名詞，根據上述，故知答案選 C。

重要字彙

glasses：(n.) 眼鏡 (恆為複數)

13. The poor boy wishes that he _____ a million dollars.

    A. could win   B. will win   C. has won   D. wins

Answer: A

重要關鍵

本題測驗重點為 "Someone wishes + that 子句" 的用法。"Someone wishes + that 子句" 表示「某人希望 / 但願……」，用於較不可能實現或與現在事實相反的希望，時態要用過去簡單式，若與過去事實相反時，則要用過去完成式。

例：I wish that I were the richest person in the world.

    (但願我是全世界最富有的人。——事實上我現在不是全世界最富有的人)

    I wish that I had apologized to Neil yesterday.

    (但願我昨天有向 Neil 道歉。——事實上我昨天沒向 Neil 道歉)

本句的時態是現在式，與現在事實相反，因此要用過去簡單式，故選 A。

14. Debby was talking on the phone _____ the doorbell rang.

    A. then   B. since   C. that   D. when

Answer: D

重要關鍵

本題測驗重點為「Someone was + V-ing + when 引導的過去式副詞子句」，表示「……時，某人正在……」，when 譯成「時」。

例：We were having dinner when the earthquake hit. (地震發生時，我們正在吃晚餐。)

題目空格前有 "Debby was talking on the phone"，空格後為過去式子句 "the doorbell rang"，故知答案應選 D。

重要字彙

doorbell : (n.) 門鈴　　　　　　　　　　**ring : (v.) 鈴響，動詞三態為 ring, rang, rung**

---

15. Here are two balloons. You can have _____ the blue one or the red one.

　　A. both　　　　　　B. also　　　　　　C. either　　　　　　D. not

Answer: C

重要關鍵

本題測驗重點為 "either...or..." 的用法。either A or B：不是 A 就是 B。

例：You can have either milk or juice. (你可以喝牛奶或果汁。)

　　I don't know either Gary or Jack. (Gary 和 Jack 我都不認識。)

空格後有連接詞 or，得知空格應置 either，故選 C。

重要字彙

balloon : (n.) 汽球

第二部份：段落填空

共 10 題，包括二個段落，每個段落各含四到六個空格。每格均有四個選項，請依照文意選出最適合的答案。

Questions 16-20

　　Most children and adults like to watch television. In fact, every child and adult has a __(16)__ cartoon. These shows don't have special effects, but they are still popular. Many children enjoy __(17)__ shows with funny or cute characters. Some adults like these, __(18)__. Many adults __(19)__ to watch older cartoons like Bugs Bunny and Daffy Duck. Adults are __(20)__ that these characters are still appearing on screen, like in the movie Looney Tunes: Back in Action. This is a movie that children and adults can enjoy together.

---

16. A. most favorite　　　B. better favorite　　　C. favorite　　　D. best favorite

Answer: C

重要關鍵

favorite 這個字的意思是「最喜愛的」，本身即具有形容詞最高級之意，所以不會說 more favorite 或 the most favorite，故本題答案要選 C。同樣類型的形容詞還有 perfect (完美的)、extreme (極度的) 等。

17. A. watching	B. to watch	C. in watches	D. watch

Answer: A

本題測試重點為動詞 enjoy 的用法。及物動詞 enjoy 表示「喜歡」，與 like 或 love 同義，但 like 或 love 後面可接不定詞或動名詞作受詞，而 enjoy 後面只可接動名詞作受詞。

例：I enjoy watching baseball games.（我喜歡看棒球比賽。）
由此可知，本題答案應選 A。

18. A. nor	B. neither	C. too	D. either

Answer: C

A. nor：(conj.) 也不，置於否定句，前面要加逗號，後面句子要倒裝。

例：Tina won't go to the party, nor will her boyfriend. (Tina 不會去參加派對，她男朋友也不會去。)

B. neither：(adv.) 也不，置於否定句，前面要加 and，後面句子要倒裝。

例：Henry isn't going to the movies tonight, and neither is Nancy.
　　(Henry 今晚沒有要去看電影，Nancy 也沒有要去。)

C. too：(adv.) 也，置於肯定句句尾，前面要加逗號。

例：Martin is from Sweden. Toby is, too. (Martin 來自瑞典，Toby 也是。)

D. either：(adv.) 也不，置於否定句句尾，前面要加逗號。

例：Vicky doesn't like potatoes, and she doesn't like carrots, either.
　　(Vicky 不喜歡馬鈴薯，也不喜歡紅蘿蔔。)

空格位於句尾，之前為肯定句，故根據上述用法，可知答案應選 C。

19. A. occur	B. regret	C. prepare	D. continue

Answer: D

A. occur to someone：某人突然想到

例：It just occurred to me that there was a better way to do the job.
　　(我突然想到還有更好方法來做這項工作。)

B. regret to V：抱歉要去做……

例：We regret to inform you that you didn't win the contest. (抱歉要通知你，你沒有贏得比賽。)

C. prepare to V：準備做……

D. continue to V / V-ing：繼續、持續做……

例：If you continue to eat this much, you will get fat soon.
　　(假如你繼續吃這麼多的話，你很快就會變胖。)

從 older 可推斷出，本句是指「許多成年人仍繼續看舊的卡通」，故答案為 D。

20. A. jealous   B. excited   C. greedy   D. surprising

Answer: B

A. jealous : (adj.) 忌妒的

B. excited : (adj.) 興奮的

C. greedy : (adj.) 貪婪的、貪心的

D. surprising : (adj.) 令人驚訝的

根據上下文語意，故答案選 B。

重要字彙

adult : (n.) 成年人

cartoon : (n.) 卡通

special effects : (n.) (電影等的) 特殊效果

popular : (adj.) 受歡迎的，**be popular with...** : 受……歡迎

例 : **Jay is popular with lots of teenagers. (Jay 受許多青少年歡迎。)**

funny : (adj.) 滑稽可笑的

character : (n.) 人物、角色

screen : (n.) (電影院的) 銀幕

Questions 21-25

Ralph likes to shop. All of his friends know that he is a picky __(21)__ . Ralph likes expensive clothes that are stylish, but he never has __(22)__ money. He is always looking for clothes that are __(23)__ sale. Ralph __(24)__ a small, but he usually buys a medium because he likes baggy clothes. At this time, Ralph has enough shirts. However, he will go to the menswear section soon to buy a few new __(25)__ of pants. Ralph will definitely make sure that they are brand-name.

21. A. seller   B. eater   C. driver   D. shopper

Answer: D

shopper : (n.) 購物者。從上文知道 Ralph 喜歡購物，可推測他應是個挑剔的購物者，故答案為 D。

22. A. many	B. much	C. few	D. lot

Answer: B

重要關鍵

本題測驗數量形容詞的用法。much 與 many 皆為「許多」之意，但前者接不可數名詞 (例如：much water)，後者則接可數名詞 (例如：many cups)。同義的 a lot of / lots of 則可接所有的名詞 (例如：a lot of fun, a lot of friends, lots of money, lots of pens)。

little 與 few 皆為「很少、幾乎沒有」之意，但前者接不可數名詞 (例如：little money)，後者則接可數名詞 (例如：few friends)。

由上可知，此題只有選項 B 符合文法。

23. A. on	B. in	C. for	D. up

Answer: A

重要關鍵

本題測驗重點為 on sale：拍賣中、減價售出、打折。

例：These gloves are on sale. (這些手套在特價。)

從前句知道 Ralph 沒有很多錢，因此可推測他總是尋找特價的衣服。

補充：for sale：待售、出售中

例：The house is for sale. (這間房子要出售。)

24. A. worn	B. wore	C. was wearing	D. wears

Answer: D

重要關鍵

wear：(v.) 穿，三態為 wear, wore, worn。本句陳述 Ralph 穿小號衣服的事實，故用現在簡單式。而從文法的觀點來看，but 連接時態一致的兩個句子，故答案須與後面的動詞 buys 時態一致，故答案為 D。

25. A. pieces	B. packs	C. pairs	D. plates

Answer: C

重要關鍵

A. piece：(n.) 一片、一件、一個、一張等，多用來修飾不可數名詞。

例：a piece of advice (一則忠告)、two pieces of baggage (兩件行李)、a piece of cloth (一塊布)、a piece of cake (一塊蛋糕)、a piece of paper (一張紙) 等。

B. pack：(n.) 一包、一群 (狼、狗等犬科動物)

例：a pack of gum (一包口香糖)、two packs of cigarettes (兩包香煙)、a pack of dogs / wolves (一群狗 / 狼) 等。

C. pair：(n.) 一對、一雙、(兩部份形成的) 一件等

例：a pair of shoes (一雙鞋)、two pairs of chopsticks (兩雙筷子)、a pair of pants (一件長褲)、three pairs of jeans (三件牛仔褲) 等。

D. plate：(n.) 盤子、一盤

例：a plate of fried rice (一盤炒飯)

本題是在講「褲子」，根據上述，故答案為 C。

shop：(v.) 購物，**go shopping**：去逛街，名詞則為「商店」之意。

補充：**shopkeeper**：店主，**shoplifter**：扒手，**shopaholic**：購物狂

picky：(adj.) 挑剔的

stylish：(adj.) 時髦的、流行的，**style**：(n.) 風格、時髦

例：**His pants are out of style.** (他的褲子過時了。)

medium：(n.) 中號 (衣服)，衣服常見的三個尺寸為 (S)-small, (M)-medium, (L)-large。

baggy：(adj.) 寬鬆似袋狀的

menswear section：男裝部門，**section**：(n.) 部門

definitely：(adv.) 肯定地、無疑地

brand-name：(adj.) 有商標、品牌的

look for...：尋找……

例：**Are you looking for your wallet?** (你在找你的錢包嗎？)

make sure + that + S + V：確定……

例：**Please make sure that everyone can come.** (請確定大家都能來。)

第三部份：閱讀理解

共 10 題，包括數篇短文，每篇短文後面有三至四個相關問題。請由四個選項中選出最適合的答案。

Questions 26-28

26. Who might go to Mama's House?

    A. David, a vegetable lover, who hates fatty foods.

    B. Sandy, who loves sugar and sweets.

    C. Harry, a meat eater, who can't live without beef.

    D. Beth, who thinks chicken is the most delicious meat.

    Answer: C

27. Mr. and Mrs. Potter visited Mama's House with Harry, their 5-year-old son, on Friday night. Mrs. Potter had a coupon from the Daily Times for their meal. How much did they have to pay altogether?

    A. $900.

    B. $850.

    C. $1,000.

    D. $1,150.

    Answer: B

28. What is NOT true about Mama's House?

    A. It is open six days a week.

    B. There are three spots in Taipei.

    C. You can eat as much as you like.

    D. You don't have to pay for your child if he or she is under 12.

Answer: D

重要字彙

steak : (n.) 牛排

coupon : (n.) 折價券

fatty : (adj.) 油膩的

beef : (n.) 牛肉

altogether : (adv.) 總共、合計 (可置於句首或句尾)

例：Altogether, you'll have to pay 50 dollars.

    = You'll have to pay 50 dollars altogether.

    (您總共需付五十元。)

seafood : (n.) 海鮮

spot : (n.) 地點

sweets : (n.) 甜食 (恆為複數)

Questions 29-31

May 12, 2013

Dear Susan,

    I haven't seen you since Dragon Boat Festival. How's school in Taichung? I'm fine here in Taipei now, but we are moving to Kaohsiung next month.

    I pack things in boxes every day. It's tiring. But I find many interesting things. Do you still remember my doll, Dora? It was a gift from my grandmother in Tainan. Her head is big. She has long hair and two big eyes. There is a butterfly on her skirt. She was our daughter when we played house. You were her father and I was her mother. It was a wonderful time. Now, we go to different schools and live in different cities. I really miss you.

    I'm sending you the doll. I think you will be happy to have it. I hope we'll always be friends.

Love,
Tammy

29. Where is Tammy?

    A. In Taichung.

    B. In Kaohsiung.

    C. In Tainan.

    D. In Taipei.

Answer: D

30. What is probably true about Susan and Tammy?

    A. Tammy is going to visit Susan on Dragon Boast Festival.

    B. Their grandmother lives in Tainan.

    C. They used to go to the same school.

    D. Susan gave the doll to Tammy when she moved to Taichung.

Answer: C

31. Why does Tammy write to Susan?

    A. To ask her not to move.

    B. To tell her she wants to give her the doll.

    C. To ask her to look for the doll.

    D. To talk about their daughter.

Answer: B

【重要字彙】

Dragon Boat Festival : (n.) 端午節

pack : (v.) 打包

butterfly : (n.) 蝴蝶

move : (v.) 搬家

tiring : (adj.) 累人的

miss : (v.) 想念

【重要片語】

play house : 玩扮家家酒

look for... : 尋找……

used to + 原形動詞 : 過去曾經……

Questions 32-35

    Emma bought a new shirt at the store yesterday. Although she really likes it, she is going to have to take it back. When she put it on, a hole ripped in the bottom of the shirt. Emma realized that the shirt was of poor quality. Emma doesn't like to complain, but she is angry because she feels like the shirt was a waste of money. Emma has decided that she will go back to the store and demand a refund. She won't put up with any excuses from the sales staff about getting her money back, and she is sure that she will not recommend this store to any of her friends.

32. Why is Emma going to go back to the store?

    A. She wants to return a shirt that is of poor quality.

    B. She wants to buy another shirt at the store.

    C. She wants to exchange the shirt for a larger size.

    D. The shirt Emma bought is too long.

Answer: A

33. According to the passage, which statement is TRUE?

    A. Emma often complains to store managers.

    B. There was a hole in the shirt before Emma put it on.

    C. Emma thinks she wasted money on the shirt.

    D. The shirt Emma bought was very cheap.

Answer: C

34. What will Emma do if the clerk tries to make any excuses?

    A. She will accept it and spend more money there.

    B. She will tell her friends to buy shirts at the store.

    C. She will not get angry.

    D. She will not stand for it.

Answer: D

35. What does Emma want the store to do?

    A. Return her money.

    B. Allow her to get a new shirt.

    C. Apologize to her and fix the hole.

    D. Offer her some free shirts.

Answer: A

重要字彙

rip：(v.) 裂開；撕 (破)、扯

例：**She ripped the letter open.** (她撕開信封。)

bottom：(n.) 底部

例：**The bottom of the cup is broken.** (這杯子的底破了。)

quality：(n.) 品質

例：**The watch is of great / poor quality.** (這個手錶品質很好 / 差。)

complain：(v.) 抱怨

例：**Monica kept complaining to me about the food.** (Monica 一直向我抱怨食物。)

waste：(n. & v.) 浪費，**a waste of money / time**：浪費金錢 / 時間

demand：(v.) 要求、請求

例：The customer demanded to see the manager. (那名顧客要求見經理。)

refund：(n.) 退款、償還金額

excuse：(n.) 藉口、理由

例：There is no excuse for your being late. (你的遲到沒有理由可說。)

staff：(n.) (全體) 職員、(全體) 工作人員，sales staff：銷售員

recommend：(v.) 推薦、介紹

例：Can you recommend me some books on this subject? (你能推薦一些有關這個學科的書給我嗎？)

exchange：(v.) 更換

accept：(v.) 接受

offer：(v.) 提供

apologize：(v.) 道歉，apologize to someone：向某人道歉

重要片語

put on...：穿上、戴上……

例：Put on your coat right now. (立刻穿上你的外套。)

take off...：脫掉……

例：Please take your shoes off before entering the room. (進門前請先脫掉鞋子。)

put up with...：忍受、容忍…… (= stand for...)

例：Kathy couldn't put up with her sister any longer. (Kathy 再也不能忍受她姊姊了。)

~ 第四回 模擬試題解答 ~

聽力 Listening

第一部份 看圖辨義	第二部份 問答		第三部份 簡短對話		第四部份 短文聽解
1. C	6. B	11. C	16. C	21. B	26. C
2. B	7. C	12. B	17. B	22. C	27. A
3. C	8. B	13. C	18. C	23. B	28. C
4. B	9. C	14. A	19. B	24. C	29. B
5. A	10. B	15. C	20. A	25. B	30. C

閱讀 Reading

第一部份 詞彙和結構			第二部份 段落填空		第三部份 閱讀理解	
1. A	6. C	11. C	16. B	21. C	26. D	31. B
2. C	7. D	12. B	17. A	22. D	27. A	32. C
3. D	8. B	13. D	18. C	23. C	28. B	33. B
4. A	9. D	14. B	19. D	24. D	29. D	34. D
5. D	10. B	15. A	20. B	25. B	30. C	35. A

第四回
聽力模擬試題解析

一、聽力測驗

本測驗分四個部份，全部都是單選題，共 30 題，作答時間約 20 分鐘。作答說明為中文，印在試題冊上並經由光碟放音機播出。

第一部份：看圖辨義

共 5 題，每題請聽光碟放音機播出的題目和三個英語句子之後，選出與所看到的圖畫最相符的答案。
每題只播出一遍。

 1. What does the picture tell us?

A. The red team has won by five points.

B. The blue team has lost by twelve points.

C. The blue team beat the red team by seven points.

```
FINAL SCORE

RED TEAM      5 points
BLUE TEAM    12 points
```

Answer: C

本題測驗重點為 win, lose, beat 及介系詞 by 的用法。win 是「贏、獲勝」的意思，beat 表示「打敗、勝過」，lose 是「輸掉」，而介系詞 by 則是表示「以……的差距」。

例：George and his partners won the science fair. (George 和他的搭檔在科展中獲勝。)

Barbara lost the race. (Barbara 輸掉比賽。)

Jim beat the other tennis player easily. (Jim 輕易地就擊敗了另一個網球選手。)

We beat the team by twenty points. (我們以二十分之差擊敗那一隊。)

從圖片中看來，Blue Team 以七分之差擊敗 Red Team，故答案為 C。

 2. Where are the people?

A. They are planting trees in the garden.

B. They are hiking in the forest.

C. They are watching a movie in the theater.

Answer: B

本題測驗疑問詞 where 引導的疑問句，用 "Where are...?" 來詢問「……在哪裡？」。從圖片中兩人身上的裝備，包括了背包和手杖，得知他們正在森林中健行，故答案選 B，hike：(v.) 健行、徒步旅行，go hiking：去做徒步旅行、去健行，forest：(n.) 森林。

重要字彙

plant：(v.) 栽種 & (n.) 植物

watch a movie：觀賞電影

3. What kind of club are the students in?

    A. A dance club.

    B. A drama club.

    C. A chess club.

Answer: C

本題在詢問圖片中的學生參加什麼樣類型的社團，kind 是「種類」，club 是「社團」，in 則有「參加、身處於」的意思。圖片中有兩個人在對弈，而旁觀學生皆熱衷的在觀看，由此可知學生們參加的是棋藝社，故答案為 C，chess：(n.) 西洋棋。

A. dance club：(n.) 舞蹈社

B. drama club：(n.) 戲劇社

4. How much do the pen and books cost?

    A. $50.

    B. $350.

    C. $300.

Answer: B

本題測驗疑問詞 how 引導的疑問句，用 "How much does something cost?" 來詢問「某物要多少錢？」。

例：How much does that wallet cost? (那個皮夾要多少錢？)

要注意，本題問的是 pen 和 books 兩種物品共多少錢，而非單一的價錢，故答案為 B。

5. What is the boy doing?

    A. Listening to music.

    B. Acting in a play.

    C. Playing a game.

Answer: A

"What is someone doing?" 是在詢問某人當下正在做什麼事，圖中男孩戴著耳機在聽音樂，故答案選 A，listen to...：傾聽 / 注意聽……。

例：Lucy likes to listen to music while jogging. (Lucy 慢跑時喜歡聽音樂。)

play：(n.) 戲劇表演，act in a play：在一場戲劇中演出

第二部份：問答

共 10 題，每題請聽光碟放音機播出的英語句子，再從試題冊上三個回答中，選出一個最適合的答案。
每題只播出一遍。

6. Do you like to take a shower in the morning?
   A. No, I don't. I like to grow vegetables.
   B. No, I prefer to take a bath.
   C. Yes, I like to take my dog for a walk.

Answer: B

 **重要關鍵**

本題測驗重點為 take a shower：淋浴。B 選項說 "No, I prefer to take a bath."（不，我比較喜歡泡澡。）
與題目問「喜不喜歡淋浴」相呼應，故選之。

prefer：(v.) 較喜歡

prefer + n. / V-ing / to V：比較喜歡……

例：I prefer walking / to walk alone.（我比較喜歡一個人蹓躂。）

prefer + n. / V-ing + to + n. / V-ing：喜歡……勝過……

例：I prefer coffee to tea.（咖啡和茶之中，我比較喜歡咖啡。）

take a bath：泡澡

重要片語

grow vegetables：種菜　　　　　　　　　　　　**take my dog for a walk：遛狗**

7. Vivian mixed blue and yellow paint.
   A. Vivian is a good artist.
   B. That will taste good.
   C. Now she has green paint.

Answer: C

重要關鍵

本題測驗重點為 mix：(v.) 使混合，paint：(n.) 油漆、塗料。將 blue 和 yellow 兩種顏料混合，可知結果為
同為顏色的 green，故答案為 C。

重要字彙

artist：(n.) 藝術家
taste：(v.) 嚐起來
例：**The steak tasted delicious.（牛排嚐起來很美味。）**

 8. Where can I try on this shirt?

    A. The bathrooms are dirty.

    B. The fitting room is over there on the left.

    C. The new pants you just bought look good.

Answer: B

重要關鍵

本題測驗重點為 try on... : 試穿 / 試戴……。shirt 是「襯衫」，可以在 fitting room (試衣間) 裡試穿，故答案為 B。

重要字彙

pants : (n.) 長褲。補充：**shorts** : 短褲，**jeans** : 牛仔褲。此類單字常以複數形出現，一件長褲為 **a pair of pants**。

 9. How did the soccer game go? Who won?

    A. I play soccer every weekend. It's great!

    B. Yes, soccer is a very interesting game.

    C. The game ended in a tie.

Answer: C

重要關鍵

本題測驗重點為 "How did...go?"，為詢問「事情進行如何？」之常用句型；"Who won?" 使用過去式，詢問 soccer game (足球比賽) 輸贏的結果，故選時態相同之 C 選項。

end in a tie : 結果平手、不分勝負。tie 亦可當動詞。

例 : The two teams tied. (兩隊平手。)

 10. How long does it take by train?

    A. I usually take the bus.

    B. It takes fifteen minutes.

    C. It costs thirty-five dollars to go there by train.

Answer: B

重要關鍵

本題測驗重點為「How long does it take by + 交通工具？」，表示「搭乘某交通工具要多久時間？」。

例 : How long does it take you to go to work by bus? (你搭公車去上班要多久時間？)

由此可知，本題答案應選 B「要十五分鐘。」。

by train : 搭火車

cost：(v.) 花 (錢)

例：It cost me NT$1,000 to buy the skirt. (我花了台幣一千元買了這件裙子。)

11. Hello, may I speak to Ms. Brown, please?

    A. Could you tell her to call me back?

    B. Yes, she can speak English.

    C. Hold on. I'll get her for you.

Answer: C

重要關鍵

本題測驗重點為電話用語。在電話中要找某人時，可說 "May / Could I speak to...?"。

例：May I speak to Sam, please? (我要找 Sam。)，以下為幾個可能的回應：

    This is Sam. / This is Sam speaking. / Sam speaking. / Speaking. (我就是。)

    Hold on, please. (請稍等。)

    Hold on. I'll get him for you. (等一下，我幫你叫他。)

    He can't come to the phone at the moment. (他目前無法過來接電話。)

    He's not here. Would you like to leave a message? (他不在。你想要留言嗎？)

    He's not here. Can I have him call you back? (他不在。需要我請他回電給你嗎？)

由此可知，故答案選 C。

12. Oh, no! The lines are so long.

    A. Please wait behind the white line.

    B. It will take us a long time to get our tickets.

    C. I can draw a line for you.

Answer: B

重要關鍵

本題測驗重點為 line：(n.) 排隊的行列，題目說「排隊的隊伍很長」，故答案選 B「我們要花很長一段時間才能買到票。」，take：(v.) 花 (時間)，take us a long time：花我們很長一段時間。

例：It took me four hours to get there. (我花了四小時才到那兒。)

A. wait behind the white line：在白線後方等候

C. draw a line：畫一條線

 13. I'm in a rush. Let's discuss this tomorrow.

    A. OK. We can cook it tomorrow.

    B. Yes, I can help you clean up tomorrow.

    C. Sure. We'll talk about it tomorrow.

Answer: C

 重要關鍵

本題測驗重點為 discuss：(v.) 討論。

例：Eric refused to discuss the problem with me.

   = Eric refused to talk about the problem with me.

   (Eric 拒絕和我討論這個問題。)

由上可知，故答案選 C。

 重要片語

in a rush：匆忙地、趕時間　　　　　　　　　　　　**clean up：打掃、整理**

 14. Should we buy a travel guide before we go to Hong Kong?

    A. Sure. Then we'll know which places to visit.

    B. Don't you have enough clothes?

    C. Yes, we need a tour guide.

Answer: A

重要關鍵

本題測驗重點為 travel guide：旅遊指南。此句話在詢問對方去香港之前是否應該先買一本旅遊指南，故答案為 A。選項 C 的 tour guide 是「導遊」之意，為陷阱選項。

 15. Dad's birthday is coming up.

    A. How could you say that?

    B. Yes, Dad is coming home soon.

    C. Yeah, what should we do to celebrate it?

Answer: C

 重要關鍵

本題是直述句，測驗重點為 be coming up：即將到來。

例：Chinese Valentine's Day is coming up. (七夕情人節快到了。)

題目說「爸爸的生日快到了。」，因此答案選 C，celebrate：(v.) 慶祝。

例：How are you going to celebrate your birthday? (你打算如何慶生？)

第三部份：簡短對話

共 10 題，每題請聽光碟放音機播出一段對話和一個相關的問題後，再從試題冊上三個選項中，選出一個最適合的答案。每段對話和問題播出一遍。

16. W: I'm worried about Jeremy.

    M: What's wrong? Isn't he in his bedroom?

    W: He is. But he never studies, and he plays video games all night.

    M: OK. I'll talk to him about it right away.

    W: Maybe I should call his teacher, too.

    Q: Who are the speakers talking about?

    　　A. Their boss.

    　　B. Their neighbor.

    　　C. Their son.

    Answer: C

重要關鍵

女子和男子在談論 Jeremy，女子說她很擔心 Jeremy，男子回應說「怎麼了？他不在臥室嗎？」女子接著說 Jeremy 從不讀書，而且整天都在打電動玩具，對話的最後男子說會和 Jeremy 談這件事，而女子則說或許應該打電話給 Jeremy 的老師，由此推測，Jeremy 應是他們的兒子，故答案選 C。

重要字彙

boss : (n.) 老闆　　　　　　　　　　　　　　　　**neighbor : (n.) 鄰居**

17. M: Hello. May I speak to Ms. Smith, please?

    W: This is she speaking.

    M: This is Maria's Bakery. Can we deliver a birthday cake to you this morning?

    W: A cake? Are you sure? I didn't order a cake.

    M: Well, it is a gift from Mr. Harrison.

    W: Oh, I see. Please have it delivered after 10:30 a.m.

    Q: Why is the woman surprised?

    　　A. She doesn't like cakes.

    　　B. She wasn't expecting a cake.

    　　C. She forgot to order a cake for Mr. Harrison.

    Answer: B

重要關鍵

從女子回應說 "A cake? Are you sure? I didn't order a cake." 得知，她沒有預期會有蛋糕送到她家，故答案為 B，expect : (v.) 預期、期待。

例 : Frank doesn't expect you to come. (Frank 沒料到你會來。)

 重要字彙

bakery : (n.) 麵包店　　　　　　　　　　**deliver : (v.) 遞送**

---

18. M: I'd like a sandwich, and my friend would like fried chicken, please.

W: Will that be all?

M: I'd also like a Coke, and my friend would like a piece of cake for dessert.

W: Both of your orders will be ready soon.

Q: What does the man's friend order?

    A. A sandwich and a Coke.

    B. French fries, a Coke, and a piece of cake.

    C. Fried chicken and a piece of cake.

Answer: C

 重要關鍵

本題為餐廳中服務生與顧客點餐的對話，題目問的是男子的朋友點了什麼，故答案為 C。

 重要字彙

sandwich : (n.) 三明治　　　　　　　　**fried chicken : (n.) 炸雞**
dessert : (n.) 甜點　　　　　　　　　　**French fries : (n.) 薯條**

---

19. M: Peter speaks French very well.

W: Yes, he studied it in high school.

M: He must have been a hardworking student.

W: Yes. Actually, he's one of the best students I've ever taught.

Q: Who is the man probably talking to?

    A. Peter's former classmate.

    B. Peter's language teacher.

    C. Peter's former student from France.

Answer: B

重要關鍵

從對話中女子說 "he's one of the best students I've ever taught" (他是我所教過最好的學生之一) 得知，
答案應選 B。

重要字彙

hardworking : (adj.) 努力的、勤勉的

20. W: Are you still coming over for dinner tonight?

M: Yeah, I'll be over in an hour.

W: Is there anything that you don't eat?

M: I don't like seafood. By the way, do you want me to rent a DVD before I come over?

W: That will be great!

Q: What will the man stop to do on his way to the woman's place?

A. Rent a DVD.

B. Buy movie tickets.

C. Pick up some seafood.

Answer: A

題目中的 stop to V 就是「停下來去做……」的意思。

例：My neighbor stopped to talk to me when she saw me on the street.

（我的鄰居在街上看見我時，停下來跟我說話。）

題目中的 "on someone's way to + 地方" 則是「在某人去某地的途中」。

例：Sam ran into a friend of his on his way to the movie theater.

（Sam 在去電影院的途中遇到一位朋友。）

對話中男子說 "do you want me to rent a DVD when I come over"（妳要我過去的時候順便租 DVD 嗎？），可知答案應選 A。

come over：順道來訪

例：**Come over any time. (隨時歡迎來坐坐。)**

21. M: Hi, Mandy. What are you doing?

W: I am studying my family tree.

M: That must be very interesting.

W: Yes. Actually, I just found out that my great-grandfather was once a general.

Q: What is the woman doing?

A. She's going camping with her family.

B. She's learning about her family history.

C. She's studying about plants and trees.

Answer: B

本題測驗重點為 family tree：家族（譜），因此答案選 B，family history：家族歷史。

 重要字彙

great-grandfather：(n.) 曾祖父　　　　　　　　　　general：(n.) 將軍

重要片語

go camping：(去) 露營。相同用法有 go jogging：(去) 慢跑，go hiking：(去) 健行，
go swimming：(去) 游泳，go bicycle-riding：(去) 騎腳踏車。

---

22. M: I don't feel very well.

W: Maybe you're coming down with a cold.

M: I think I'll go home and rest.

Q: What is the woman saying?

　A. The taxi is downstairs.

　B. The man should put on a sweater.

　C. The man might be getting sick.

Answer: C

重要關鍵

本題測驗重點為 come down with...：染上……(病)。

例：Dave didn't go to school because he came down with a bad cold.

　(Dave 沒有去上學，因為他得了重感冒。)

對話中女子說男子或許 coming down with a cold (得了感冒)，故知答案應選 C，get sick：生病。

重要字彙

downstairs：(adv.) 在樓下，upstairs：(adv.) 在樓上，兩字皆可當名詞、形容詞及副詞。
sweater：(n.) 毛衣

---

23. M: Do you like my new cell phone?

W: Yes, it's nice. Was it expensive?

M: Not really. I got it for fifty percent off.

W: Really? Where did you buy it?

Q: What does the man say about the cell phone?

　A. It was free.

　B. It was on sale.

　C. It was a gift from his parents.

Answer: B

重要關鍵

對話中男子說他用 fifty percent off 買到他的手機，就是「打對折」的意思，因此答案選 B「它在特價。」。

on sale：特價

例：These shoes are on sale.（這些鞋子在特價。）

 24. W: That woman is looking at you.

    M: What woman?

    W: The one in the pink dress.

    M: She's a stranger to me. I don't remember seeing her before.

    Q: What does the man say about the woman in the pink dress?

       A. He met her once before.

       B. He used to work with her.

       C. He doesn't know her.

Answer: C

重要關鍵

stranger (n.) 是「陌生人」的意思，男子說「她對我來說是陌生人。」，意即「我不認識她。」的意思，因此答案選 C。

重要字彙

once：(adv.) 一次；曾經

 25. M: The five-day holiday is coming up.

    W: What are you going to do?

    M: I think I'll just watch TV.

    W: You shouldn't waste time like that.

    M: Well, maybe I will go on a trip to Kenting.

    Q: What are the people discussing?

       A. The woman's trip.

       B. The man's holiday plans.

       C. Their vacation in Kenting.

Answer: B

重要關鍵

本題為朋友或同事間，談論男子五天假期要做什麼的情況，關鍵句是第二句女子所說的 "What are you going to do?"，所以答案選 B。

第四部份：短文聽解

共 5 題，每題有三個圖片選項。請聽光碟放音機播出的題目，並選出一個最適合的圖片。每題播出一遍。

 26. Please look at the following three pictures.

Tiffany's mother is talking to her neighbor. What is Tiffany learning to do?

I'm so proud of Tiffany. She's growing up so fast. I took off her training wheels, and she learned how to ride on two wheels in just one afternoon! She kept falling in the beginning, but I made sure she wore a helmet so she wouldn't get hurt. It's exciting how quickly she's learning.

A   B   C

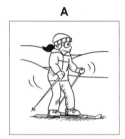

Answer: C

重要關鍵

我為 Tiffany 感到驕傲。她成長得好快。我拿掉她的輔助輪，然後她只花了一個下午就學會騎在兩輪上！一開始她一直跌倒，但是我確認她有戴安全帽，才不會受傷。她這麼快就學會，真讓人感到很興奮。

由此可知，Tiffany 在學騎腳踏車。

重要字彙

proud：(adj.) 驕傲的，**be proud of...**：為……驕傲、以……為榮
wheel：(n.) 輪子
helmet：(n.) 安全帽

27. Please look at the following three pictures.

Listen to the following short talk. What activity does the couple enjoy?

Harry and I are busy most mornings. We like to go outside and exercise together. We're not the most athletic. We don't run that fast. But while we jog, we like to talk about what's happening in our lives. It's really a fun way to exercise.

A	B	C

Answer: A

Harry 和我大部份的早晨都很忙。我們喜歡一起去外面運動。我們不是最活躍靈敏的。我們沒有跑得那麼快。但是當我們慢跑時，我們喜歡談談生活中發生的事。這樣運動真的很有趣。

由此可知，這對夫婦喜歡慢跑。

重要字彙

exercise : (v.) 運動
athletic : (adj.) 行動敏捷的、擅長運動的
jog : (v.) 慢跑

28. Please look at the following three pictures.

Listen to the following message for Paul. What is wrong with Tony?

Hello, Paul. It's Tony. Thanks for coming to visit me. I'm usually pretty bored in here because I can't really move around. Sometimes I read or watch TV, but usually I just lie here and think. I really like getting visitors. It helps me forget that I'm stuck in this room.

A	B	C
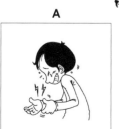	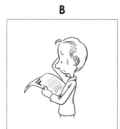	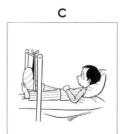

Answer: C

哈囉，Paul。我是 Tony。謝謝你來看我。我在這裡通常都很無聊，因為我不能四處走動。有時候我會讀點書或是看電視，但是通常我只是躺在這裡想東想西。我真的很高興有訪客來。這能讓我暫時忘記我被困在這房間裡。

由此可知，Tony 腿受傷了不能動。

重要字彙

bored : (adj.) 無聊的

visitor : (n.) 探病者、探訪者

stick : (v.) 困住，三態為 stick, stuck, stuck，be stuck in... : 被困在……

 29. Please look at the following three pictures.

Listen to the following short talk. What does Pam like to do?

Ever since Pam was a kid, she has loved reading so much. Before she went to school, she would read. After class, she would read her textbooks, and then read more of her favorite novels. She even keeps a pile of books next to her bed so she can read before she falls asleep.

A	B	C
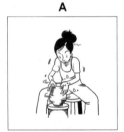		

Answer: B

重要關鍵

從 Pam 還是個孩子時，她已經非常喜歡閱讀了。在她上學前，她會讀個書。放學後，她會先唸課本，然後再多讀幾本她最愛的小說。她甚至放了一堆書在她的床邊，這樣她就可以在睡前讀書了。

由此可知，Pam 喜歡閱讀。

重要字彙

textbook : (n.) 課本　　　　　　　　　　　　　　　pile : (n.) 一堆，a pile of... : 一堆……

重要片語

fall asleep : 睡著

30. Please look at the following three pictures.

Listen to the following short talk. What class is the boy in?

When you're done using that, may I borrow it? I need it to make my sculpture. I think it will really make the face look good. I think I already did a good job making the body. What are you making? It looks so beautiful. Do you know what color you'll paint it later?

A   B   C

Answer: C

當你用完那個後,可以借我嗎?我需要用它來做我的雕塑。我想它真的會讓臉看起來很棒。我覺得我已經把身體做得很好了。你在做什麼?看起來好美。你想好等一下要上什麼顏色了嗎?

由此知,男孩在上美術課。

重要字彙

sculpture : (n.) 雕塑品

第四回
閱讀模擬試題解析

二、閱讀能力測驗

本測驗分三部份，全部都是單選題，共 35 題，作答時間 35 分鐘。

第一部份：詞彙和結構

共 15 題，每個題目裡有一個空格。請從四個選項中選出一個最適合題意的字或詞作答。

---

1. Billy is too _____ to ask any questions in class. He always asks his sister for help after school.

    A. shy   B. brave   C. polite   D. talkative

Answer: A

重要關鍵

A. shy：(adj.) 害羞的

例：Some people think that Emily is rude, but she's just shy.

    (有些人認為 Emily 很沒禮貌，但她只是害羞而已。)

B. brave：(adj.) 勇敢的

C. polite：(adj.) 有禮貌的

D. talkative：(adj.) 話多的

"too + adj. + to V" 表示「太……而不 (能)……」。

例：This article is too difficult for Tom to understand. (這篇文章對 Tom 來說太難了，他看不懂。)

根據上下文意，故答案選 A。

---

2. My grandmother is starting to learn how to use a computer, and she just got an e-mail _____.

    A. garage   B. object   C. address   D. block

Answer: C

重要關鍵

A. garage：(n.) 車庫

B. object：(n.) 物體

C. address：(n.) 住址、地址；位址

D. block：(n.) 街區

本題測驗重點為 e-mail address：電子郵件信箱，故答案為 C。

3. Have you _____ the new movie playing at the theater downtown?

    A. tried   B. gone   C. looked   D. seen

Answer: D

重要關鍵

本題測驗「看電影」的用法：

see a movie：看一場電影 (= watch a movie)

例：How often do you see a movie? (你多常去看電影？)

go to the movies：去看電影

例：Jim can't go to the movies with us tonight. (Jim 今晚沒辦法和我們去看電影。)

由此可知，本題答案應選 D。

重要字彙

theater：(n.) 電影院 (美式)。在英國則稱電影院為 **cinema**。

downtown：(adv.) 城市的商業區、市中心

4. Mr. Brown loves traveling. He has _____ England, Canada, Egypt, and Brazil, and he is in Japan right now.

    A. been to   B. had to   C. gone to   D. went to

Answer: A

重要關鍵

本題測驗重點為 have been to 與 have gone to 的區別：

"have been to + 地方" 表示某人「曾去過某地」，但現在人不在某地。

例：Have you been to Disneyland before? (你去過迪士尼樂園嗎？)

＊ 問經驗，現在人不在迪士尼。

"have gone to + 地方" 則表示某人「已經前往或抵達某地」，也就是現在人在某地或在去某地的途中。

例：Willy has gone to Germany. (Willy 已經去德國了。)

＊ 現在人在德國或前往德國的途中。

根據用法及上下文語意，可知答案應選 A。

重要片語

right now：現在

5. The spicy food Mike _____ at the restaurant yesterday is giving him a very bad stomachache now.

    A. is eating   B. will eat   C. eat   D. ate

Answer: D

重要關鍵

本題測驗重點為時態。句中有表過去時間的 yesterday，因此動詞要用過去式，故答案為 D。

重要字彙

spicy：(adj.) 辛辣的   stomachache：(n.) 胃痛

6. Catherine _____, but he lost it in just one day.

    A. to Henry lent her book

    B. for Henry to lend her book

    C. lent her book to Henry

    D. lent her book from Henry

Answer: C

重要關鍵

本題測驗重點為動詞 lend (借出、借給，動詞三態為 lend, lent, lent) 的用法：

lend something to someone：把某物借給某人 (= lend someone something)。

例：My brother seldom lends his car to me. (我哥哥很少會把車借給我。)

    Can you lend me 20 dollars? I want to buy some ice cream. (可以借我二十塊錢嗎？我想買冰淇淋。)

比較 borrow (借入) 的用法：

borrow something from someone：向某人借某物

例：Can I borrow a pen from you? (我可以向你借一枝筆嗎？)

由此可知，本題答案應選 C。

7. During the summertime, my cat likes to _____ on the floor to keep himself cool.

    A. lying   B. laid   C. lay   D. lie

Answer: D

重要關鍵

本題測驗重點為動詞 lie：(v.) 躺、臥，動詞三態變化為 lie, lay, lain，動名詞及現在分詞為 lying。

例：I'm so tired. I have to lie down. (我好累，我必須躺下來。)

    The little boy was lying on the floor crying. (那個小男孩正躺在地上哭。)

lie 另有「說謊」之意，動詞三態變化為 lie, lied, lied，動名詞及現在分詞也是 lying。

例：Don't ever lie to me again. (永遠別再對我說謊。)

lay 也可以做原形動詞，表示「放置」，動詞三態變化為 lay, laid, laid。

例：Lay the blanket down on the grass so we can start our picnic.

(把毯子放在草地上，我們就可以開始野餐了。)

空格前有不定詞的 to，因此 A、B 不可選。lay 及 lie 均為原形動詞，但根據上下文語意，故答案選 D。

重要片語

keep...cool：使……保持涼爽

「**keep + 名詞 + 形容詞**」表示「**使……保持某種狀態**」的意思。

例：**This jacket will keep you warm. (這件夾克會使你暖和。)**

另一種用法為「**keep + 名詞 + V-ing**」。

例：**I'm sorry to keep you waiting. (我很抱歉讓你等這麼久。)**

8. One of Sandy's dreams _____ around the world before she turns 35 years old.

    A. are traveling   B. is to travel   C. will travel   D. travels

Answer: B

重要關鍵

本題測驗不定詞片語置於 be 動詞後作主詞補語的用法。

名詞如 dream (夢想、理想)、goal (目標)、plan (計劃)、wish (願望) 等，都是表示一種未完成或想要完成的事情，因此這類名詞作主詞，且之後有 be 動詞時，應接 to 引導的不定詞片語作主詞補語。

例：Harold's dream is to be a baseball player. (Harold 的夢想是當一名棒球選手。)

Jenny's goal is to lose three kilograms. (Jenny 的目標是瘦三公斤。)

根據用法及上下文語意，故答案應選 B。要注意的是，本句的主詞為 One of Sandy's dreams，真正的主詞為 One 而非 Sandy's dreams，因此為第三人稱單數主詞。

重要片語

travel around the world：環遊世界

9. All of the students went on the field trip _____ for Bill, who came down with the flu today.

    A. in addition   B. as well   C. including   D. except

Answer: D

重要關鍵

A. in addition 後須與 to 並用：

in addition to + n. / V-ing：除了……以外

例：In addition to cleaning the bathroom, we also have to clean the kitchen.

    (除了打掃浴室之外，我們還得清理廚房。)

B. as well 後須與 as 並用，形成 as well as... (以及……) 的用法。

例：Andy is smart as well as handsome. (Andy 很聰明，人也長得帥。)

C. including：(prep.) 包括 / 包含……

例：Everyone has to help clean the classroom, including you. (每個人都要幫忙打掃教室，包括你。)

D. except for... : 除了……之外 (for 可省略)

例：All of the girls except for Joanna went swimming. (除了 Joanna，所有的女孩都去游泳。)

根據用法及上下文語意，故答案選 D。

重要字彙

field trip : (n.) 校外教學

10. Kevin really _____ his father. He always turns to his father for help when in trouble.

    A. makes up for   B. looks up to   C. puts up with   D. hangs up on

Answer: B

重要關鍵

A. make up for... : 彌補 / 補償……

例：What can we do to make up for your loss? (我們能做什麼來彌補你的損失？)

B. look up to someone : 尊敬 / 敬重某人，look down on someone 則是「輕視 / 瞧不起某人」。

例：We all look up to Mark because he is a good leader.

    (我們全都很尊敬 Mark，因為他是一位好的領導者。)

C. put up with... : 容忍 / 忍受……

例：Anna can't put up with her lazy boyfriend anymore. (Anna 再也無法忍受她懶惰的男友了。)

D. hang up on someone : 掛某人電話

例：I can't believe Kent just hung up on me. (我不敢相信 Kent 剛剛竟然掛我電話。)

根據上下文語意，故答案選 B。

重要片語

turn to someone for help：向某人求助　　　　　　　　　　　　in trouble：有麻煩

---

11. You need to click on the button in order _____ to the music on this stereo.

    A. listening　　　　　　B. that listens　　　　　　C. to listen　　　　　　D. will listen

Answer: C

重要關鍵

本題測驗重點為 in order to 後接原形動詞的用法。

in order to + 原形動詞：為了……(的目的)

例：She worked hard in order to study abroad next year. (她努力工作為了明年可以出國讀書。)

in order 後若為 that 時，則需接主詞加動詞，in order that + 主詞 + 動詞：以便……。

例：Mr. Lee works hard in order that he may give his family a better life.

   (李先生努力工作好讓家人生活過得好一點。)

根據上述，故知答案應選 C。

重要字彙

button：(n.) 按鈕　　　　　　　　　　　　　　　　　　stereo：(n.) 立體聲音響

重要片語

click on...：用滑鼠點……

例：If you want to open a file, click twice on the icon for it. (如果想要開啟檔案，點這個圖像兩次。)

---

12. _____ money is more difficult than I realized.

    A. Save　　　　　　B. Saving　　　　　　C. That saves　　　　　　D. By saving

Answer: B

重要關鍵

本題測驗動名詞作主詞的用法。動詞不可直接作句中的主詞，一定要變成動名詞後才能作主詞，且動名詞視為第三人稱單數，須搭配單數動詞。

例：Smoking is bad for you. (抽菸對你有害。)

根據上述，故答案應選 B。

重要字彙

realize：(v.) 了解

第四回閱讀模擬試題解析

重要片語

A is more + adj. + than + B：A 比 B 更為……

例：The red dress is more expensive than the blue one. (這件紅色洋裝比藍色那件還貴。)

---

13. Roger would like to try _____ like rock climbing or skydiving.

    A. excited something

    B. something excited

    C. exciting something

    D. something exciting

Answer: D

重要關鍵

本題測驗重點為 something 與形容詞的位置：

形容詞若與 something, nothing, anything, everything 等並用時，該形容詞須置於這些字的後面。

例：Nancy bought something nice for her children. (Nancy 買了些好東西給她的小孩。)

    I didn't do anything wrong. (我沒有做錯事。)

選項 B 及選項 D 均符合上述原則，但 excited 是「感到興奮的」，用來修飾人，無法用來修飾事物，故 B 不可選；exciting 則是「令人感到興奮的、刺激的」，可用來修飾事物，故答案為 D。

重要字彙

rock climbing：(n.) 攀岩　　　　　　　　　　　　　**skydiving：(n.) 高空跳傘**

---

14. Michael is about _____ to junior high school.

    A. go   B. to go   C. going   D. goes

Answer: B

重要關鍵

本題測驗重點為 "be about to + 原形動詞"，表示「即將／快要 (做某事)」。

例：The program is about to begin. (節目即將要開始了。)

因此答案選 B。

15. Bill walked so fast that I couldn't _____ up with him.

   A. catch   B. run   C. hold   D. pick

Answer: A

 重要關鍵

本題測驗重點為 catch up with someone：趕上某人。

例：I had to run really fast to catch up with Nancy.（我得跑很快才能趕上 Nancy。）

由此可知，本題答案為 A。

第二部份：段落填空

共 10 題，包括二個段落，每個段落各含四到六個空格。每格均有四個選項，請依照文意選出最適合的答案。

Questions 16-20

    Billy wants to play a practical joke on Mrs. Brown. He decides to wrap up a spider as a gift and __(16)__. Billy knows that Mrs. Brown is afraid __(17)__ spiders, and he thinks that it will be very funny. Mrs. Brown screams when she opens the gift, and she __(18)__ Billy to stand in the corner as a punishment. Now, the rest of Billy's class is worried that Mrs. Brown won't be their teacher __(19)__. So, they decide to __(20)__ her a special party and buy her some flowers.

16. A. give her to it   B. give it to her   C. to her give it   D. for her to give

Answer: B

 重要關鍵

本題測驗授與動詞 give（給予）的用法：

give something to someone：將某物給某人 (= give someone something)。

例：Beth gave ten dollars to the beggar.

    = Beth gave the beggar ten dollars.

    (Beth 給了那乞丐十塊錢。)

由此可知，答案選 B。

17. A. of   B. in   C. to   D. at

Answer: A

重要關鍵

本題測驗 "be afraid of..." 的用法。be afraid of...：害怕……、對……感到害怕。

例：The child is afraid of being left alone in the big house.（這孩子怕一個人留在那間大房子裡。）

由此可知，故答案為 A。

18. A. carries   B. invites   C. orders   D. argues

Answer: C

 重要關鍵

A. carry：(v.) 攜帶

B. invite：(v.) 邀請

C. order：(v.) 命令，order someone to V：命令某人做⋯⋯

例：The police officer ordered me to stop my car.（警察命令我把車停下來。）

D. argue：(v.) 爭辯、爭吵

例：Stop arguing with your parents.（別再跟你父母爭論了。）

根據上下文語意及用法，故答案選 C。

19. A. anything   B. anywhere   C. anyone   D. anymore

Answer: D

 重要關鍵

本題測驗 "not... anymore" 的用法。not...anymore 表示「不再⋯⋯、再也不⋯⋯」。

例：He doesn't work anymore.（他不再工作了。）

由此可知，故答案為 D。

20. A. gather   B. throw   C. make   D. create

Answer: B

 重要關鍵

本題測驗 throw someone a party：為某人舉辦派對（口語）。

例：Are your parents going to throw you a birthday party this year?

（今年你父母會為你舉行生日派對嗎？）

根據上述，故答案選 B。

重要字彙

practical joke：(n.) 惡作劇，**play a practical joke on...**：對⋯⋯惡作劇

spider：(n.) 蜘蛛

scream：(v.) 尖叫

punishment：(n.) 處罰、懲罰

rest：(n.) 剩餘部份、其餘的人，常做 **the rest of...**

例：**The rest of the eggs have gone bad.**（剩餘的雞蛋都壞掉了。）

wrap up... : 把……包裝起來,wrap : (v.) 包、纏繞

例:**Diane wrapped up her friend's birthday gift in colorful paper.**
(**Diane** 用彩色包裝紙把她朋友的生日禮物包起來。)
She wrapped a scarf around her neck. (她把一條圍巾圍在脖子上。)

Questions 21-25

Families are different around the world. In some countries, such as Taiwan, it is common for three __(21)__ to live in the same house. On the other hand, young people in the United States often __(22)__ away from home when they finish school. They try __(23)__ on their parents. __(24)__ they don't live at home, they are still close with their family. They __(25)__ their family a visit often. Parents often like the change, too. They feel like they have a new life and often begin new activities.

21. A. nations	B. stations	C. generations	D. directions

Answer: C

A. nation : (n.) 國家
B. station : (n.) 車站
C. generation : (n.) 世代,three generations 意指「三代」
D. direction : (n.) 方向
根據上下文語意,故答案選 C。

22. A. leave	B. jump	C. climb	D. move

Answer: D

本題測驗重點為 move away from home : 搬離家中,故答案選 D。

23. A. not depend	B. to not depending	C. not to depend	D. depending not

Answer: C

本題測驗重點為 to 引導的不定詞片語與否定副詞 not 的位置:
"to + 原形動詞" 形成的不定詞片語與 not 並用時,not 要放在 to 之前。
例:**The teacher told the students not to cheat.** (老師叫學生不要作弊。)
由此得知,答案應為 C。

24. A. If	B. Before	C. Ever since	D. Even though

Answer: D

A. if : (conj.) 如果、假如

B. before : (conj.) 在……之前

C. ever since : (conj.) 自……之後，後面接過去式的子句，修飾完成式的主要子句。

例 : Ted has gained a lot of weight ever since he got married. (自從結婚後，Ted 胖了不少。)

D. even though... : (conj.) 即使、雖然……

例 : Even though the ticket is expensive, I still want to buy it. (雖然票價很貴，我還是想買。)

空格後面兩個子句的語意相對：they don't live at home (他們不住在家裡)、they are still close with their family (他們和家裡還是很親密)，唯一符合語意和文法的連接詞為 even though，故選 D。

25. A. call	B. pay	C. drop	D. bring

Answer: B

本題測驗重點為 pay someone a visit : 拜訪某人。

例 : Paul plans to pay his uncle a visit this weekend. (Paul 打算這個週末去拜訪他叔叔。)

"pay someone a visit" 為固定用法，因此答案選 B。

重要字彙

common : (adj.) 普通、常見的

close : (adj.) 親密的、密切的

activity : (n.) 活動

重要片語

around the world : 全世界

such as... : 像是……

on the other hand : 另一方面

depend on... : 依賴……、依靠……

例 : **Ray doesn't like to depend on other people. (Ray 不喜歡依賴別人。)**

共 10 題，包括數篇短文，每篇短文後面有三至四個相關問題。請由四個選項中選出最適合的答案。

Questions 26-28

Help Wanted

Looking for a new, exciting career in radio?

106.7 FM is looking for a DJ to host a live on-air talk show.

- *Must have at least two years of experience in radio or television.*

- *You must also have a fun personality and a strong speaking voice.*

Send your resume and a demo tape to Chad at fun1067@pmail.com.

---

26. What is 106.7 FM looking for?

    A. Someone to hold a party.

    B. Someone to play music.

    C. Someone to read the news.

    D. Someone to host a radio show.

    Answer: D

27. What must you have to apply for the job?

    A. At least two years of work experience.

    B. A good knowledge of music.

    C. To be able to speak quickly.

    D. A good education.

    Answer: A

28. How do you apply for the job?

    A. Mail your demo tape to the station.

    B. Send a resume by e-mail.

    C. Call Chad at the station.

    D. Fill out a form at the station.

    Answer: B

重要字彙

career : (n.) 職業
live : (adj.) 現場的
experience : (n.) 經驗
resume : (n.) 履歷
knowledge : (n.) 知識

host : (v.) 主持
on-air : (adj.) 現場直播的
personality : (n.) 個性
demo : (n.) 試聽帶
education : (n.) 教育

重要片語

look for... : 尋找……
at least... : 至少……
hold a party : 舉辦派對
apply for... : 申請、請求……，apply for a job : 應徵工作、求職
fill out... : 填寫……
例 : To get a passport, you have to fill out all these papers. (要辦護照必須填寫這些文件。)

Questions 29-31

September 15, 2013

Dear Emma,

    I love to go to new places every summer. This summer I went to a water park with my mom, dad, and brother. We went on the first weekend in August. I got to ride many water rides. My favorite was the big water slide. My brother and my dad went on the ride, too. My mom was too scared to go on the ride. She just watched us and took pictures. At the end of the day, we ate hot dogs and watched the sun go down. I hope I can go back there soon. It was so much fun! How about you? Where did you go this summer?

Sincerely yours,
George

29. What is George's letter about?

    A. A place he goes every year.

    B. A place he wishes to go to.

    C. A place that his family owns.

    D. A place he visited in the summer.

Answer: D

30. What is George's favorite thing at the water park?

    A. The sunset.

    B. The large pool.

    C. The big slide.

    D. The food and drinks.

Answer: C

31. What does George say about his mother?

    A. She prepared hot dogs for everyone.

    B. She feared to go on the ride.

    C. She didn't like the water park.

    D. She couldn't go on the trip.

Answer: B

重要字彙

ride：(v.) 搭乘、乘坐 & (n.) 遊樂設施，**go on a / the ride**：搭乘遊樂設施

favorite：(adj.) 最喜歡的

slide：(n.) 滑道、滑梯

scared：(adj.) 害怕的

hot dog：(n.) 熱狗

sunset：(n.) 日落，**sunrise**：(n.) 日出

pool：(n.) 水池

Questions 32-35

Ben went to visit Leah at the end of last summer. After seeing that Leah hadn't done anything all summer but watch TV, he was disappointed in her. He decided to plan some fun activities for the last week before school. First, they went to the Taipei Water Park, but it was closed. The next day, they went to the zoo with Leah's little sister, but she disappeared. They spent the whole day looking for her. Finally, they took a three-day trip to the beach. Just as they arrived, a typhoon hit. It ruined the entire trip. It seemed like everything went wrong!

32. Why was Ben disappointed in Leah?

    A. Leah didn't enjoy watching TV.

    B. Ben thought she didn't like him anymore.

    C. She hadn't done anything all summer.

    D. She didn't want to see Ben before school.

Answer: C

33. What happened to Leah's sister at the zoo?

    A. She fell down and got hurt.

    B. Ben and Leah could not find her.

    C. She had a great time at the zoo.

    D. Leah and Ben made her go home.

Answer: B

34. Which of the following is NOT true?

    A. Leah watched TV all summer.

    B. The story took place during the week before school began.

    C. The Water Park was not open.

    D. The typhoon struck before they went to the beach.

Answer: D

35. What is a good title for this story?

    A. What an Unlucky Week

    B. How to Prepare for a Typhoon

    C. Having Fun at the Water Park

    D. A Wonderful Trip to the Zoo

Answer: A

重要字彙

disappointed：(adj.) 失望的，be disappointed in... : 對⋯⋯感到失望

例：Beth was disappointed in Mark because he forgot her birthday.

    (Beth 對 Mark 感到很失望，因為他忘記她的生日。)

plan：(v.) 計畫

activity：(n.) 活動

zoo：(n.) 動物園

disappear：(v.) 消失、不見

beach：(n.) 海邊

typhoon：(n.) 颱風

entire：(adj.) 全部的、整個的

ruin：(v.) 破壞、毀壞

unlucky：(adj.) 不幸運的、倒楣的

 重要片語

not do anything but + 原形動詞 = do nothing but + 原形動詞：除了……外，什麼都沒做

例：He did nothing but play video games all day. (他整天除了打電動以外，什麼都沒做。)

spend + 時間 + V-ing：花時間在……上

例：I spent a lot of time cleaning my room. (我花很多時間打掃我的房間。)

look for...：尋找……

take a trip：去旅行

go wrong：出差錯

take place：發生

prepare for...：為……作準備

~ 第五回 模擬試題解答 ~

聽力 Listening

第一部份 看圖辨義	第二部份 問答		第三部份 簡短對話		第四部份 短文聽解
1. A	6. B	11. B	16. C	21. B	26. B
2. B	7. A	12. A	17. A	22. C	27. A
3. C	8. B	13. B	18. C	23. A	28. C
4. A	9. A	14. C	19. A	24. C	29. A
5. C	10. C	15. A	20. C	25. B	30. C

閱讀 Reading

第一部份 詞彙和結構			第二部份 段落填空		第三部份 閱讀理解	
1. B	6. D	11. B	16. D	21. C	26. B	31. C
2. C	7. C	12. C	17. A	22. D	27. A	32. D
3. B	8. B	13. B	18. B	23. B	28. D	33. A
4. D	9. D	14. D	19. A	24. D	29. B	34. B
5. C	10. C	15. C	20. C	25. A	30. A	35. C

第五回
聽力模擬試題解析

一、聽力測驗

本測驗分四個部份，全部都是單選題，共 30 題，作答時間約 20 分鐘。作答說明為中文，印在試題冊上並經由光碟放音機播出。

第一部份：看圖辨義

共 5 題，每題請聽光碟放音機播出的題目和三個英語句子之後，選出與所看到的圖畫最相符的答案。
每題只播出一遍。

1. What is the boy doing?
   A. Crossing the street.
   B. Entering a store.
   C. Chasing the dog.

   Answer: A

重要關鍵

"What is someone doing?" 以現在進行式的方式詢問某人當下正在做什麼事，或從事什麼樣的事務。
從圖片看來，這個男孩正在穿越斑馬線，故答案為 A，cross：(v.) 穿越、經過。
例：Ted helped an old lady cross the street. (Ted 幫忙一位老太太過馬路。)

enter：(v.) 進入   chase：(v.) 追逐

2. Where is the bookstore?
   A. Inside the junior high school.
   B. Next to the bank.
   C. Across from the library.

   Answer: B

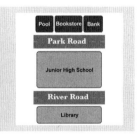

重要關鍵

本題考的是位置的說法。圖中的 Bookstore (書店) 在 Bank (銀行) 旁邊，Junior High School (國中) 的對面，故知 B 項為正確答案，next to...：在……旁邊。
A. inside：(prep.) 在……裡面
C. across from...：在……對面

3. If Sam leaves home at 9:00 p.m., which show will he be able to see?
   A. The 7:00 p.m. one.
   B. The 8:50 p.m. one.
   C. The 10:15 p.m. one.

Answer: C

Show Times
7:00 pm
8:50
10:15

由圖可得知，表演的時間分別是晚上七點、八點五十分及十點十五分，如果 Sam 晚上九點才出門的話，他只能看到十點十五分的表演，故答案為 C。

4. What is true about the picture?
   A. The phone is ringing.
   B. It is noon.
   C. There is a computer.

Answer: A

本題測驗「關於圖片，何者為是？」，由圖可知，牆上的時鐘正指著一點半的時間，桌上有一本書或筆記本，且電話在響，故答案選 A，ring：(v.) 鈴響 & (n.) 鈴聲。
另一個須注意的是，一點半已經是下午了，而非選項 B 中的 noon：正午時分。

5. How many people are there in the classroom?
   A. The boy feels bored.
   B. He is studying hard in his room.
   C. There is one boy in the classroom.

Answer: C

本題測驗重點是 how many，用來詢問「……的數量」。題目問「教室裡有幾個人？」，因此答案選 C。
A「這男孩覺得很無聊。」是男孩的狀態，問句應是 "How does the boy feel?"。
bored：(adj.)（人）感到無聊的、厭煩的
B「他正在房間裡用功讀書。」是指動作，問句應是 "What is the boy doing?"。

第二部份：問答

共 10 題，每題請聽光碟放音機播出的英語句子，再從試題冊上三個回答中，選出一個最適合的答案。每題只播出一遍。

6. How long have we been walking? I am so tired.

    A. Walking is my favorite kind of exercise.

    B. I don't know, but it's time to take a break.

    C. We need to work hard and play hard.

Answer: B

本題測驗重點為 "How long has someone been + V-ing?"，用來詢問「某人持續做某事多久時間了？」。

例：A: How long has Alison been working here? (A: Alison 在這裡工作多久了？)

    B: She has been working here for three years. (B: 她已經在這裡工作三年了。)

故答案選 B，it's time to V：該是……的時候了；take a break：休息。

7. Why are you so lazy?

    A. I don't think I am. I just like to relax.

    B. You're right. I'm pretty busy.

    C. What? I'm not crazy!

Answer: A

本題用 "Why is someone...?" 來詢問「某人為什麼……？」。測驗重點為 lazy：(adj.) 懶惰的。題目問 "Why are you so lazy?" (你怎麼這麼懶惰？)，因此答案選 A「我不覺得自己懶。我只是喜歡放輕鬆。」。relax：(v.) 放鬆。

例：You need to relax and clear your mind. (你需要放鬆，把思緒清空。)

 8. Do you eat in this restaurant often?

　　A. Yes, I've been here once.

　　B. Yes, I come here a lot.

　　C. Yes, I wish I could come.

Answer: B

重要關鍵

本題測驗重點為頻率副詞 often (經常)。題目問「你經常來這間餐廳吃飯嗎？」，因此答案選 B「是的，我很常來這裡。」

A「是的，我來過這裡一次。」則不合邏輯，應要說「沒有，我只來過一次。」才對。

C「是的，我希望我能來。」則答非所問。

 9. Kevin is in the hospital.

　　A. What happened? Is he sick?

　　B. He must be very hungry.

　　C. Are you feeling better now?

Answer: A

重要關鍵

本題是直述句，測驗重點是 in the hospital，是「在醫院」的意思。

例：Cathy had to stay a night in the hospital. (Cathy 必須住院一天。)

題目說「Kevin 現在在醫院。」，因此答案選 A「怎麼了？他生病了嗎？」。

B「他一定很餓。」及 C「你現在覺得好點了嗎？」均答非所問。

 10. Excuse me, sir. Do you have the time?

　　A. No, I don't have time right now.

　　B. Yes, it's Friday today.

　　C. Sure. It's 10:30.

Answer: C

重要關鍵

本題測驗重點為向別人詢問時間的用法。"Do you have the time?" 意思為「請問現在幾點？」，也可說 "What time is it?"，因此回答應是「現在幾點鐘」或「現在幾點幾分」，故答案為 C。

A「不，我現在沒空。」則答非所問。

B「是的，今天是星期五。」的問句應是 "What day is today?" 或 "What day is it today?"。

11. My mother was angry because I got mud on the floor.
   A. That's terrible you dropped ice cream on the floor.
   B. Well, did you help clean up the floor?
   C. Why did you go to the second floor?

Answer: B

本題是直述句，測驗重點為 mud：(n.) 泥土，floor：(n.) 地板，因此答案用選項 B 中的 clean up the floor
(清理地板) 來回應。

12. I have to buy groceries tonight.
   A. Good idea. We need more food.
   B. There's a drugstore on the corner.
   C. I think you have enough clothes.

Answer: A

本題是直述句，測驗重點為 groceries：(n.) 食品雜貨 (恆為複數)。句子說「我今晚必須買一些食品雜貨。」
因此答案選 A「好主意。我們還需要多一點食物。」。
B「轉角那兒有家藥局。」及 C「我認為你的衣服夠多了。」均答非所問。

重要字彙

drugstore：(n.) 藥局

重要片語

on the corner：在轉角處

13. Who is that tall, beautiful woman in pink?
   A. She is talking to Mr. Lee.
   B. She is our new teacher.
   C. She is angry with me.

Answer: B

本題測驗重點是 who，聽到以 who 開頭的問題，就要注意答案應和人的身分或姓名有關，因此答案為
B「她是我們的新老師。」。題目中的 in pink 是「穿著粉紅色衣服」的意思。
A「她正在和李先生說話。」是指動作，並非適當的回應。
C「她在生我的氣。」是指情緒，亦非適當的回應。

 14. When will you send me that important package?

    A. The package weighs two pounds.

    B. I will take the bus tomorrow.

    C. I will deliver it myself tomorrow.

Answer: C

重要關鍵

本題測驗重點為 package：(n.) 包裹，send someone a / the package：寄送包裹給某人。題目說「你什麼時候會把那個重要的包裹寄給我？」，因此答案選 C「我明天會親自送過去。」，deliver：(v.) 運送、投遞。

例：Can you deliver this pot to my house?（可以把這個鍋子送到我家嗎？）

重要字彙

weigh：(v.) 重達，weight：(n.) 重量

例：**How much does the baby weigh?（小寶寶多重？）**

    The man weighs 110 pounds.（那男人重一百一十磅。）

 15. What happened when you got a bad cold last month?

    A. I had to stay in bed for a week.

    B. They invited me back.

    C. It has been cold for the past month.

Answer: A

重要關鍵

本題測驗重點為 "What happened?"（發生何事？）。題目問「你上個月感冒時發生何事？」，因此答案選 A 來回應最適當，stay in bed：在床上休息。

get a bad cold：得了重感冒，亦可說 have a bad cold，染上感冒則是說 catch a cold。

第三部份：簡短對話

共 10 題，每題請聽光碟放音機播出一段對話和一個相關的問題後，再從試題冊上三個選項中，選出一個最適合的答案。每段對話和問題播出一遍。

16. M: I really enjoyed the meal at that restaurant.

W: Me, too. Oh, no.

M: What's the problem?

W: I think I may have left my purse there.

Q: Where is the woman's purse?

    A. In her left hand.

    B. At her home.

    C. At the restaurant.

Answer: C

重要關鍵

本題測驗重點為 leave : (v.) 遺留，三態為 leave, left, left，left 亦可作形容詞，表示「左邊的」。

例：Mandy left her insurance card at the hospital. (Mandy 把健保卡留在醫院了。)

題目問「女子的錢包在哪裡？」，關鍵句在男子開頭所說的 "I really enjoyed the meal at that restaurant." (剛剛在那家餐廳吃的食物我很喜歡。)，由此可知，他們剛剛在餐廳吃飯，而女子說 "I think I may have left my purse there." (我想我可能把錢包遺留在那裡了)，故知答案為 C。

17. M: Why don't you come and eat dinner with us?

W: Thanks for the invitation, but I already have plans tonight.

M: Come on!

W: Maybe next time.

Q: Is the woman going to join them?

    A. No, she can't go out for dinner with them.

    B. Yes, but she is going to be a little late.

    C. She will change her plans and join them.

Answer: A

重要關鍵

本題測驗重點為 "I already have plans" (我已經有計劃了) 以及 "Maybe next time." (或許下次吧。)，這都是婉拒別人邀約時常用的話，故答案選 A。

重要字彙

invitation : (n.) 邀請，Thanks for the invitation. : 謝謝邀請。

例：Tina turned down my movie invitation. (Tina 拒絕了我的電影邀約。)

 18. M: So, what does your father do?

    W: He owns a furniture shop downtown.

    M: Oh? Does he sell sofas?

    W: He sells all kinds of furniture.

    Q: What does the woman's father sell?

      A. Only sofas.

      B. Everything but sofas.

      C. Many types of furniture.

Answer: C

重要關鍵 💡

all kinds of... 是「各種的 / 各式各樣的……」之意，女子說自己的爸爸販售各式各樣的傢俱 (furniture)，因此最適合的答案為 C「很多種類的傢俱。」。

A「只賣沙發。」和 B「除了沙發之外的任何傢俱。」皆不符語意。

 19. W: Hey, where are you going?

    M: I have to mail my mom a package.

    W: I can do that on my way to the supermarket if you want.

    M: Thanks. I appreciate it.

    Q: Who is going to mail the package?

      A. The woman.

      B. The man.

      C. Both the man and woman.

Answer: A

重要關鍵 💡

對話中男子說要寄包裹給母親，而女子提議說，她可以在去超市的途中幫他寄包裹，由男子的回應 "Thanks. I appreciate it." (謝謝。我很感激。) 可知，女子會幫男子寄包裹，故答案為 A。

重要字彙

mail : (v.) 寄送 (包裹或郵件)

package : (n.) 包裹

appreciate : (v.) 感激、感謝

例：I really appreciate your help. (我很感激你的協助。)

20. W: Why does it take you an hour to get to work?

M: I live far away from my office.

W: What time do you have to get up every morning?

M: I usually get up at 6:30 and leave home at 7: 00.

Q: Why does the man have to get up early?

　　A. He goes to work on foot.

　　B. He usually has a meeting at 7:00.

　　C. He does not live near his company.

Answer: C

本題測驗重點為 far away from... : 距離……很遙遠。

例 : My school is far away from my house. (我的學校離我家很遠。)

題目問「為何男子必須早起？」，關鍵句是男子所說 "I live far away from my office." (我住的地方離辦公室很遠。)，故知答案應選 C「他不住在公司附近。」。

near : (prep.) 在……附近，company : (n.) 公司。

on foot : 走路、步行

例 : **Stella went to the MRT station on foot. (Stella 走路去捷運站。)**

 21. M: I bought this cell phone yesterday.

W: Good for you.

M: Well, something is wrong with it.

W: Are you sure? You should take it back then.

Q: What does the man say about his cell phone?

　　A. It works really well.

　　B. There's a problem with it.

　　C. He spent a lot of money on it.

Answer: B

本題測驗重點為 something is wrong with... : ……不太對勁、有問題。

例 : Something's wrong with my scooter. It's making a strange noise.

　　(我的機車不太對勁，它發出很奇怪的聲音。)

因此答案選 B「它有問題。」。

重要片語

Good for you. : 你那樣做很好。通常用於肯定、鼓勵對方的所作所為。

例：A: I work at a hospital for free every week. (A: 我每週都在醫院當義工。)

　　B: Good for you. (B: 那樣很好。)

 22. M: Mom, can you give me one hundred dollars?

　　W: Forget it!

　　M: Please! I will help do the dishes tomorrow.

　　W: OK. But you have to take out the garbage, too.

　　Q: What does the boy have to do to get the money?

　　　　A. Do the dishes every day.

　　　　B. Help his mother collect garbage.

　　　　C. Wash the dishes and take out the garbage.

Answer: C

重要關鍵

本題關鍵為男孩所說「拜託嘛！我明天會幫忙洗碗盤。」及下一句他媽媽所說「好吧。那你還要倒垃圾。」，do the dishes : 洗碗盤 (= wash the dishes)，take out the garbage : 倒垃圾，故知答案選 C。

重要片語

Forget it! : 別想！(忘掉這件事吧！)

 23. M: What are you doing with the table?

　　W: I'm throwing it away.

　　M: What? Why are you doing that?

　　W: Because it is really ugly.

　　M: Why don't you just give it to me? Mine broke yesterday.

　　Q: Why is the woman throwing out the table?

　　　　A. It is not nice to look at.

　　　　B. She has a new one.

　　　　C. The man broke it.

Answer: A

重要關鍵

題目詢問「女子為什麼要扔掉桌子？」，原因就在倒數第二句「因為它真的很難看。」，ugly 是「醜陋的；難看的」之意，也就是選項 A 的 "It is not nice to look at."。

重要字彙

break：(v.) 弄壞；打破，三態為 break，broke，broken。broken 可當形容詞，壞掉的。

例：These headphones don't work. I think they are broken.（這副耳機不能用，我想它壞了。）

24. W: My favorite actor's new movie is playing now.

M: Sorry, but I'm not interested.

W: Come on! I think you would like it.

M: Uh, I doubt it.

Q: What does the man say about the movie?

　　A. He already saw it, and it's quite interesting.

　　B. He is too busy to see it.

　　C. He doesn't think he would like it.

Answer: C

重要關鍵

本題測驗重點為 doubt：(v.) 懷疑。

例：I doubt that Ted can get up early tomorrow morning.（我懷疑 Ted 明天早上能不能早起。）

由對話的最後兩句，女子說「來嘛！我覺得你會喜歡那部電影。」男子說「呃，我很懷疑。」可以得知男子「不覺得自己會喜歡那部電影。」，所以答案為 C。

 重要字彙

interested：(adj.) 感興趣的　　　　　　　　　　　interesting：(adj.) 有趣的

25. M: Hello, I'd like to speak to Betty.

W: There's no one by that name here.

M: Is this 2577-2324?

W: No, this is 2577-2327.

M: Oops! I'm so sorry.

Q: Why can't the man speak to Betty?

　　A. Because she forgot to bring her phone.

　　B. Because he called the wrong number.

　　C. Because her line is busy.

Answer: B

重要關鍵

本題關鍵句為 "Is this 2577-2324?"（這支電話是 2577-2324 嗎？），以及下一句的 "No, this is 2577-2327."（不是，是 2577-2327。），故知男子打錯電話，因此答案選 B。

a person by that name：叫那名字的人

Oops!：喔噢！糟了！（不小心說錯話或犯下小錯時，所發出的口頭語。）

someone's line is busy：某人電話忙線

例：**I called you several times, but your line was busy.**（我打給你好幾次，但是電話都忙線中。）

第四部份：短文聽解

共 5 題，每題有三個圖片選項。請聽光碟放音機播出的題目，並選出一個最適合的圖片。每題播出一遍。

 26. Please look at the following three pictures.

Lucy left a message on Mark's answering machine. What is wrong with Katie?

Hi, Mark. This is Lucy. I'm sorry, but I can't go to the movies with you tonight. I have to stay home to take care of my sister, Katie. She was climbing a tree, and she fell. A branch scratched her arm pretty badly. I hope you can find someone else to go with you. Bye!

A	B	C

Answer: B

嗨，Mark。我是 Lucy。很抱歉今晚不能和你去看電影了。我得留在家照顧我妹妹 Katie。她爬樹，結果摔了下來。她的手臂被一根樹枝劃傷得很嚴重。希望你可以找到別人和你一起去。再見！

由此可知，Katie 手臂受傷了。

branch：(n.) 樹枝　　　　　　　　　　　　　　　　**scratch**：(v.) 劃傷、劃破

27. Please look at the following three pictures.

Listen to the following news story. What is the speaker talking about?

An old shipwreck was found on the ocean floor yesterday by a local woman who was out diving for fun. She decided to go to a spot in the ocean she had never been before and swam toward a large group of fish. When she got closer, she saw that they were swimming near a sunken ship.

A	B	C
		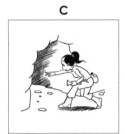

Answer: A

 重要關鍵

昨天一名本地女子外出潛水遊玩時，在海底發現一艘古老的沉船。她一開始決定去一個海裡她從未去過的地點，並游向一大群魚。當她靠近時，她看到魚群正游在一艘沉船附近。

由此可知，說話者談的是潛水。

重要字彙

shipwreck : (n.) 失事船的殘骸　　　　　　　　local : (adj.) 本地的、當地的
dive : (v.) 潛水　　　　　　　　　　　　　　spot : (n.) 地點
sunken : (adj.) 沉入水中的

 28. Please look at the following three pictures.

Listen to the following message for Tina. What class is Ted talking about?

Hi, Tina. It's Ted. I didn't see you in class yesterday. Do you want to see my notes? The lecture was pretty difficult. It was about all the different parts of the brain. Our test will be about which parts of the brain control certain parts of the body. Good luck with your studying.

A	B	C
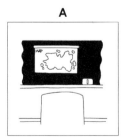	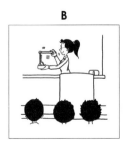	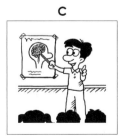

Answer: C

 重要關鍵

嗨，Tina。我是 Ted。我昨天在課堂上沒有看到妳。妳想看我的筆記嗎？那堂課相當難。它是有關腦部所有不同的部位。我們的考試題目則是有關我們身體的某些部份是由腦部的哪個部位所控制的。祝妳好運了！

由此可知，上的是跟大腦有關的課。

重要字彙

note : (n.) 筆記　　　　　　　　　　　　　　lecture : (n.) 授課

brain : (n.) 腦、大腦　　　　　　　　　　　control : (v.) 控制

---

29. Please look at the following three pictures.

Listen to the following short talk. Who is the speaker talking about?

That's too bad you had a bad flight. My flight was great. It was really long, but the service was excellent. I never went thirsty because the attendant kept giving us drinks. Also, she was very polite and helped me whenever I asked.

Answer: A

 重要關鍵

很遺憾你這趟飛行不順利。我這次的航程很棒。飛行時間真的很長，但服務非常好。我都不會覺得渴，因為空服員總是不斷給我們飲料。此外，當我有問題時，她總是很有禮貌的幫助我。

由此可知，講的是空服員。

重要字彙

flight : (n.) 飛行航程　　　　　　　　　　　excellent : (adj.) 很棒的

attendant : (n.) 空服員　　　　　　　　　　polite : (adj.) 有禮貌的

30. Please look at the following three pictures.

Listen to the following short talk. Where is the man?

Hi, I have a few things I'd like to take care of. First, I would like to deposit this check. Also, I'd like to take out $100 in cash. Lastly, I just came back from vacation, so I have some extra foreign money I'd like to exchange.

A	B	C

Answer: C

嗨，我有一些事情想處理。首先，我想要存這張支票。另外，我想要領一百元現金。最後，因為我剛度完假回來，所以我有一些多出來的外幣想要兌換。

由此可知，男子在銀行。

重要字彙

deposit : (v.) 存 (款) & (n.) 存款

extra : (adj.) 額外的

check : (n.) 支票

exchange : (v.) 兌換

全民英檢
初級聽力
L
5

第五回
閱讀模擬試題解析

二、閱讀能力測驗

本測驗分三部份，全部都是單選題，共 35 題，作答時間 35 分鐘。

第一部份：詞彙和結構

共 15 題，每個題目裡有一個空格。請從四個選項中選出一個最適合題意的字或詞作答。

---

1. Mom is having a conversation with Aunt Molly _____ the phone.

    A. in   B. on   C. to   D. by

Answer: B

本題測驗重點為 on the phone：講電話。

例：Terry has been on the phone with Ruth for three hours. (Terry 和 Ruth 講電話已經講了三個小時。)
根據上述，故知答案為 B。

have a conversation with someone：與某人談話

---

2. The author's new novel is great. It is _____ as I expected.

    A. the most interesting

    B. more interesting

    C. as interesting

    D. so interesting

Answer: C

本題測驗重點為同等比較 "as...as..." 的用法。在 "as...as..." 的結構中，第一個 as 是副詞，表「一樣地」，之後接形容詞或副詞，第二個 as 是連接詞，表示「和」。

as + adj. / adv. + as...：和……一樣地……

例：Ted is as tall as his father. (Ted 和他爸爸一樣高。)

    This car runs as fast as that one. (這輛車跑得和那輛車一樣快。)

否定用法則為 not as + adj. / adv. + as...：不像……一樣……。

例：My parents aren't as patient as yours. (我的父母不像你父母那麼有耐心。)

本題為肯定句，空格前為 be 動詞 is，空格後有 as I expected，根據上述，空格應選 "as + adj."，故答案為 C。

author : (n.) 作者　　　　　　　　　　　　　　　　　　novel : (n.) 小說

expect : (v.) 預期、期待

---

3. My grandfather fell down the _____ last night. Luckily, he didn't get hurt.

   A. faucets　　　　　B. stairs　　　　　C. drawers　　　　　D. blankets

   Answer: B

A. faucet : (n.) 水龍頭

B. stair : (n.) 樓梯、階梯，fall down the stairs : 跌下樓梯

例 : Gary fell down the stairs and hurt his knees. (Gary 跌下樓梯摔傷了膝蓋。)

C. drawer : (n.) 抽屜

D. blanket : (n.) 毛毯

根據前後文語意及用法，故答案選 B。

luckily : (adv.) 幸運地

---

4. My brother likes to paint. He is a great _____.

   A. businessman　　　　B. customer　　　　C. partner　　　　D. artist

   Answer: D

A. businessman : (n.) 商人

B. customer : (n.) 顧客

C. partner : (n.) 搭檔、伙伴

D. artist : (n.) 藝術家

題目前一句說「我哥哥喜歡繪畫。」，由此可知，他應是個「藝術家」，故答案選 D。

---

5. Jimmy doesn't like eating vegetables. He thinks they _____ terrible.

   A. act　　　　　B. spell　　　　　C. taste　　　　　D. boil

   Answer: C

重要關鍵

A. act：(v.) 行動、舉動

例：Why are you acting so strangely? (為何你的舉動那麼怪異？)

B. spell：(v.) 拼 (字)

例：Cathy spelled my name wrong. (Cathy 把我的名字拼錯了。)

C. taste：(v.) 嚐起來，之後接形容詞。

例：The steak tastes really good. (這牛排真好吃。)

D. boil：(v.) 烹、煮

例：It only takes a few minutes to boil an egg. (把蛋煮熟只需要幾分鐘的時間。)

空格後為形容詞 terrible，選項中只有 taste 之後可接形容詞作主詞補語，故答案選 C。

---

6. It took six weeks for Mike's _____ leg to heal.

　　A. breaking　　　　B. break　　　　C. broke　　　　D. broken

Answer: D

重要關鍵

本題測驗重點為動詞 break 的過去分詞 broken 作形容詞用。

broken：(adj.) 斷掉的；壞掉的

例：Henry couldn't ride his bike because of his broken arm. (Henry 因為手臂斷掉，所以無法騎腳踏車。)

空格前有所有格 Mike's，後面為名詞 leg，因此空格應選形容詞來修飾 leg，根據上述，故知答案為 D。

重要字彙

heal：(v.) 復原、治癒

---

7. I'm lost. I don't know which way _____.

　　A. gone　　　　B. going　　　　C. to go　　　　D. goes

Answer: C

重要關鍵

本題測驗疑問詞引導的名詞片語用法。

名詞片語的形成方式為「疑問詞 (which, what, where, when, how 等) + 不定詞片語 (to V)」，名詞片語與名詞子句一樣，在句子中可作主詞、及物動詞或介系詞的受詞。

例：Sherry couldn't decide which dress to wear to the wedding.

　　(Sherry 無法決定穿哪件洋裝去參加婚禮。)

　　Where to hold the party is not decided yet. (在哪裡舉行派對尚未決定。)

根據上述，故知答案應選 C 選項的不定詞 to go。

8. I can't find my glasses, but I am sure they must be _____ in the room.

    A. where   B. somewhere   C. everywhere   D. anywhere

Answer: B

重要關鍵

A. where：(adv.) 在哪裡

B. somewhere：(adv.) 某處、某個地方

例：Abby lost her purse somewhere in the supermarket. (Abby 把錢包掉在超市的某個地方了。)

C. everywhere：(adv.) 到處、各地

例：Oil prices are going up everywhere. (各地的油價都在上漲。)

D. anywhere：(adv.) 任何地方

例：Tammy couldn't find her cell phone anywhere. (Tammy 到處都找不到她的手機。)

根據前後文語意，故知答案應選 B。

9. Nobody knows what _____ in the future.

    A. happen   B. going to happen   C. happening   D. will happen

Answer: D

重要關鍵

本題測驗重點為 in the future 與時態的搭配用法。future 表示「未來、將來」，in the future 指「在未來、在將來」，因此要用未來式。

例：Skip promises that he will study hard in the future. (Skip 承諾他將來會用功讀書。)

根據上述，故知答案為 D。

10. The police are not sure _____ the man is the killer or not.

    A. why   B. what   C. whether   D. however

Answer: C

重要關鍵

本題測驗重點為 whether...or not：是否……。

whether 是連接詞，表示「是否」，常與 or not 並用，or not 可置於 whether 之後，也可以置於句尾，甚至可以省略。

例：I can't tell whether that's a real Prada bag or not. (我分辨不出那個 Prada 包是否為真品。)

題目句尾有 or not，根據上述，可知空格內應置 whether，故答案為 C。

11. I don't know if I should buy _____ sunglasses.

    A. a little   B. these   C. this   D. a

Answer: B

重要關鍵

本題測驗重點為可數名詞與不可數名詞之前的形容詞。

A. a little + 不可數名詞

例：I only have a little money in my pocket. (我口袋裡只有一點錢。)

B. these + 複數可數名詞

例：These boys are so noisy. (這些男孩真吵。)

C. this + 單數名詞

例：This dress is so beautiful. (這件洋裝真漂亮。)

D. a + 單數可數名詞

例：I saw a strange man in the school yesterday. (我昨天在學校看到一個奇怪的男子。)

sunglasses (太陽眼鏡) 為複數可數名詞，故選 B。

12. My grandparents usually take a walk _____ the river after breakfast.

    A. in   B. over   C. along   D. through

Answer: C

重要關鍵

A. in : (prep.) 在……內

B. over : (prep.) 在……上方

C. along : (prep.) 沿著……

例：You can find the flower shop along the street. (沿著這條街你就可以找到那家花店。)

D. through : (prep.) 穿過……

例：They went through the forest. (他們穿過了森林。)

根據前後文語意，故知答案應選 C。

 **重要片語**

take a walk : 散步

例：**My father usually takes a walk after dinner. (我爸爸通常晚餐後會去散步。)**

13. The rich man decided to give away his wealth and live _____.

    A. clearly   B. simply   C. locally   D. recently

Answer: B

 重要關鍵

A. clearly : (adv.) 清楚地

B. simply : (adv.) 簡單地、簡樸地，live simply : 過簡樸的生活 (= live a simple life)

C. locally : (adv.) 在當地

D. recently : (adv.) 最近

根據前後文語意及用法，故知答案應選 B。

重要字彙

wealth : (n.) 財富

重要片語

give away... : 贈送……

14. My neighbor's dog barked all night. He almost _____ me crazy!

    A. blew   B. chased   C. shouted   D. drove

Answer: D

 重要關鍵

A. blow : (v.) 吹動，三態為 blow, blew, blown

B. chase : (v.) 追逐

例 : The dog chased after me for a long time. (那隻狗追了我好久。)

C. shout : (v.) 喊叫

D. drive someone crazy : 把某人逼瘋

例 : All that noise is driving me crazy. (那噪音要把我逼瘋了。)

本題測驗重點為 drive someone crazy 的固定用法，故答案選 D。

 重要字彙

bark : (v.) 吠

例 : I was scared when the dog barked at me. (那隻狗對著我叫的時候，我嚇到了。)

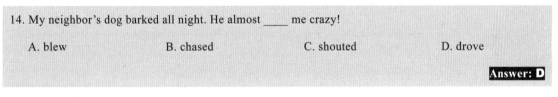

15. When you hold the baby, you must be _____.

A. sudden   B. positive   C. gentle   D. fair

Answer: C

A. sudden : (adj.) 突然的

B. positive : (adj.) 積極的、正面的

C. gentle : (adj.) 輕柔的、溫和的

例 : He is gentle and nice. (他個性溫柔和善。)

D. fair : (adj.) 公平的

根據前後文語意，故知答案應選 C。

第二部份：段落填空

共 10 題，包括二個段落，每個段落各含四到六個空格。每格均有四個選項，請依照文意選出最適合的答案。

Questions 16-20

It's true when they say that big things come in small packages. Just look at Taroko National Park. It is not big. It is not __(16)__ Taiwan's biggest national park. However, many people think it's the best __(17)__. It is popular with tourists from __(18)__ Taiwan and abroad. Since Taroko isn't big, you can see the best __(19)__ in one day. You can travel around it by tour bus, by car, or by scooter. You can even travel __(20)__ foot!

16. A. always   B. only   C. sometimes   D. even

Answer: D

A. always : (adv.) 總是、一直，not always... : 並非總是……

B. only : (adv.) 只、僅僅

C. sometimes: (adv.) 有時候

D. even : (adv.) 甚至 (強調用法)

例 : My little brother can't even walk on his own. (我弟弟甚至連自己走路都還不會。)

本句說「太魯閣不是台灣最大的國家公園」，由此可知，這裡需要一個加強語氣的副詞，用來強調「最大的」，故答案為 D。

17. A. one	B. other	C. ones	D. another

Answer: A

 重要關鍵

單數可數名詞在句中出現兩次時，為避免重複，可用 one 代替，ones 則代替複數名詞。

例：I don't like the blue car; I like that black one. (我不喜歡這輛藍色的車子；我喜歡黑色的那輛。)

They are tearing down old buildings and building new ones. (他們正在拆除老舊的建築，建造新的。)

因此答案選 A，the best one = the best national park。

18. A. either	B. both	C. not only	D. as well as

Answer: B

 重要關鍵

A. either A or B：不是 A 就是 B (表示「兩者擇一」)

B. both A and B：A 和 B 兩者 (都……)

例：Wilson speaks both Chinese and Japanese. (Wilson 會說中文和日文。)

C. not only A but (also) B：不僅 A 而且 B

D. A as well as B：A 以及 B

空格後有 and，故本題測驗重點為 "both A and B" 的用法，故答案應選 B。

19. A. parts	B. piles	C. plans	D. prices

Answer: A

 重要關鍵

A. part：(n.) 部份

B. pile：(n.) (一) 堆

C. plan：(n.) 計劃

D. price：(n.) 價格

本句是指因為太魯閣不是很大，可以在一天之內看完最美的「部份」，故本題答案選 A。

20. A. with	B. by	C. on	D. at

Answer: C

重要關鍵

本題測驗重點為 on foot：步行。

例：She usually goes to school on foot. (她通常步行上學。)

由此可知，本題答案應選 C。

重要字彙

package : (n.) 包裹，"Big things come in small packages." 是一句俗諺，表示「大不見得好 / 小兵立大功。」之意。

national park : (n.) 國家公園

popular : (adj.) 受歡迎的，**be popular with...** : 受……歡迎

例：This kind of lipstick is popular with young girls. (這款口紅很受年輕女孩歡迎。)

abroad : (n.) 海外

tour bus : (n.) 觀光巴士

scooter : (n.) 機車

Questions 21-25

Debbie and Sue are friends from high school. Now, they are at __(21)__ ten-year class reunion. They are happy to know that they live near __(22)__ . Sue wants to contact Debbie soon. Debbie tells Sue that she can reach her at home or at her office. __(23)__ Debbie leaves, she tells Sue to get in touch with her soon. Sue tells Debbie that she __(24)__ out of town next week. __(25)__ , she will give her a call when she returns.

21. A. they're	B. theirs	C. their	D. them

Answer: C

they're 是 they are 的縮寫，theirs 是所有格代名詞，等於 "their + 名詞"，their 為所有格，them 為受格。空格後的 ten-year class reunion 為名詞，因此前面只可加所有格 their，故本題答案為 C。

22. A. each one	B. one other	C. another one	D. each other

Answer: D

本題測驗重點為代名詞 each other 的用法。

each other 表示兩人之間的「互相」。

例：Zack and Sarah trust each other. (Zack 和 Sarah 互相信任。)

三人或三人以上則用 one another。

例：The kids are chasing one another around the room. (孩子們在房間裡互相追逐。)

本文主角為 Debbie 和 Sue 兩人，故本題答案為 D。

注意：each other 與 one another 在美語中已逐漸通用，均可表示兩人或三人以上的彼此。

23. A. Because	B. Before	C. After	D. Although

Answer: B

 重要關鍵

A. because : (conj.) 因為
B. before : (conj.) 在……之前
C. after : (conj.) 在……之後
D. although : (conj.) 雖然

根據語意，應是在離開「之前」，Debbie 告訴 Sue 要盡快跟她聯絡，因此答案選 B。

24. A. was	B. would be	C. went	D. will be

Answer: D

 重要關鍵

本句的句尾有時間副詞 next week (下星期)，因此時態應用未來式，故答案為 D 選項的 will be。

25. A. Therefore	B. Besides	C. Already	D. Or

Answer: A

 重要關鍵

A. therefore : (adv.) 因此、所以
B. besides : (adv.) 此外、而且
C. already : (adv.) 已經
D. or : (conj.) 否則

本文最後兩句有因果關係，空格前的 "she will be out of town next week" (她下星期會出遠門) 為「因」，空格後的 "she will give her a call when she returns" (她回來的時候會打電話給她) 為「果」，因此須填入表示「結果」的副詞 therefore，故答案選 A。

重要字彙

reunion : (n.) 團聚、重聚，class reunion : 同學會　　　　contact : (v.) 聯絡
reach : (v.) 聯絡；到達

重要片語

get in touch with someone : 聯絡某人
give someone a call : 打電話給某人

第三部份：閱讀理解

共 10 題，包括數篇短文，每篇短文後面有三至四個相關問題。請由四個選項中選出最適合的答案。

Questions 26-28

Old Joe's Restaurant

99 Park Road

Open 24 hours, even on holidays!

Pizza	$2 / piece
Spaghetti	$6.49
Onion rings	$1.59
Soda or Coke	$1

Apple or Cherry Pie

Free with every meal!

26. When is Old Joe's Restaurant open?

    A. Only on holidays.

    B. All the time.

    C. Only on weekends.

    D. Every day except holidays.

    Answer: B

27. What is the most expensive thing on the menu?

    A. The spaghetti.

    B. The pizza.

    C. The pie.

    D. The onion rings.

    Answer: A

28. What do you get with every meal?

    A. A toy.

    B. Some fruit.

    C. A drink.

    D. Free dessert.

    Answer: D

open : (adj.) 營業的

spaghetti : (n.) 義大利麵

pie : (n.) 派

except : (prep.) 除了……之外

menu : (n.) 菜單

holiday : (n.) 假日

onion : (n.) 洋蔥，onion rings : 洋蔥圈

free : (adj.) 免費的

expensive : (adj.) 昂貴的

dessert : (n.) 甜點

重要片語

all the time : 一直、總是

Questions 29-31

August 19, 2013

Dear Diary,

Today was not my day. First, I woke up late and didn't have time for breakfast. On my walk to school, it started raining, and I didn't have my umbrella, so I got wet. In math class, Mr. Jones gave us a surprise quiz. I just know I didn't do well.

But the worst thing happened at lunch. I was walking to my seat when I tripped and fell. My lunch landed on the floor. I was so sad that I cried. And I felt hungry all afternoon. At least I am home now. I can go to sleep and forget this awful, no good, very bad day.

Anita

29. What kind of day did Anita have?

A. A wonderful day.

B. A terrible day.

C. A lucky day.

D. An interesting day.

Answer: B

30. How did Anita get to school?

　　A. She went to school on foot.

　　B. She took the train.

　　C. She rode her bike to school.

　　D. She took the bus.

Answer: A

31. What happened to Anita at lunch?

　　A. She felt sick.

　　B. She didn't have a seat.

　　C. She fell and dropped her lunch.

　　D. She didn't have enough money.

Answer: C

 重要字彙

diary : (n.) 日記
seat : (n.) 座位
land : (v.) 落下、著陸
awful : (adj.) 極糟的

quiz : (n.) 小考
trip : (v.) 絆倒
hungry : (adj.) 饑餓的
lucky : (adj.) 幸運的

重要片語

wake up : 醒來
on foot : 步行

at least : 至少

Questions 32-35

Camping in Taiwan can be a lot different from camping in North America. One time, I decided to camp at Yang Ming Mountain with some friends. I brought my tent but was surprised to find that the place already had tents set up. We enjoyed a barbecue, and I suggested we build a fire before dark. But the people working at the campground said fires were not allowed. The most important part of camping was the same in Taiwan, though. I was able to enjoy some time in nature with some good friends.

32. What is the main idea of the passage?

　　A. Camping in America is fun.

　　B. There are great places to camp in Taiwan.

　　C. It's always better to camp with friends.

　　D. Camping in Taiwan is not the same as in the West.

Answer: D

33. How is camping in Taiwan different from camping in North America?

    A. Tents are set up in Taiwan.

    B. Most camp areas are in the mountains in Taiwan.

    C. People enjoy barbecues in Taiwan.

    D. Camping is not popular in Taiwan.

    Answer: A

34. Why didn't the author build a campfire at the campground?

    A. She wanted to go to sleep.

    B. Workers at the campsite wouldn't let her.

    C. She didn't know how to.

    D. Other campers invited her to share their fire.

    Answer: B

35. What does the author say is the same about camping in Taiwan and North America?

    A. She can go camping anywhere she wants.

    B. She can meet some new people.

    C. She can spend time outdoors with friends.

    D. She can take a hike.

    Answer: C

R

初級全民英
閱讀檢
5

重要字彙

camp : (v.) 露營 & (n.) 營地，go camping : 去露營
different : (adj.) 不同的，be different from... : 和……不同
tent : (n.) 帳篷
suggest : (v.) 建議
allow : (v.) 允許
popular : (adj.) 受歡迎的
outdoors : (adv.) 在戶外

North America : (n.) 北美洲
decide : (v.) 決定
barbecue : (n.) 烤肉
campground : (n.) 營地 (= campsite)
campfire : (n.) 營火
share : (v.) 分享

重要片語

set up... : 搭建……

be able to V : 能夠做……

~ 第六回 模擬試題解答 ~

聽力 Listening

第一部份 看圖辨義	第二部份 問答		第三部份 簡短對話		第四部份 短文聽解
1. A	6. A	11. A	16. B	21. A	26. C
2. B	7. B	12. C	17. A	22. B	27. A
3. A	8. C	13. B	18. B	23. C	28. A
4. B	9. B	14. A	19. A	24. B	29. C
5. A	10. C	15. B	20. C	25. C	30. A

閱讀 Reading

第一部份 詞彙和結構			第二部份 段落填空		第三部份 閱讀理解	
1. A	6. A	11. C	16. C	21. B	26. D	31. D
2. B	7. D	12. D	17. B	22. C	27. A	32. A
3. C	8. B	13. A	18. A	23. A	28. C	33. D
4. D	9. C	14. D	19. C	24. D	29. B	34. B
5. C	10. B	15. B	20. D	25. B	30. C	35. C

第六回
聽力模擬試題解析

一、聽力測驗

本測驗分四個部份，全部都是單選題，共 30 題，作答時間約 20 分鐘。作答說明為中文，印在試題冊上並經由光碟放音機播出。

第一部份：看圖辨義

共 5 題，每題請聽光碟放音機播出的題目和三個英語句子之後，選出與所看到的圖畫最相符的答案。
每題只播出一遍。

1. What can we say about the man?
   A. He can hardly put up with the woman.
   B. He is talking loudly to the woman.
   C. He is having a nice chat with the woman.

Answer: A

重要關鍵

題目問 "What can we say about the man?"（我們可以說男子如何？）。在圖片中，女子正大聲的對著男子說話，而男子則皺起眉頭將耳朵搗住，代表他幾乎無法忍受這名女子的聲音，故答案應選 A。

hardly : (adv.) 幾乎不

例：Speak louder. I can hardly hear you.（講話大聲點。我幾乎聽不到你在說什麼。）

put up with... : 忍受……

例：My grandfather can't put up with the noise in the city.（我爺爺無法忍受城市裡的噪音。）

重要字彙

loudly : (adv.) 大聲地

chat : (n.) 聊天，have a nice chat with someone : 和某人聊得很愉快

2. Where is the money?
   A. In the boy's pocket.
   B. On the ground.
   C. In the sky.

Answer: B

重要關鍵

本題測驗疑問詞 where 引導的疑問句，用 "Where is...?" 來詢問「……在哪裡？」。圖中的鈔票及錢幣在地上男孩的腳邊，故答案選 B。

重要字彙

pocket : (n.) 口袋

sky : (n.) 天空

3. What is the man doing?

    A. Dialing a number.

    B. Buying a phone.

    C. Hanging up.

Answer: A

 重要關鍵

本題測驗疑問詞 what 引導的疑問句,用 "What is someone doing?" 來詢問「某人正在做什麼?」。由圖可知,男人正在打電話,故答案選 A,dial:(v.) 撥打 (電話號碼),dial a number:撥電話號碼。

 重要片語

hang up:掛斷電話、把聽筒掛上

4. What is true about the woman?

    A. She is in a shop.

    B. She is at a meeting.

    C. She is on a date.

Answer: B

 重要關鍵

本題測驗「關於女子,何者為是?」,由圖可知,女子正在其他人面前做簡報,因此可以說女子正在和其他人開會,因此答案選 B,at a meeting:在會議中。

重要字彙

shop:(n.) 商店   **date:(n.) 約會,on a date:約會中**

5. What is true about the boy?

    A. He is telling a lie.

    B. He is wearing glasses.

    C. He is eating a cookie.

Answer: A

 重要關鍵

題目問「關於男孩,何者為是?」,由圖可知,戴眼鏡 (wear glasses) 的是男子,男子問男孩有沒有拿餅乾 (cookie),男孩把餅乾藏在背後,然後回答男子說他沒拿,可知男孩在說謊,故答案為 A,tell a lie:說謊。

第二部份：問答

共 10 題，每題請聽光碟放音機播出的英語句子，再從試題冊上三個回答中，選出一個最適合的答案。
每題只播出一遍。

6. Jane made a big mistake at work today.
   A. Really? What did she do wrong?
   B. Yeah! She's really responsible.
   C. Great! She really needs the money.

Answer: **A**

重要關鍵

本題是直述句，測驗重點為 make a mistake：犯錯。

例：Sam made a lot of dumb mistakes. (Sam 犯了很多愚蠢的錯誤。)

題目說「Jane 今天在工作上犯了一個大錯。」，故答案選 A「真的嗎？她做錯了什麼？」來回應最適當。

重要字彙

responsible：(adj.) 負責的

7. What does the red one taste like?
   A. It smells like chicken soup.
   B. It tastes like strawberries.
   C. It looks like chocolate.

Answer: **B**

本題測驗重點為 taste like...：嚐起來像……。

例：This cookie tastes like pumpkin pie. (這塊餅乾吃起來像南瓜派。)

題目問「紅色那個嚐起來像什麼？」，故答案應選 B「嚐起來像草莓。」，strawberry：(n.) 草莓。

A. smell like...：聞起來像……

例：The perfume smells like roses. (這香水聞起來像玫瑰。)

C. look like...：看起來像……

例：The toy looks like a real camera. (那個玩具看起來像真的照相機。)

 8. Oh, no! I forgot my ticket at home!

    A. It's OK. They sell food there.

    B. I thought you could read without it.

    C. They won't let you on without it.

Answer: C

重要關鍵 💡

本題是直述句，測驗重點為 forget someone's ticket：忘了帶某人的票。

題目說「我把車票忘在家裡了！」，因此回答說 "They won't let you on without it." (沒有票，他們不會讓你上車。)，故答案為 C。

 9. Does Robert keep a pet?

    A. No, he only has a son.

    B. Yes, he has two dogs.

    C. No, he takes the bus.

Answer: B

重要關鍵 💡

本題測驗重點為 keep a pet：養寵物，keep...as a pet：養……當寵物。

例：We're not allowed to keep a pet in our new apartment. (我們的新公寓不准養寵物。)

    Billy keeps a frog as a pet. (Billy 養了一隻青蛙當寵物。)

題目問「Robert 有養寵物嗎？」，故答案選 B「有。他養了兩隻狗。」

 10. If we don't leave now, we'll be late!

    A. No, I haven't bought a ticket yet.

    B. So we're going to the movies tomorrow?

    C. Don't worry. We still have ten more minutes.

Answer: C

重要關鍵 💡

本題是直述句，測驗重點為 leave：(v.) 離開，late：(adj.) 遲到的。

題目說「如果我們現在不出發，我們就會遲到。」，因此用選項 C「別擔心。我們還有十分鐘。」來回答最適當。

11. Can I clean my room later on, Mom?
   A. No, you have to do it now.
   B. Thanks for cleaning it up.
   C. Yes, I cleaned it.

Answer: A

本題測驗重點為 later on : 待會、等一下。

例 : I'll e-mail you these photos later on. (我稍後會把這些照片用電子郵件傳給你。)

題目問「媽,我可以等一下再打掃我的房間嗎?」,故答案應選 A「不行,你現在就要去做。」。選項 B
「謝謝你打掃它。」和選項 C「對,我打掃過了。」皆不符題意。

12. What time did you get home last night?
   A. By train.
   B. Near a park.
   C. Around 10:30 p.m.

Answer: C

本題測驗重點為 what time,用來詢問時間「幾點幾分」,因此回答也要用時間「幾點幾分」。

例 : May: What time did you get up this morning? (May : 妳今天早上幾點起床?)
   Jane: At 6:30. / Around seven o'clock. (Jane : 六點半。 / 大約七點鐘。)

題目問「你昨天晚上幾點回到家?」,故知答案為 C「大約十點半。」。

A「搭火車。」的問句與交通工具有關,而 B「在公園附近。」的問句則與地方有關。

13. Hey! Why did you push me?
   A. I didn't talk to you.
   B. Sorry. I didn't mean it.
   C. I thought you were hungry.

Answer: B

本題測驗重點為 push : 推。

例 : I didn't mean to push him. (我不是故意要推他的。)

題目說「嘿!你為什麼推我?」,因此用 "Sorry. I didn't mean it." (抱歉。我不是故意的。) 來回答,
故答案為 B "I didn't mean it.",表示「我不是故意的。」,通常是做錯事想要道歉、表示懺悔時所說的話。

 14. Did you book our train tickets?

    A. Yes, we leave at 7:00 p.m.

    B. No, I haven't had a chance to read it.

    C. I gave it back already.

Answer: A

 重要關鍵

本題測驗重點為 book : (v.) 預訂 & (n.) 書，book a train ticket：預訂火車票。

例：I just booked two movie tickets online. (我剛剛在網路上訂了兩張電影票。)

題目問「你訂火車票了嗎？」，故知答案應選 A「訂了。我們晚上七點出發。」。

 15. Be careful! You shouldn't touch that dog.

    A. Did you give him any food today?

    B. Why? Will he bite me?

    C. I wish I had enough money to buy it.

Answer: B

重要關鍵

本題為直述句，測驗重點為 "Be careful!"，用來請對方「小心！」，以及 touch : (v.) 觸摸、觸碰。

例：Be careful! You shouldn't touch that knife. It's very sharp. (小心！你不該碰那把刀。它很銳利。)

題目說「小心！你不該碰那隻狗。」，故選 B 反問「為什麼不行？牠會咬人嗎？」，bite : (v.) 咬、啃。

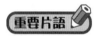 **重要片語**

I wish (that) + S + V：我希望……，表示與現在事實相反的假設或不可能達成的願望時，後面要接過去式動詞。

例：I wish Steven was here with me. (我希望 Steven 跟我一起在這裡。)

第三部份：簡短對話

共 10 題，每題請聽光碟放音機播出一段對話和一個相關的問題後，再從試題冊上三個選項中，選出一個最適合的答案。每段對話和問題播出一遍。

16. M: Maggie, are you coming to my birthday party?

W: What party? I wasn't invited.

M: Sure you were. I e-mailed you.

W: Oh, I never check my e-mail.

Q: What did the man send Maggie?

    A. A letter in the mail.

    B. A letter on the computer.

    C. A birthday card.

Answer: B

重要關鍵

本題測驗重點為 e-mail : (v.) 傳電子郵件，亦可當名詞，為「電子郵件」之意。

題目問「男子寄什麼給 Maggie ？」，故知答案應選 B。

重要字彙

invite : (v.) 邀請   **check : (v.) 檢查**

17. M: I heard you were sick last week.

W: Yeah, I had a bad cold.

M: How are you now?

W: I've recovered. Thanks.

Q: How does the woman feel now?

    A. She feels better.

    B. She still feels bad.

    C. She feels worse.

Answer: A

重要關鍵

本題測驗重點為 recover : (v.) 恢復健康、復原。

例 : Resting enough will help you recover sooner. (充分休息有助你儘早復原。)

題目問「女子現在感覺如何？」，關鍵句在女子所說 "I've recovered." (我已經復原了。)，故知答案為 A。

 18. M: I heard Danny is good at soccer.

W: Yes, but he doesn't pass enough.

M: You should tell him that.

W: I already have.

Q: What doesn't Danny do?

    A. Run fast enough.

    B. Give the ball to others.

    C. Get enough points.

Answer: B

 重要關鍵

本題測驗重點為 pass：(v.) 傳球。

題目問「Danny 沒有做什麼？」，關鍵句在女子所說 "he doesn't pass enough"（他傳球傳得不夠），故答案選 B「把球傳給別人。」。

重要字彙

soccer：(n.) 足球　　　　　　　　　　　　　　　**point：(n.) 分數、得分**

重要片語

be good at...：擅長⋯⋯

 19. M: Hello! May I help you?

W: Yes, I'd like to return this dress, please.

M: Sure. What seems to be the problem?

W: It was a gift. It doesn't fit me.

Q: Why does the woman return the dress?

    A. It is the wrong size.

    B. She doesn't like the color.

    C. She has too many dresses already.

Answer: A

重要關鍵

本題測驗重點為 fit：(v.) 合⋯⋯身。

例：Those shoes don't fit me. They are too small.（這雙鞋我穿起來不合腳。太小了。）

題目問「為何女子要退回洋裝？」，關鍵句在女子所說 "It doesn't fit me."（我穿起來不合身。），故答案為 A「洋裝的尺寸不對。」。

重要字彙

return：(v.) 歸還、退回　　　　　　　　　　　**dress：(n.) 洋裝**

20. M: Yeah! I am so excited!

W: Why are you so happy?

M: I got a role in the school play!

W: Wow, that's great! Congratulations, Andrew!

Q: Why is Andrew so happy?

    A. He is writing a play.

    B. He got tickets for a play.

    C. He is acting in a play.

Answer: C

重要關鍵

本題測驗重點為 role：(n.) 角色。

例：Tim is going to play the role of the king in the movie. (Tim 將在這部電影裡扮演國王這個角色。)

題目問「Andrew 為什麼很開心？」，關鍵句在男子所說 "I got a role in the school play!" (我得到學校話劇裡的一個角色！)，因此答案選 C「他要在話劇中演出。」，act：(v.) 演出、扮演。

重要字彙

excited：(adj.) 感到興奮的   **play：(n.) 戲劇**

congratulations：(n.) 恭喜、祝賀

21. W: Hey Simon, are you going to the meeting?

M: No, Amy. I have to see the dentist.

W: Well, you may miss something important.

M: Will you tell me what is discussed?

Q: What does Simon ask Amy to tell him?

    A. What they talk about in the meeting.

    B. Where they hold the meeting.

    C. Who is at the meeting.

Answer: A

重要關鍵

本題測驗重點為 discuss：(v.) 討論 (= talk about...)。

例：I don't like to discuss politics with others. (我不喜歡和別人討論政治。)

題目問「Simon 要 Amy 告訴他什麼？」，關鍵句在 Simon 所說 "Will you tell me what is discussed?" (妳可以告訴我討論的內容嗎？)，因此答案為 A「他們會議中所討論的事情。」。

重要字彙

meeting：(n.) 會議   **dentist：(n.) 牙醫**

miss：(v.) 錯過   **hold：(v.) 舉行**

L

初級全民英檢聽力

6

 22. W: Ben wants to go for a bike ride.

M: That's a good idea. Will you go with him?

W: I want to, but our bikes aren't in the basement.

M: Oh, look in the yard beside the fence.

Q: Where will the woman likely find the bikes?

　A. In the basement.

　B. Next to the fence.

　C. Outside the yard.

Answer: B

重要關鍵

本題測驗重點為 beside：(prep.) 在……旁邊，相當於 next to 的意思。

題目問「女子可能在哪裡找到腳踏車？」，關鍵句在男子所說 "look in the yard beside the fence"
(去院子裡的圍籬旁看看。)，故知答案應選 B。

重要字彙

basement : (n.) 地下室　　　　　　　　　　　**yard : (n.) 院子**

fence : (n.) 圍籬、籬笆　　　　　　　　　　　**outside : (prep.) 在……外面**

23. W: Who's that girl over there?

M: Oh, that's Melissa. She is our new neighbor.

W: She is so slender.

M: Yes, she is. She is also tall and beautiful.

Q: What does the woman say about Melissa?

　A. She's pretty.

　B. She's tall.

　C. She's thin.

Answer: C

重要關鍵

本題測驗重點為 slender：(adj.) 纖細的、苗條的。

例：My new friend, Sophie, is tall and slender. (我的新朋友 Sophie 又高又瘦。)

題目問「這名女子說了關於 Melissa 什麼事？」，女子在對話中說 "She is so slender." (她好苗條。)，

相當於 thin 之意，故知本題答案應選 C。

24. W: What would you like to order, sir?

M: Do you have any spaghetti?

W: Sorry. We are all out.

M: OK. I'll have pizza instead.

Q: Who is the woman?

    A. She is a customer.

    B. She is a waitress.

    C. She is the man's secretary.

Answer: B

題目問「女子是誰？」，由對話內容 order (點餐)、spaghetti (義大利麵) 和 pizza (披薩) 可推知，對話發生在餐廳，故知女子應為女服務生 (waitress)，因此答案選 B。

重要字彙

customer : (n.) 顧客   secretary : (n.) 秘書

25. M: That was a great movie.

W: I know! Thanks for the ticket.

M: Anytime. I laughed so hard.

W: Me, too.

Q: What kind of movie did the man and woman watch?

    A. A boring movie.

    B. A sad movie.

    C. A funny movie.

Answer: C

初級全民英檢聽力 6

本題測驗重點為 laugh so hard，表示「笑得很開心」之意。

題目問「男子和女子看的是哪一種電影？」，關鍵句在男子所說 "I laughed so hard."（我笑得好開心。），由此可知，這部電影應該是好笑的、有趣的，故答案選 C，funny : (adj.) 好笑的、滑稽的。

重要字彙

boring : (adj.) 無聊的   sad : (adj.) 傷心的

第四部份：短文聽解

共 5 題，每題有三個圖片選項。請聽光碟放音機播出的題目，並選出一個最適合的圖片。每題播出一遍。

26. Please look at the following three pictures.

Listen to the following short talk. Where is the man?

My doctor prescribed me this medicine. Please hurry up and give it to me. I'm feeling absolutely terrible. It's tiring for me just to stand up right now. I just want to go home, take some pills, and fall asleep.

A 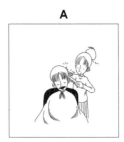 B 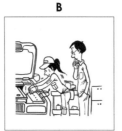 C

Answer: C

我的醫生開了這個藥方給我。請快點把藥給我。我現在覺得很不舒服。現在光是站著，我都覺得累。我只想要回家，吃個藥，然後睡覺。

由此可知，男子在藥局。

重要字彙

prescribe : (v.) 開藥方   absolutely : (adv.) 絕對地、完全地

tiring : (adj.) 累人的   pill : (n.) 藥丸

重要片語

hurry up : 趕快   fall asleep : 入睡

27. Please look at the following three pictures.

Listen to the following short talk. What will the boy have for lunch?

I don't feel like having a big meal today, so that's why I'm having this. I love eating it with lots of mustard and a little ketchup. That's it. I don't need any other toppings, like pickles or onions. Best of all, I can just eat it with my hands.

A   B   C

 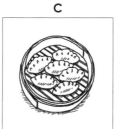

Answer: A

重要關鍵

我今天不想吃很多，這就是為什麼我現在在吃這個。我喜歡在上面加很多芥末和一點點番茄醬吃。就這樣，我不需要任何其他的配料，像是醃黃瓜或洋蔥。最棒的是，我可以用手拿著吃。

由此可知，男孩中餐要吃熱狗。

重要字彙

mustard：(n.) 芥末
topping：(n.) 加在食物上的配料
onion：(n.) 洋蔥

ketchup：(n.) 番茄醬
pickle：(n.) 醃黃瓜

28. Please look at the following three pictures.

Listen to the following message for Tom. What is broken?

Hi, Tom. This is Nick. The thing that keeps me cool in my apartment is broken. It's been so hot recently, and I don't have an air-conditioner. Now is the worst time for it to stop working. I think I'm going to melt at home. Can I go to your place now? Thanks.

A   B   C

Answer: A

重要關鍵

嗨，Tom。我是 Nick。讓我在公寓內保持涼爽的東西壞掉了。最近一直都很熱，而我又沒有冷氣。現在這個壞掉真的是最糟糕的時候了。我想我就快要融化在家裡面了。我現在可以去你家嗎？謝啦。

由此可知，電風扇壞掉了。

重要字彙

apartment : (n.) 公寓
recently : (adv.) 最近
air-conditioner : (n.) 冷氣機

---

 29. Please look at the following three pictures.

Listen to the following short talk. What did Mary and her friend do yesterday?

I had a great time with my friend yesterday. The main actor is so handsome! The story wasn't great, but I didn't care. My friend didn't seem to have such a good time, though. He didn't like the actors or the story!

A	B	C

Answer: C

重要關鍵

我昨天和朋友過得很愉快。主角實在太帥了！故事沒有很精采，但我不介意。我朋友似乎就沒這麼開心了。他不喜歡裡面的演員也不喜歡故事情節。

由此可知，Mary 和她朋友昨天去看電影了。

重要字彙

main : (adj.) 主要的
handsome : (adj.) 英俊的
care : (v.) 介意、在乎

30. Please look at the following three pictures.

Susan is leaving a message on Mark's answering machine. What happened to Bill?

Hi, Mark. Do you know what happened to Bill? This morning, I was outside playing when he rode his bike in front of me. Then he must have hit a rock or something, and he fell flat on his face. He's at home right now because he doesn't want anybody to see him.

A	B	C

Answer: A

嗨，Mark。你知道 Bill 發生什麼事嗎？今天早上，當我在外面玩時，他騎腳踏車從我面前經過。然後他一定是撞到石頭或什麼東西，於是他就臉朝下摔倒在地上了。他現在正在家裡，因為他不想要讓任何人看到他。由此可知，Bill 摔車了。

重要字彙

answering machine : (n.) 電話答錄機
ride : (v.) 騎 (腳踏車、機車)
rock : (n.) 石頭
flat : (adv.) 俯伏地，fall flat on someone's face : 直挺挺面朝下地倒下

重要片語

leave a message : 留言　　　　　　　　　　　　in front of... : 在……前面

199

第六回

閱讀模擬試題解析

二、閱讀能力測驗

本測驗分三部份,全部都是單選題,共 35 題,作答時間 35 分鐘。

第一部份:詞彙和結構

共 15 題,每個題目裡有一個空格。請從四個選項中選出一個最適合題意的字或詞作答。

---

1. The snake was still _____ even after it was run over by the car.

    A. alive   B. basic   C. legal   D. instant

Answer: A

重要關鍵

A. alive:(adj.) 活的

例:Everybody was happy that the missing boy was still alive. (每個人都很慶幸那失蹤的男孩還活著。)

B. basic:(adj.) 基本的

C. legal:(adj.) 合法的

D. instant:(adj.) 即刻的、立即的

例:I got an instant reply from Jim. (Jim 立即給我回覆。)

根據前後文語意,故知答案應選 A。

重要字彙

snake:(n.) 蛇

重要片語

be run over:被輾過

例:The dog was almost run over by a car. (那隻狗差點被車子輾過去。)

---

2. Johnny, it's ten o'clock. It's time for you _____ to bed.

    A. went   B. to go   C. going   D. will go

Answer: B

重要關鍵

本題測驗重點為 It's time for someone to V:該是某人……的時候了。

例:It's time for Bill to get a haircut. (Bill 該去理髮了。)

由此可知,空格應選不定詞,故答案為 B。

3. The good thing about traveling is _____ you can leave your worries at home.

   A. so   B. after   C. that   D. whether

Answer: C

本題測驗重點為引導名詞子句的連接詞 that。that 可引導名詞子句，形成方式如下：

在任何一個主詞起首的完整句前面加 that，即成 that 子句。

例：The word is that Jack broke up with Carrie. (聽說 Jack 和 Carrie 分手了。)

名詞子句在句中可作主詞、及物動詞的受詞、或置於 be 動詞之後作主詞補語。

根據上述用法，故知答案應選 C。whether (是否) 雖然也可引導名詞子句，但在本句中語意不合而不可選。

4. Geography is my _____ subject. I like it best.

   A. private   B. painful   C. funny   D. favorite

Answer: D

A. private：(adj.) 私人的，相反詞為 public：(adj.) 公開的、公共的。

例：Don't ask me about my family. That's private. (別問我有關家人的事情，那是私事。)

B. painful：(adj.) 痛苦的

C. funny：(adj.) 好笑的

D. favorite：(adj.) 最喜愛的

例：Titanic is my favorite movie. (《鐵達尼號》是我最喜歡的電影。)

題目第二句說 "I like it best." (我最喜歡它。)，可知答案應為 D。

geography：(n.) 地理   **subject：(n.) 科目**

like...(the) best：最喜歡……

5. Remember to turn _____ the light when you leave the room.

    A. around   B. over   C. off   D. in

Answer: C

重要關鍵

A. turn...around：使⋯⋯轉過來、將⋯⋯向後轉

B. turn over...：將⋯⋯翻轉；移交⋯⋯

C. turn off...：關掉電視、收音機、電燈等電器的電源，相反詞為 turn on（打開）。

例：He turns on the computer as soon as he gets home.（他一回到家就開電腦。）

D. turn in...：繳交⋯⋯

根據前後文語意，可知本題答案應選 C。

6. There are usually traffic _____ on this busy road during rush hour.

    A. jams   B. crowds   C. errors   D. bases

Answer: A

重要關鍵

A. jam：(n.) 壅塞、堵塞，traffic jam：塞車，為可數名詞。

例：I was stuck on the road because of a traffic jam.（因為塞車，所以我被困在路上。）

B. crowd：(n.) 群眾

C. error：(n.) 錯誤

D. base：(n.) 基地；總部

本題測驗重點為表「塞車」的固定用法，故答案為 A。

重要字彙

busy：(adj.) 交通繁忙的   rush hour：(n.) 上下班尖峰時間

7. Yellow diamonds are _____. That's why they're so expensive.

    A. ordinary   B. plenty   C. usual   D. rare

Answer: D

重要關鍵

A. ordinary：(adj.) 普通的

B. plenty：(adj.) 很多的

C. usual：(adj.) 通常的、平常的

D. rare：(adj.) 稀少的、罕見的

例：There are some rare flowers in the garden.（花園裡有些罕見的花卉。）

根據前後文語意，可知因為「稀少」，所以價格昂貴，故答案為 D。

that's why + S + V：那就是⋯⋯的原因，用來解釋原因。

例：Buses are always crowded. That's why I don't take buses.

（公車總是很擠，那就是我不搭公車的原因。）

8. Mother's Day is on the _____ Sunday of May.

A. two　　　　　　　B. second　　　　　　C. double　　　　　　D. twice

Answer: B

重要關鍵

A. two 為基數，表示「兩個」，後面接複數名詞，如：two people（兩個人）。

B. second 為序數，表示「第二的」。

例：Kent's birthday falls on the second Saturday in November this year.

（今年 Kent 的生日在十一月的第二個星期六。）

This is my second time in Hualien.（這是我第二次造訪花蓮。）

C. double：(adj.) 加倍的、兩倍的

D. twice 為倍數詞，表示「兩次、兩倍」，即等於 two times。

例：I called twice before Marie answered.（我打了兩次之後，Marie 才接電話。）

本題測驗重點為序數詞的用法，故本題答案應選 B。

9. The son of your brother or sister is your _____.

A. niece　　　　　　B. cousin　　　　　　C. nephew　　　　　　D. grandson

Answer: C

重要關鍵

A. niece：(n.) 姪女、外甥女

B. cousin：(n.) 表（堂）兄弟姐妹

C. nephew：(n.) 姪子、外甥

D. grandson：(n.) 孫子

兄弟的兒子稱為姪子，姊妹的兒子稱為外甥，故答案為 C。

10. When summer comes, the beach is always _____ of people on weekends.

    A. able   B. full   C. huge   D. sure

Answer: B

重要關鍵

A. able：(adj.) 能夠的，be able to V：能夠做……
B. full：(adj.) 充滿的，be full of...：充滿……
例：This pond is full of fish.（這個池塘裡都是魚。）
C. huge：(adj.) 極大的、巨大的
D. sure：(adj.) 確定的、確信的，be sure of...：確定……、確信……
根據前後文語意，可知本題答案應選 B。

重要字彙

beach：(n.) 海灘

11. The power failure in this area _____ the typhoon.

    A. was caused   B. caused by   C. was caused by   D. has caused in

Answer: C

重要關鍵

本題測試被動語態的用法。
被動語態的基本句型為：「主詞 + be 動詞 + p.p. + by + 實行動作的對象」。
例：Computers are used by many people.（電腦為很多人所使用。）
空格前的主詞為 power failure（停電），空格後有 typhoon（颱風），「停電」應是被「颱風」造成的，故本題答案選 C。

重要字彙

power failure：(n.) (意外) 停電   **typhoon：(n.) 颱風**

12. Amy was sad because she didn't receive _____ gifts on her birthday.

    A. all   B. few   C. some   D. any

Answer: D

重要關鍵

A. all 表示「所有的」，置入空格後不合語意，故不可選。

B. few 表示「沒幾個」，之後要接複數名詞，由於 few 本身就有否定的涵義，故不可再與 not 並用。

例：Bill only has few friends. (Bill 沒什麼朋友。)

C. some 表示「一些」，之後可以接複數名詞或不可數名詞，但只用於肯定句，而不與 not 並用。

例：Irene gave me some tips on how to make coffee. (Irene 傳授我一些煮咖啡的秘訣。)

　　Jill put some fruit in the refrigerator. (Jill 把一些水果放在冰箱裡。)

D. any 表示「任何的」，與 not 並用，not any 等於 no，之後可接單數名詞、複數名詞或不可數名詞。

例：This hotel doesn't have any rooms available. (這間飯店已經沒有空房了。)

　　Sorry, but I don't have any money to lend you. (抱歉，我沒有錢可以借你。)

句子的空格前有 didn't，故知答案應選 D。

---

13. You cannot _____ your car in the middle of the street.

　　A. park　　　　　　B. pick　　　　　　C. pull　　　　　　D. push

Answer: A

重要關鍵

A. park：(v.) 停放 (車輛)

例：Jack forgot where he had parked his car. (Jack 忘記自己把車停在哪兒了。)

B. pick：(v.) 挑選

例：Helen picked a good book for her son. (Helen 為她兒子挑選了一本好書。)

C. pull：(v.) 拔、拉

例：The dentist pulled Alan's tooth out. (牙醫把 Alan 的牙齒拔出來。)

D. push：(v.) 推 (擠)

例：Hey! Please don't push me. (嘿！請不要推我。)

由本句後半 in the middle of the street (街道的中間) 可推知，本題答案應選 A。

---

14. People in Taiwan are _____. They are always happy to help others.

　　A. dizzy　　　　　　B. noisy　　　　　　C. lonely　　　　　　D. friendly

Answer: D

重要關鍵

A. dizzy：(adj.) 暈眩的

B. noisy：(adj.) 吵鬧的

C. lonely：(adj.) 寂寞的

D. friendly：(adj.) 友善的

例：Warren is friendly to other people. (Warren 對他人很友善。)

從第二句 "They are always happy to help others." (他們總是樂於助人。) 可推知，本題答案應選 D。

15. You have to pay a tip for the waiter's _____ at this restaurant.

    A. system   B. service   C. solution   D. sample

Answer: B

重要關鍵

A. system：(n.) 系統

B. service：(n.) 服務

例：The service in that coffee shop is excellent. (那家咖啡廳的服務很棒。)

C. solution：(n.) 解決方法

例：Larry came up with a solution to the problem. (Larry 想出一個解決這個問題的方法。)

D. sample：(n.) 樣品、試用品

例：The store is giving away free samples. (那家商店正在分發免費試用品。)

根據前後文語意，故知答案為 B。

重要字彙

tip：(n.) 小費，pay a tip：給小費   **waiter：(n.) 服務生**

第二部份：段落填空

共 10 題，包括二個段落，每個段落各含四到六個空格。每格均有四個選項，請依照文意選出最適合的答案。

Questions 16-20

    There once lived an old dog. When he was young, he was loved by his owner __(16)__ because he was the greatest hunter. But when he got old, he __(17)__ weak and slow.

    One day, the old dog and his owner __(18)__ in the forest when they saw a wild pig. The dog began to chase it. Finally, he caught the pig __(19)__ the ear. Unfortunately, __(20)__ his teeth were weak, the pig easily pulled away. The dog was worried that his owner would be angry.

16. A. very   B. lot   C. very much   D. so many

Answer: C

重要關鍵

本題測驗重點為修飾動詞的副詞用法。

在四個選項中，只有 very much (非常) 可置於句尾用來修飾動詞，very, lot, so many 則不可，故答案為 C。

17. A. changed	B. became	C. started	D. made

Answer: **B**

本題測驗重點為不完全不及物動詞 become 的用法。

become (變成) 為不完全不及物動詞，後面需接名詞或形容詞作主詞補語。

例：Damon wants to become famous one day. (Damon 想要有一天能成名。)

He became a doctor when he was only 25 years old. (他二十五歲的時候就成為醫生。)

空格後為形容詞 weak and slow (衰弱及緩慢)，根據上述，故知答案應選 B。

18. A. were walking	B. would walk	C. have walked	D. was walking

Answer: **A**

本題測驗重點為「S + was / were+ V-ing + when 引導的過去式副詞子句」，表示「……時，……正在……」，when 譯成「時」。

例：Henry was watching TV when the power went out. (停電時，Henry 正在看電視。)

空格後有 when 引導的過去式副詞子句 "when they saw a pig"，故知空格應置過去進行式，因本句主詞有兩個：the old dog and his owner，故答案為 A。

19. A. for	B. over	C. by	D. at

Answer: **C**

本題測驗重點為 catch...by + 某部位：抓住……的某部位。

例：The policeman caught the robber by the arm. (警察抓住搶匪的手臂。)

根據上述，故知本題答案為 C。

20. A. if	B. although	C. before	D. since

Answer: **D**

A. if : (conj.) 如果

B. although : (conj.) 雖然

C. before : (conj.) 在……之前

D. since : (conj.) 因為、由於

例：Since you can't make a decision, I will decide for you. (由於你無法做出決定，我來幫你。)

根據上下文語意，本題答案應選 D。

owner : (n.) 主人

forest : (n.) 森林

unfortunately : (adv.) 不幸地

hunter : (n.) 獵犬、獵人

chase : (v.) 追捕、追趕

easily : (adv.) 輕易地

pull away : 脫身

Questions 21-25

Daniel is reading a book about English names. He is interested __(21)__ changing his name. He thinks the name "Daniel" is __(22)__. In Taiwan, people get to choose their own English names. Daniel __(23)__ his name for himself when he started to learn English two years ago. In other words, "Daniel" is not his __(24)__ name. Daniel's friends think it's great that he can choose any name. Daniel's friend, Skip, wants him to __(25)__ his name in the book. He jokes that "Skip" must mean "super handsome"!

21. A. at	B. in	C. by	D. on
			Answer: B

本題測驗重點為 be interested in... : 對……有興趣。

例 : Susan was very interested in cooking. (Susan 對烹飪很有興趣。)

由此可知，本題答案應選 B。

22. A. bored	B. excited	C. boring	D. exciting
			Answer: C

上文說 Daniel 想換名字，由此可知 Daniel 不滿意他原來的名字，因此應選含有負面意思的 boring 或是 bored。

boring 表示「無趣的、令人感到無聊的」。

例 : The basketball game is boring. (那場籃球賽很無聊。)

而 bored 表示「感到無聊的」。

例 : Tina feels bored because she has nothing to do. (Tina 覺得很無聊，因為她沒事可做。)

由此可知，本題答案應選 C。

23. A. selected   B. filled   C. counted   D. ordered

Answer: A

重要關鍵

A. select：(v.) 選擇

B. fill：(v.) 裝滿、填滿

C. count：(v.) 數、計算

D. order：(v.) 命令；點餐

本句意思是 Daniel 自己「選」名字，因此答案選 A。

24. A. family   B. new   C. right   D. real

Answer: D

重要關鍵

real：(adj.) 真的。本句意思是："Daniel" 不是他「真的」名字，故答案選 D。

補充：選項 A 的 family name 是指一個人的「姓」，也等於 last name，而 first name 則是指一個人的「名」。

例：Mary Wang，first name 是 Mary，family / last name 是 Wang。

25. A. look at   B. look up   C. look after   D. look down

Answer: B

重要關鍵

A. look at...：看、注視……

例：He is looking at a beautiful painting. (他正在看一幅漂亮的畫。)

B. look up...：查看……

例：Eric looks up a difficult word in the dictionary. (Eric 在字典裡查一個困難的單字。)

C. look after...：照料……

D. look down：往下看，為不及物動詞片語，後面不可加受詞。

例：Jimmy dared not look down while he was riding the roller coaster.

    (Jimmy 搭雲霄飛車的時候不敢往下看。)

本句意思為「Skip 要 Daniel 在那本書『查看』他名字的含意。」，故答案選 B。

重要字彙

own：(adj.) 自己的

super：(adv.) 非常地、極度地

例：**I am super tired! I am going to bed.** (我累斃了！我要去睡覺了。)

handsome：(adj.) 英俊的

R

初級全民英檢閱讀 **6**

in other words：換句話說、也就是說

例：Everyone makes mistakes. In other words, no one is perfect.

（每個人都會犯錯。換句話說，沒有人是完美的。）

第三部份：閱讀理解

共 10 題，包括數篇短文，每篇短文後面有三至四個相關問題。請由四個選項中選出最適合的答案。

Questions 26-28

Attention

Cougars have been seen in this mountain area for the past few weeks. Cougars usually eat small animals, but if they can't find them, they'll eat larger animals. So, keep children and pets close to you, or they could become a cougar's food!

If you see a cougar, follow these rules:

- ☻ Pick up small children first.
- ☻ Face the animal and walk backward slowly—NEVER run.
- ☻ Don't take your eyes off the animal.
- ☻ Shout or throw stones at the animal—it may get scared and run away.

26. What would be a cougar's first choice for food?

   A. A tall, heavy man.

   B. A bear.

   C. An elephant.

   D. A rabbit.

Answer: D

27. What shouldn't you do if you see a cougar?

 A. Turn around and run quickly.

 B. Shout loudly.

 C. Keep the cougar in sight.

 D. Throw small rocks at it.

Answer: A

28. What is the main purpose of this notice?

 A. To welcome people to this mountain area.

 B. To encourage people to hike in this mountain area.

 C. To warn people of danger in this mountain area.

 D. To give people directions to this mountain area.

Answer: C

重要字彙

cougar：(n.) 美洲獅

face：(v.) 面對

backward：(adv.) 向後地，**walk backward**：後退著走

shout：(v.) 喊叫

scared：(adj.) 害怕的

bear：(n.) 熊

elephant：(n.) 大象

rabbit：(n.) 兔子

loudly：(adv.) 大聲地

rock：(n.) 石塊 (可指小石子，亦可指大石塊)

notice：(n.) 公告、告示

encourage：(v.) 鼓勵，**encourage someone to V**：鼓勵某人……

warn：(v.) 警告，**warn someone of something**：警告某人某事

danger：(n.) 危險

directions：(n.) 行路指引

重要片語

take someone's eyes off...：將某人的視線從……移開

turn around：轉身

keep...in sight：使……保持在視線內、看住 / 盯著……

Questions 29-32

To: wendy@bbc.com.tw

From: lucylin@coolnet.com

Sub: Trip to Spain

Sent: December 20, 2013

Dear Wendy,

How's your summer going?
I'm sad that I don't see you at the office anymore. I'm studying Spanish here in Taiwan since I am going to visit you in Spain during the Chinese New Year. What's it like there? Do you like your classes? When we meet up there, we can have dinner. You choose the restaurant, and I'll pay. Make sure that you choose somewhere with nice Spanish food.

I'll stay at a hotel near your school. I'll arrive on January 29, but it will be late at night. So, you can give me a call the next day. Oh, I got a new cell phone! My new number is 0911-234-567.

See you soon.

Lucy

---

29. Why does Lucy write to Wendy?

A. She hopes Wendy to give her new number to her.

B. She wants to get together with Wendy.

C. She hopes to pick the restaurant for their dinner.

D. She wants Wendy to teach her Spanish.

Answer: B

30. How do Lucy and Wendy know each other?

A. They went to the same school.

B. They are teacher and student.

C. They worked together.

D. They met each other in Spain.

Answer: C

31. How does Lucy get in touch with Wendy?

    A. She calls her on her cell phone.

    B. She sends her a postcard.

    C. She visits her school.

    D. She sends her an e-mail.

Answer: D

32. What do we know from this letter?

    A. Lucy will treat Wendy to dinner.

    B. Wendy will call Lucy on January 29.

    C. Wendy will return to Taiwan this Chinese New Year.

    D. Lucy wants to stay with Wendy when she visits Spain.

Answer: A

 重要字彙

Spanish : (n.) 西班牙語 & (adj.) 西班牙的   **Spain**: (n.) 西班牙 (國名)
postcard : (n.) 明信片

重要片語

give someone a call : 打電話給某人
get together with someone : 和某人相聚
get in touch with someone : 和某人聯絡
treat someone to something : 招待某人某事物

Questions 33-35

David likes to ride his bike to school. He thinks it is the best way to get to school. He can avoid all the cars and get to school early. David doesn't like the pollution in his city, though. It makes him hard to breathe when he rides his bike. Sometimes drivers don't watch out for bike riders. David tries to tell all of his friends to be careful when they drive. If they don't watch for bike riders, they might cause a lot of trouble!

33. Why is David able to get to school early?

    A. His friends drive him every day.

    B. His scooter is really fast.

    C. He lives close to his school.

    D. He doesn't have to worry about traffic.

Answer: D

34. What doesn't David like about riding to school?

    A. It makes him tired.

    B. Air pollution is a problem.

    C. Other people drive too fast.

    D. There is a lot of traffic.

Answer: B

35. Which of the following is TRUE?

    A. Pollution is a problem for David's friends.

    B. Most of David's friends are careful drivers.

    C. Drivers sometimes don't pay attention to bike riders.

    D. David always rides his bike carelessly.

Answer: C

重要字彙

ride : (v.) 騎 (腳踏車、機車)

pollution : (n.) 污染

cause : (v.) 造成

carelessly : (adv.) 不小心地、魯莽地

avoid : (v.) 避開

breathe : (v.) 呼吸

scooter : (n.) 小型機車

重要片語

get to + 地方 : 抵達某地

watch out for... : 注意 / 留神…… (= watch for...)

worry about... : 擔心……

pay attention to... : 注意……